A Different Mix

Andy Bracken

A Morning Brake Book

Copyright © 2021 Andy Bracken

All rights reserved.

ISBN: 9798518060746

First (and probably only) Edition.

ANDY BRACKEN

For C & R. With love.

x

This is for the DJs and dreamers amongst you!

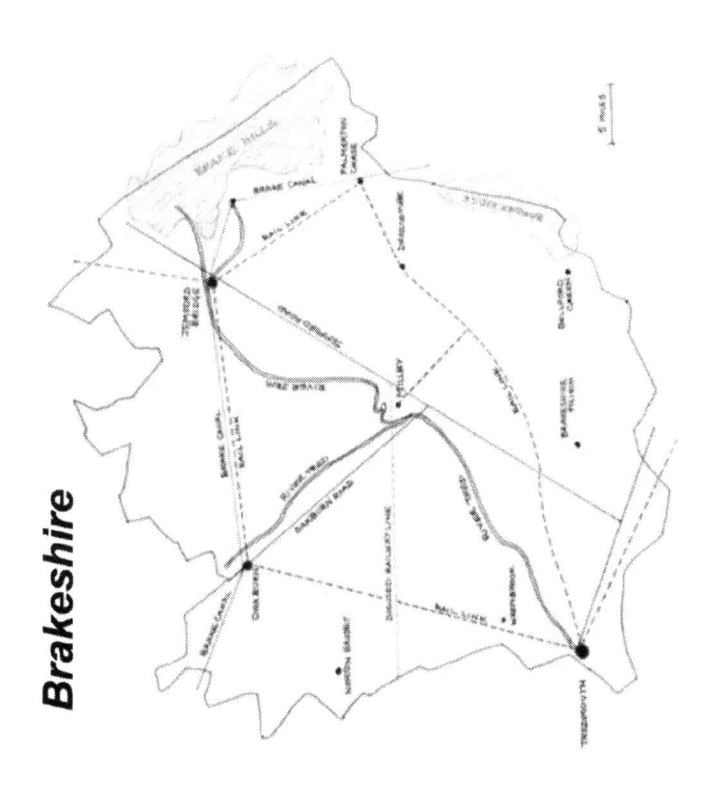

A DIFFERENT MIX

1.

It was a punt; a bit of a gamble. You never know, it could be something rare and valuable.

Though my gut tells me it isn't going to be.

Value comes from supply and demand - literally, more people want it than there are copies available.

Scarcity is different. There might only be one, but if nobody covets it, it's largely worthless.

It was ninety-nine pence, the record, tucked in a box of singles similarly priced. The rest were tat; sifted through prior to being made available to the public.

I saw the record shop owner doing precisely that, as he took each seven-inch and glanced at it. A slightly distasteful expression accompanied the ninety-nine pence rejections.

A little smile and a widening of his eyes greeted any he deemed worthy of further exploration.

He greeted me with a similar mien. I think he recognised me. He was certainly old enough to remember when I was something of a minor local celebrity.

But what of this record?

Did he play it?

He must have done, because there's no other indication as to what it contains. I guess it wasn't familiar, so he dismissed it.

There's a certain arrogance in that; to ignore something on the grounds of it not being known.

He probably dropped the stylus in the middle of the track, and gave it a count of five or ten, before the distasteful look soured his face.

In contrast, it makes me smile to simply hold it, and to be able to call it mine. Besides, perhaps he was wrong, the man in the shop.

Not that it matters. The truth is, I like discovering. Its potential uniqueness appeals to me. As does the mystery that comes with it.

Years from now, someone not yet a global sensation might admit to it being an early song they cut for the artist's brother to give to a mate of a man he knew at a record label.

In the meantime, it'll sit in the small section of my collection, alongside the other 'unknowns' I always seem to be drawn to.

From time to time I look for them on the internet - unknown artist on an acetate or white label. It's surprising how often they come up for sale.

They intrigue me. How did they come to be? What happened? After all, the trouble was taken, and the money spent, to record and press a record that nobody now recognises - nobody values - except me.

The needle descends to the beginning.

I stand and listen, my mind clearing as a calmness settles within me. Music can do that.

All of my stresses fall away. For I am stressed. Constantly, it seems, I'm anxious about something or other.

It's a simple song. Three notes on a piano. Sad notes. It's strange that something so melancholy should lift my mood.

There's a familiarity in the melody, but nothing I can put my finger on. And despite feeling quite contemporary, there's a classical flavour to it.

I can imagine it playing over a scene in a film, as an accompaniment to a poignant moment.

And I know the scene would probably make me want to cry. I wouldn't though, because I'm a man of a certain generation, and any emotion of that type is best kept in check.

No, I'd cough and think happy or sexy thoughts to move my mind on and not go there.

At least, that's what I do when observed.

Alone is different.

Only when I'm alone can I be true to myself.

2.

The song continues from one side to the other, building as it goes - morphing and darkening, but remaining essentially the same. I got lucky, I think, chancing on the first side first, as there's no indication. It feels right to play it this way round.

It's beguiling; it draws me in and holds me, as it invites me to reflect.

Reflect: Throw back an image of. Embody or represent. To think deeply about.

No sooner is it finished than I begin it again. As the sound of a wave washes through me, I hit a switch and plunge the room into near blackness. Only the lights on the amp emit a comforting glow.

Until, after a few seconds, my eyes adjust, and I become aware of fingers of brittle moonlight reaching in through the pleats in the curtains. They point accusingly.

A more unnatural yellow light, warmer and somehow denser, thrusts an arm through the gap at the edge of the door. It's as if it's attempting to pull me away to safety.

It isn't difficult to resist, as the music has a firmer grip on me.

Reflecting.

Does a reflection exist in the dark? If I stand in front of a mirror in absolute pitch blackness, am I still there looking back at myself?

No, I don't think I am. I have a sense that light makes it possible.

Can a shadow cast a shadow?

What a thing to think!

I'm not drunk, and I've definitely taken no drugs. I've had a solitary beer, but am used to that. After all, it's what I do to kill the time every evening of my life.

Never too much. I've never been a big drinker.

A coffee has subsequently balanced me, and fended off the tiredness alcohol brings - particularly since my sixties appeared in front of me and crooked a beckoning finger.

Routine is how I survive and cope. Every day largely the same, distinguished by small differences, such as the ready-meal I have for my tea, or the freshness of the bread I consume.

It's not worth cooking for one. Why dirty a pan and peel something? Occasionally I put some frozen chips in the oven, but tend to rely on the microwave for most things, eaten from the plastic trays they come in to save soiling a plate.

I eat late - around nine in the evening. My work dictates it all.

My work.

It was a full-time job for years. Most of the time was spent planning and listening to submissions that would arrive by the sack-load.

They stopped coming at some point about a decade ago. Perhaps longer.

Most days I get a batch of emails that invite me to visit a website and download MP3s. I usually do, because I still hang on to a weedy thread of hope that one of them will contain 'the new thing' - the next great seismic music shift that will render everything else redundant almost overnight.

I'm desperate to discover it. Is that so I might ride off on its coattails and not be redundacised by it?

A mouse-click and a wait, while megabytes of data download onto my tired computer. And in the minute or two it takes for that to happen, I dare to dream!

Hope rises within my core; a romantic sense of being on the brink of discovery sends the tiniest shiver of expectation scurrying along the back of my hairline.

Shiver me timbers!

I'm like a lookout on a sailing ship - straining to see undiscovered land on the horizon.

Those are the best couple of minutes of my day.

'Heard it all before,' I mutter to myself, and log out.

There's no originality. That's the most soul-destroying part.

Has everything been done before?

Or have people given up on originality, and switched over to a path more clearly marked and popular? And did they do that because it's the only way to get on?

I'm too old. I've listened too much. My memory is too good.

If I could erase it all, that vast bank of music played and absorbed, I could hear it all again with fresh ears and an open mind.

The same could be said of life.

My life, I mean.

Are things as bad as I think they are, or am I a curmudgeonly jaded man?

It begs the question - what is it I want?

Or, rather, what is it I feel I don't have?

A freshness.

Staleness has crept in to my world, and I see and hear no beauty in anything stale. All I see is a gathering rot and decay, and ultimately death and dust.

I've always been a discoverer, impatient for the next page in the story - the next record in the pile - the next relationship.

As a result, I rarely appreciated what I had until after I'd moved on and lost it.

It also attracted me to people who were of a similar mind. But it never once occurred to me that they would tire of me as soon as something perceived to be better came along.

Somewhere in all of that is why I bought this record for ninety-nine pence - a record I flip over and begin again as soon as it's finished.

I feel as though I could continue doing this perpetually.

3.

"Morning Dave."
Dave's my Producer.
"Alright Nick? Good days off?"
"Spectacular. You?" I ask him.
"Yep."
Dave's been producing my show for nigh on twenty years. I suppose we're friends, even though we don't see much of each other outside the studio.
"What have we got today?" I ask brightly.
"The usual shit."
Dave says shit a lot. As well as other un-broadcastable words.
"What year are we doing on the oldies hour?" I plough on.
"It's seventies this week."
"Oh, right."
"1974 today. It's shit."
"Oh dear."
"Mind you, it's not as shit as the current shit."
I spend a long time getting my chair set to a comfortable position. Not too comfy though, lest I should nod off.
"Want a coffee?" Dave asks through the comms.
"From the machine?"
"Yes."
"No thanks."
"I might have one," he says.
Sometimes he has too much coffee. It gives him the shits. Still, he's a professional, and won't leave the desk.
I've been doing this show for the best part of a decade. Prior to then, I had the DriveTime slot - a prime gig. And

I'd sometimes stand in on the breakfast show - the primest gig of all.

Now I get the graveyard stint. Two hours between two and four in the morning, Monday through Thursday, when listenership is at its lowest. For years, the talk has been about playing pre-recorded music and doing away with any personality.

I feel duty-bound to take the show in that inevitable direction.

A love of music got me into the business, DJing University gigs, and running a mobile disco through the first half of my twenties.

It was Amanda who got me in at Tred FM. I suppose I owe her for that.

Ultimately, she took all she was owed, and then some.

And I loved it back then. There was freedom to play whatever I liked. Yes, the current hits had to be spun, but they were tolerable. When was that? 1984 was my first year on the air hosting my own show. I was twenty-six, and local county radio was merely a steppingstone for me. I'd get spotted by one of the nationals, and move to London or Manchester or somewhere. The BBC was my aim!

It never happened, though. And come the new millennium, everything changed.

Controlled playlists took over commercial radio; all major label releases - a deal done by the parent company that bought Brakeshire Radio Ltd. I was left with one free choice an hour.

I say 'free choice', but only if it existed in the database of digitised music it had to be selected from.

Now I don't even get that.

Still, I have 1974 to look forward to this morning. I was sixteen that year. Well, fifteen for half of it.

Forty-four years ago. All the fours, Diana Dors!

Is that where I'll end up, bloody bingo calling? Even that's probably automated now. And on-line.

I don't know what I'd do if I didn't do this for a living. That's despite not particularly enjoying what I do.

It's better than nothing.

I thought by now that it wouldn't be an issue - I'd have enough tucked away to see me through to pension claiming. I'd still be working, but only because I wanted to.

Amanda made sure that wasn't going to happen. I was 'Diana Dors' at the time, and didn't have the will.

I've been floating ever since, like a fatty turd, waiting for a change in the current that will propel me to somewhere else.

Well, either that, or for someone to chance along, piss all over me, and pull the chain.

Dave's back.

"What are you thinking about?" his voice booms in my headphones.

"Diana Dors."

"Why?"

"Bingo. Forty-four."

"They don't say that any more."

"Don't they?"

"No. Droopy Drawers now," he solemnly informs me.

"Really?"

"Really."

"And you know this, how?"

"Right, three minute warning," he says, changing the subject.

"No, no, no. How do you know that?"

"I do a bit," he replies quietly.

"A bit of what?"

"Bingo calling."

"What? When? Where?"

"Saturdays. It's for charity."

"You've never mentioned it."

"Haven't I?"

"No. I'd remember. Do you get paid?"

"No, it's for charity."

"You don't agree with charity," I remind him.

"I subscribe to some charities."

"What's it in aid of?"

"This and that."

"Dave, I'll find out."

"You're on in two minutes," he says, and fiddles with his control board.

4.

- Ed Sheeran's latest single taking us up to the news.
- We'll be back with the oldies in a few minutes. And this morning, we're going back, back, back in time, and delving down, down, deeper on down into 1974 - sponsored by Knight & Day antique timepieces.
- So, slide your flares over your platform shoes, hook your thumbs through your belt loops, and get ready to let your hair down!

"That wasn't the new Ed Sheeran," Dave says through my headphones.

"Wasn't it?"

"No. It's all on the computer screen right in front of your face."

"It sounded like Ed Sheeran."

"Everyone sounds like Ed Sheeran because he's really fucking popular."

"Who was it?"

"It doesn't matter. The moment's gone. Besides which, we played the new Ed Sheeran three songs ago."

"Did we?"

"Yes."

"Nobody will notice," I say hopefully.

"There's nobody to notice," Dave replies more realistically.

"How long have I got?"

"Two minutes."

Removing my headphones, I stand and walk the small studio a few times to restore circulation to my legs.

What do I remember about 1974? IRA bombings, three-day week, power cuts, strikes, plane crashes, disasters, racial unrest, ABBA winning Eurovision.

It was a grim year.

That said, I attended my first proper gig!

Marc Bolan and T. Rex in Birmingham. It was late-January, and I was fifteen. And drunk.

Nerves did for me, as I went with Sharon, a girl a year my senior. A school year, I mean. She was closer to two years older in real time, with me being born in the summer.

In other ways, she was bordering on being a different generation.

It was a fluke, my being there.

Bolan was yesterday's man come 1974, but Sharon had adored him since 'Ride A White Swan'. Her friend had pulled out of the gig in favour of an Alvin Stardust poster on her bedroom wall, leaving her with a spare ticket.

Sharon lived near me in Tredmouth, so we'd often walk home together.

That's not strictly true. It was more that I'd follow her whenever I could, and pretend it was coincidence.

A couple of years of that led to her sometimes acknowledging my existence.

I'll never forget the first words she ever said to me. In her sultry voice, she asked, "why are you following me, you weird little prick?"

She had curly blonde hair, glittery makeup, a curvy body and really full lips. Those lips pouted earnestly when she promised my mum she'd make sure nothing bad would happen to me.

That sealed it. Despite being a school night, I could have her spare ticket for free. It had cost one whole pound for the rear stalls. All I needed to do was pay my coach fare and cobble together a bit of spending money. For an orange squash and some sweets.

Sod that for a game of soldiers!

I took my own orange squash in my plastic toy army canteen, and sweets from Woolies pick'n'mix, and saved my cash for more exciting delights.

That was how I ended up drunk on a bottle of vodka Sharon and I shared to keep the cold out.

She picked it up on our arrival in Birmingham after we pooled our cash reserves. We decanted it into my plastic army canteen, and I smuggled it in the venue in the ripped lining of my coat. Despite lots of bombs going off, they didn't search me very well.

We both thought Marc was brilliant that night. Mind you, I had no point of comparison, and in Sharon's eyes, he could do no wrong.

I decided there and then to have my hair permed. It took me months to grow it long enough, and when it was done, I looked like Leo bloody Sayer.

Ah, but that night, as we ran to make the coach back to Brakeshire!

Hand in hand, as she reached out and seized mine in hers, and pulled me along, keeping me upright, my feet not doing what I wanted them to do.

I see her misty breaths as she turned and smiled at me, her pouty lips parting to show her wide front teeth shining in the streetlight glow...

A tapping on the glass brings me back to the here and now, Dave pointing at the desk while rotating his other hand.

He flashes me a splayed palm - five seconds until I'm back on.

Whatever happened to the teenage dream?

5.

- *'Long Live Love' by Olivia Newton John, the highest new entry, straight in at number twenty-eight this very week forty-four years ago.*
- *the highest climber on the chart comes to us courtesy of The Carpenters, up from forty to number nineteen, with 'Jambalaya'. Oh me oh my oh!*

"Dave, are you awake?"

"I am, unfortunately."

"What was your first gig?"

"School hall, late-July, 1971."

"Who?"

"No, they were too big by then."

"Who?"

"Yes."

"You saw Yes in your school hall?" I ask incredulously.

"What the fuck are you talking about?"

"Who... What band did you see?"

"My band."

"How old were you?"

"Fifteen. Sixteen."

"What were you called?"

"Dave Grave & The Exhumers."

"What was your role?"

"Front man. Singer. And I wrote the songs."

"Really?"

"Don't sound so fucking surprised!"

"Well... What kind of music did you play?"

"Goth, before anybody had thought of it. Prog-goth, I suppose. But we didn't know that back then. We were too ahead of our time. Add on twelve years, and we'd have been perfect."

"Did you ever release anything?"

"No. Someone recorded something on an open-reel tape, but fuck knows what happened to it."

"I never knew that, Dave."

"No, well, not much to say really. You're back on in sixty seconds."

"What did you wear on stage?"

"See, the thing was, all the popular acts were going down the glam route. Shoulder pads and sequins were coming in. We were the anti-whatsit to that. So I wore black, head to toe."

"Black what?"

"The boys dressed like Victorian grave diggers. All working class collarless shirts and flat caps. We'd rub dirt in the shirts to make them look right. I'd be front and centre in a black burial gown, with a black veil and whatnot."

"Bloody hell."

"Thirty seconds."

"Was this when you were living down south?"

"That's right. Down in Dorset."

"And you haven't got anything I can hear?" I ask again.

"No. Not from that band."

"That band?"

"I had other bands."

"Such as?"

"By '74 I was fronting up Dave Redd and The Reddlemen. We were more proto-punk, I suppose."

"What did you wear?"

"Why are you so interested in what I wore?"

"I don't know."

"Ten seconds. To answer your question, not a lot. I'd be largely naked and coated in red ochre. Three, two, and one..."

- *Karen and Richard Carpenter with 'Jambalaya', up twenty-one places to number nineteen this week in 1974, the year Producer Dave formed his band Dave Redd & The Reddlemen!*

- *What were you doing at the time? It was the year I went to see T. Rex in Birmingham! Drop us an email or text, and let us know.*

- *You're listening to Nick Cherry, picking the ripest hits just for you - the pip of the pops - four days a week between two and four. There's fog around, so be careful out there if you're on the road.*

- *We'll pick our way through the top ten singles when we come back, after these few messages.*

"I saw T. Rex in '72," Dave says.

"Nice one. How were they?"

"Dunno. I was stoned out of my box. Saw David Bowie, too."

"And?"

"Can't remember anything about the night."

"Right. Did you ever have a record out, Dave?"

"Define 'out'."

"Released. Available for purchase."

"Ah, no, it never quite got that far."

"Well, how far did it get?"

"Hang on - we have an email!" Dave announces with mock surprise.

"Excellent. Who from?"

"It's from our old friend Timbo Quimbo. You know, I don't think that's the name Mr and Mrs Quimbo gave him."

"Oh god, what does he say?"

"He says, 'Morning Dick and Knave. In 1974 I was sucking on my mum's tit, you old wankers.'"

"That's nice."

Dave suggests, "you could read it out and add, 'so was I. Don't tell the man you call daddy.'"

"Any others?"

"A couple of 'love the show' types. A handful of requests which we can't play. And several hundred from people wanting your credit card information."

"Send me the 'love the show' ones."

"Most of them added 'so far'."

"What happened with your music career?" I push on.

"Chemisette Records wanted to sign us up. That was what first brought me to Brakeshire," Dave says as he forwards me the emails just about worth bothering with.

"When was that?"

"Late '76. They were looking to cash in on the punk thing."

"That must have been exciting."

"Not really. By the time we got to the studio at Norton Basset, we'd changed to a more minimalist three-piece. That quickly became a one-piece when the other two fucked off back to Dorset."

"Why did they do that?"

"Bryan Adams."

"Bryan Adams stole your band?"

"Don't be a tit! One quit, and the other got married. It was the winter of '76."

"What did you do?"

"Thirty seconds. I re-imagined myself as Dave Grave's Empty Sarcophagus, and did the audition. It was just me and a 1950s Beat Frequency Oscillator wired to a monitor speaker."

"That was brave. How did it go?"

"Not great. Patrick Oggy Ogden was in the chair. I took the frequency to an audio range that induced him to have some kind of seizure."

"They didn't sign you up?"

"What do you fucking think? No. But Baz Baxter offered me a job which led to me getting into the radio production side of things. Three, two, one..."

6.

- Ah, the good old Wombles, with 'The Wombling Song', down three places to number ten on the countdown from March of 1974. The single peaked at number four. Prior to that they were an underground band!
- We'll be back after these messages with the one and only Freddie Starr! Don't go anywhere. I'm presuming you can't!

"I did warn you it was terrible," Dave says.

"What's number one?"

"Paper Lace, 'Billy Don't Be A Hero'."

"Good grief."

"Forty-three minutes to go."

"How many seconds is that?" I ask him.

"Two-thousand, five-hundred and eighty... seventy-nine.. seventy-eight..."

"Oh, god. You count them?"

"Every show."

"When am I next on?"

"Freddie goes on for three minutes plus."

"Doesn't he do a talkie voice bit?"

"Oh yes!"

"I might go and strain my greens."

"Have one for me."

I stand at the urinal and recall needing a wee on the coach back from Birmingham. There wasn't a toilet onboard in those days, so we finished the vodka and orange in my canteen, and I filled it back up.

It was Sharon's idea.

Half an hour on, and she needed to go. To that end, I poured the canteen contents out the coach window. Only some of it blew back in.

On the back seat, she removed her jeans and undies as I kept watch. There were only a dozen people on the coach, and we had the rear third to ourselves.

"You're going to have to hold it for me," she whispered.

"I didn't realise girls had to do that," I replied.

"What?"

"Nothing," I muttered taking the canteen she held out.

It only had a small opening. I suppose it was about half an inch across.

I held it upright on the felt seat, and she squatted over it with her feet either side. We were both drunk and giggly.

Most of her wee went in it, but some ran down the sides and warmed my hands.

She let me dry them on her undies, which I thought was very kind, before she used them to wipe herself and clean up. She then stuffed them down the back of the seat.

With her jeans back on, we moved forward a couple of rows, me closest to the window.

"Thanks for letting me piss in your army thing," she said, and kissed me to show how grateful she really was.

I can still feel how her gorgeous fleshy lips were on mine that night.

"You're my 20th Century Boy!" she said afterwards.

In the glow from headlights and the couple of functioning overhead lights, I smiled at her.

"Do you want to be my toy?" she added, and I didn't know what to say.

I wash my hands, sliding my ring up my finger, and work the lavender scented soap into the skin exposed beneath it.

It was a squally Monday night in late-January of 1974, on a tired coach trundling along the slow lane of the motorway, my head woozy on vodka and pick'n'mix, her head resting on my lap, her legs stretched out across the aisle.

My eyes picked out patterns cast in the grime on the window, as her brimmed lips enveloped me and I tried to hold myself in check.

To no avail.

I think I could have had sex with Sharon that night on the bus, had I not erupted after twelve seconds of oral stimulation.

It took us both by surprise.

Sharon more than me, I'd wager, judging by the sounds she made.

"Sorry," I mumbled.

Sharon didn't say anything. She made a motion with her hands.

"It's just that you're so beautiful," I tried to explain.

Her scrabbling around became more frantic.

Looking back, I can appreciate the words 'plastic army canteen' are quite difficult to say without moving your tongue to the back of your teeth.

I got there in the end, and unscrewed the top for her in a gentlemanly way.

"Bloody hell, Nicky," she eventually said, "how long have you been saving that up?"

Stupidly, I replied, "only since this morning."

Shit, how long have I been standing here washing my hands?

I wipe them on my trousers as I jog back to the studio.

Dave has covered for me by running a jingle and moving straight on through Paul McCartney & Wings. As a result, I get back in time to introduce The Bay City Rollers' 'Remember (Sha-la-la-la)'.

"Where have you been?" Dave hisses in my ears.

"Sorry. Something I ate."

"You alright?"

"Yes, I'm fine now."

"No harm done."

"Thanks for covering. Hey, I picked up a record yesterday. Another of those 'unknown artist, unknown song' ones."

"Any good?"

"I think so. I couldn't stop playing it, to be honest."

"It must be a shock to the system coming in here after that," Dave suggests.

"It was only ninety-nine pence."

"Where from?"

"That place down the bottom of Tredmouth. Under the railway bridge, and tucked away in a side street."

"Shit shop."

"I don't go there often, but I fancied a stroll."

"Was Malcolm there?" Dave asks.

"Who's Malcolm?"

"The owner. Miserable fucker. Face like a ball of tinfoil."

"Yes, he was there."

"He's a good mate of mine."

"It's funny," I say, "I have an urge to go home and listen to it again."

"I'm not surprised, given what we play here."

"No, I'm being serious. I can't explain it. There was something about it - something that made me think about my life."

"It's called music, Nick. It's what it's supposed to do."

"Then why doesn't it? Why are we sneering at the hits from 1974? Why do we have no attachment to the current chart fodder?" I ask rhetorically.

Dave doesn't do rhetorically.

He girds up his cheeks before answering. "Because we're broken. We're old and past it. So, whereas we used to dream and aspire, now we scoff and resent. We hang on to a thread of belief, that if we'd only had the breaks, we could do a better job. Essentially, we've turned into our parents.

"We're musically bitter, because we never made it. I never got a recording deal, and toured the world, and shagged loads of women.

"You never got poached by the BBC, and did the Road Show, and shagged loads of women.

"We're here, on local radio in Brakeshire, doing a show next to nobody gives a shit about.

"Think about it. We're on air for two hours. About an hour and a quarter of that is spent playing music we don't like, and you talk for approximately ten minutes - when you're not in the toilet. The rest is adverts for things we don't understand or give a shit about, the weather that anyone up at this hour of the day either doesn't give a shit about, or is actually out in and knows better than we do, and the news everyone knows anyway from the internet.

"We serve no worthwhile purpose. We're dinosaurs. Obsolete. Fuddy-duddy wankers, sitting here pretending we're conveyers of good taste and vital information, every single bit of which is at people's fingertips in a much more convenient way. And, unlike with us, they can skip the tracks they don't like and listen to the ones they do, all whilst checking the weather, news, and researching

products they're actually fucking interested in. You're back on in thirty."
"You make it all sound so romantic, Dave."
"It was. Once."
"What happened?"
"Shit happened."
"So, why do we continue to do it?"
He thinks about his response. "Money, in a word. And because, honestly - what the fuck would we do if we didn't?"
"Oh, and because we love it. This - being on the air, spinning the shit tunes, having the banter. There's nothing better. Five seconds."
Suzi Quatro's 'Devil Gate Drive' could almost be described as a few minutes of welcome respite, before Ringo's 'You're Sixteen'. Thereafter, Charlie Rich assaults our ears with 'The Most Beautiful Girl'.
Of course, I don't say that on the air.
Eventually, we reach Paper Lace. I sign off before the track can play, so I might remove my headphones and not have to listen to it.
"What have we got tomorrow, Dave?"
"Same shit. And the oldies are from the chart in March of 1976."
"It has to be better."
"Don't you bloody believe it."
"Well, what was the highest new entry?"
"Brotherhood Of Man. 'Save Your Kisses For Me'."
"Shit me backwards."

7.

It's just after six in the morning as I leave the building. Another fifteen minutes and the sun will rise.

It will rise, because I can see it lurking beneath the horizon, showing silver on the otherwise leaden sky.

Anticyclone Hartmut and Storm Emma have passed on, and it feels comparatively balmy, as I ride home on the 1984 metallic-blue Vespa I bought with my first radio wages.

Home.

It's a small semi in a quiet cul-de-sac in the north of Tredmouth, a few miles from the radio station building and the city centre.

It's the kind of place where everyone keeps an eye open for everyone else, but never has anything to do with anyone else. That, I think, was what drew me to it.

It was a little beyond the limit of what I could afford. Fifteen years on, and it remains so.

I'll be sixty in three months. Sixty!

Four more years until the mortgage is cleared.

I took a pay cut a few years ago to keep my job. It was in the aftermath of the financial crisis. Advertising dried up. I sensed my options were to take what was offered, or be let go.

What was offered was the two hour graveyard stint four mornings a week.

Despite telling myself that I did it for Dave, I did it for myself first and foremost. It defines me, my work. Without it, I'm Nick Cherry. With it, I'm The DJ Nick Cherry.

The bloke who used to do the DriveTime show.

There are twenty houses in the cul-de-sac; ten almost coupled pairs. They end at a strip of scrubby grass, on the far side of which a line of trees follow the bank of the river Tred.

Tredmouth is something of a misnomer, as such places are generally located at the coast. The 'mouth' of this river is formed by the fact it merges quite violently with a more significant waterway half a mile to the southwest.

Plenty have drowned in the undercurrents caused by such a meeting.

We walked along the river bank from the bus depot in Tredmouth, Sharon and I. We held hands and gabbled about the gig and how brilliant it was.

And we giggled as we relived pissing in my canteen, and the shenanigans we'd got up to on the coach home.

"I'm sorry about what happened," I told her.

"Do you really think I'm beautiful?" she asked, and it was the first time I'd witnessed any shyness in her, as she turned away and peered down off the bridge into the raging torrent of the river-merging.

Her show of vulnerability encouraged me. "I've loved you since I first saw you," I informed her meekly, speaking to her back.

"What are you going to do when you leave school?" she asked evasively.

"I'm going to be a Disc Jockey."

"What? On the radio, you mean?"

"Yes," I said with absolute certainty. "I make radio shows in my bedroom, on my cassette recorder. It has a microphone built in, so I speak into it, and record songs from records."

"What do you do that for?"

"It's practice, I suppose."

"Do you send them to people?"

"No. They're just for me. Anyway, I usually end up recording over what I've done, because tapes are quite expensive."

"Will you make one for me?"

"Yes. Of course," I happily told her.

"Shit, what do you think the time is?"

I looked up at the moon. "Not far off midnight."

She looked where I looked. "You can tell the time from the moon?"

I nodded as we walked on. Slowly. I didn't want the night to end.

"How? Isn't it in a different place every night?"

"Yes. It's not exact. But I know roughly from where it is."

"Do you have some kind of chart on your wall?"

Shaking my head, I smiled. "I have a picture of Marc Bolan on my wall."

I didn't tell her that I climbed out of my bedroom window most dry nights, and sat on the flat roof looking up at the sky.

Had I told her that, she would have asked me why.

And I couldn't have lied to Sharon, because I did genuinely love her. If you genuinely love someone, you should never lie to them.

Just as you should never come home from the pub and hit them, so they have to wear long sleeves and skirts all the time to hide the bruises, and tell the doctor that they've always been clumsy and are always banging into things and tripping over stuff.

And if you do that, the doctor tests your eyes, and decides you need glasses. That's why she was so clumsy. That explained it.

Mum was happy with her glasses and their broad tinted lenses. They covered up the bruises she sometimes had on her clumsy face.

Besides which, they stopped him punching her there, in case he should break the lenses and do some real damage.

No, I didn't want to tell Sharon any of that, and that I climbed out on the roof so I wouldn't have to hear it all going on.

"What fucking time do you call this?" my dad asked after Sharon had kissed me goodnight at the gate.

"Sorry. The bus was late."

"It's a fucking school night. If I'd have known, you wouldn't have gone."

"Sorry. Mum said it was okay."

"Who's the fucking boss in this house?"

"You are."

"And don't you forget it, you scrawny little shit," he growled in my face, his finger pointing.

I shook my head. I'd never forget that.

"Have you been drinking?" he then asked, as he snatched the canteen, unscrewed the top, sniffed it, and took a little sip.

He pulled a face and gave it back. "Is that bloody Dandelion And Burdock? Can't stand the stuff."

Mum popped her head round their bedroom door as I made my way to my room.

"Did you have a nice time, lovey?" she asked in her kindly way.

"It was brilliant, mum," I beamed back.

She smiled then, happy that I was happy.

And I felt her wince a little when I gave her a kiss and a hug goodnight.

8.

I play the unknown record as I stand at the window and watch the sun buff the day to a silver sheen.

Others might say grey, but I see silver.

That's optimism; that's a bit of hope.

It's not solid silver of a sterling type. It's silver plate that will tarnish and uglify if left exposed and neglected. But a bit of maintenance - an occasional polish - will keep it bright and cheerful enough to fool any casual observers.

My spirit in the sky!

Sharon blanked me at school the next day. That was okay, she was just being cool in front of her peers. After all, I saw the little playful twist of her mouth when I passed her and her gang in the corridor.

After school I ran from class to make sure I was ahead of her. And I walked slowly once I was, pausing to look at nothing of interest, as I waited for her to catch me up.

"Alright, Sharon?" I said when she did.

"Alright?" she replied.

I went to take her hand.

"What are you doing?" she snapped, pulling away.

"Nothing. I just thought... I thought we were together. I thought we might be boyfriend and girlfriend."

"Don't be daft," she said, but not nastily.

"But last night..."

"It was a laugh. That was all."

"But we're friends, right?" I almost pleaded.

She smiled and nodded. "Yes, but don't tell anybody."

And we walked on together.

I'd make her a tape - my radio show. I'd grow my hair and get a spiral perm like Marc Bolan. I'd try to get us tickets for another gig.

Strike while the iron's hot! Hot love! Get it on!

Despite being tired, I made a start on the show that very evening. To that end, I ate my tea and headed up to my room 'to do my homework'.

It was homework of sorts, now I look back on it, flicking through a cardboard box of singles I'd picked up or inherited, and spinning the A and B sides in search of tracks she'd like.

And when I had my playlist selected, I placed my cassette recorder in front of the speakers hooked up to my record player, and prepared to begin.

Dad was home from work, and he was shouting again. I couldn't record my show in that din, so I played the records anyway to drown it out, and thought about what I wanted to say - what I wanted to say to Sharon through them.

Many were from the fifties and sixties, given to me by my uncle Russ - my mother's brother - after he upgraded to LPs. He caught me looking through them on a visit to his house with mum.

They'd talk in hushed voices in the kitchen as they drank tea. It wasn't anything I should hear, so I'd be deposited in the sitting room with a fizzy drink from his SodaStream machine. I'd pick a different flavour every time, and I know the day I got the records I went for lime.

"Nicky, you shouldn't touch things without asking," mum said making me jump.

"He's alright," uncle Russ said.

"He does like his music. He must get it from our side of the family."

"You can have them, if you want. I never play them now."

"Really?" I asked with amazement.

He nodded. "Your birthday's coming up. Have them as a present."

"Thanks, uncle Russ."

There were a hundred and twelve records in total, which I carried home in the box they lived in. That would have been in 1971, when I turned thirteen. He methodically wrote his first name on each, either on the label or the paper sleeve.

So I played through my choices - The Beatles 'I Want To Hold Your Hand', and Yardbirds 'For Your Love', and T. Rex '20th Century Boy' to remind her that I was her toy.

As I did, I lay on the carpeted floor, and put my face where the tape recorder should have been, to drown out the noise. Not too loudly, though, so as not to incur his wrath.

And I waited to hear the thud of the front door slamming, indicating he'd finished his food and was heading to the pub, offering us three hours of respite.

Three hours in which to record an hour of tape, thirty minutes per side, hoping I'd worked the song lengths about right to neatly fill them.

Thud!

My finger went to work, manually winding the tape forward until the brown of the recordable part just began to show through the gap in the top.

In it went, the clunky play and record buttons pressed down in unison, before instantly sliding left and hitting the pause button.

Good to go.

The Beatles were cued up on my record player, the worn out needle descending - crackles and a pop, like uncle

Russ's SodaStream - and releasing the pause as I let the music play the show in.

Watching and listening, as the stylus worked its way, knowing the track so well that I knew precisely when to turn the volume and speak into the built-in microphone, every breath captured atmospherically, as my broken but occasionally fluctuating voice announced:

- *The Beatles with 'I Want To Hold Your Hand', starting off this show especially for Sharon. She knows why I played that one! This is Nicky 'Cherry Picker' Cherry, and next we have The Yardbirds, and 'Love Me Do'... fuck it, fuck it, fuck it. 'For Your Love'!*

Stop.

Rewind.

Being that early in proceedings, it was simpler to begin again than attempt to edit over my error. I wrote the bands and song titles in my book to help eradicate mistakes. And so I wouldn't duplicate when I made her shows in the future.

I was nervous, having never recorded anything other than for myself before. It was for Sharon, and it had to be perfect.

On I went, finding a bit of a rhythm, probably saying a similar thing between every track, the time passing so quickly - oblivious to its passage, thanks to my total absorption in my task.

The phone rang at some point, picked up by the mic, forcing me to begin that track again. Not quite lining things up correctly, clipping off the last couple of seconds of Bowie's 'Andy Warhol'.

She wouldn't notice.

An hour and a half after starting, I neared the end of side one. Removing the cassette, I thought there would be enough room for The Who's 'I Can't Explain'.

There wasn't.

I covered it with an instrumental - 'Wonderful Land' by The Shadows - which I faded out when my nerve got the better of me, counting down the ninety seconds of space I had left.

- *Sharon's show continues on the other side. See you there!*

A tap came on my door.

"Hey, bedtime," mum said, and smiled at me so her cheeks pushed out like a hamster's. "Come on. You had a late night last night."

I switched everything off as mum went and stood by my window.

By the time I'd used the loo and brushed my teeth, I expected her to be gone, but she was still there. She was holding my notebook. I blushed at her seeing what I'd written. Most of it was about Sharon. I usually hid it in the lid of my record player.

With her back to me as she faced the window, she said, "are you happy, Nicky?"

"Yes," was my instant reply.

I was. In that moment, I was so blindly happy. The previous night with Sharon was tangibly fresh in my mind, hanging around in my mouth like a boiled sweet after you've eaten it. I'd been to see T. Rex. I'd had almost-sex with the most beautiful girl at school.

What was there not to be happy about?

"You wouldn't want to move away, would you?" she asked next.

"Away from Tredmouth?"

"Yes," she confirmed.

"No. I've got my exams soon. And all my friends are at school."

Sharon, Sharon, Sharon...

"I know," she agreed, and laid my notebook gently on top of my record player. "Come on, get into bed, cheeky lad."

She, too, seemed happy in that moment.

"Who was on the phone?" I asked her, remembering the call from half an hour or so before.

"Nobody. Wrong number," she shrugged, and leant down to kiss me goodnight.

"I love you," she added, but I didn't respond because I was fifteen, and all the love I had to offer was Sharon's alone.

Mum flicked off the light as she left my room, and I lay there wondering if it might have been Sharon on the phone.

Tiredness caught up and overtook me. For once, I didn't hear dad come home from the pub. If there was any arguing between them, I was, unusually, oblivious to it.

Rather, the steady thrum of a coach on a damp road lulled me, and in my mind's eye, I looked down myself to see Sharon's lips slipping up and down me.

When I awoke, it was morning. I got up, washed and dressed, ate my cereals and headed off to school, just as I did on any other day.

Except that day would be like no other day.

9.

Lying in bed, I listen to the sounds of activity outside as the day-lit world continues without me.

I don't bother to put the radio on.

The time after arriving home was whiled away by routine. A cup of instant coffee at half past seven; another with food an hour on. Two hours were spent checking email and tinkering around on the internet, all of which could have been accomplished in five minutes.

At eleven, I headed upstairs, my alarm set for seven in the evening. Eight hours set aside for sleep, because I can't think of a better use for a third of my time on this earth.

The reality is, I sleep for perhaps five or six of those hours. The remainder are used up in attempting to pinpoint the precise moment at which my life went awry.

The song on the unknown record lingers in my head; the simple three note melody is now ingrained. From that, a fourth note is added, and the harmonious part is revealed to me as a result.

In an attempt to shake it from my mind, I force myself to think of another song. But I can't get a fix on anything, and the unknown remains hauntingly to the fore.

It was a Wednesday, the day after I began the radio show for Sharon. As a result, the afternoon was allocated to sport. Being winter, more precisely, it was given over to rugby.

I stood on the wing, avoiding the fifteen opposing players, as I waited for the ball to be thrown to me. Ninety percent of the time, I'd manage to catch it without fumbling and knocking on. And when I did, I'd run - because one thing I could do was run.

I'd run until an opponent got too close and threatened to make a tackle, at which point I'd blindly toss the ball infield, nearly always managing to avoid a forward pass. I knew most of the rules.

Sometimes, more often than one might imagine, my team would score a try, or otherwise gain advantage through that. Further, once every other match, I'd score a try if no opposition player got close enough. Thus, I was considered a handy winger to have on your side.

I was never picked first from the line of lads stood shivering on the touchline. But neither did I remain there to the stage where captains are asking the teacher if they can play a man short rather than take what's left.

Being January 30th, there was barely a blade of grass on the field. The wet start to the year, and almost daily use, had resulted in a quagmire, particularly in the middle of the pitch. It meant I was set to see plenty of the ball.

It was my most glorious day in a striped jersey. I glided to a hat-trick, as heavy-legged lads twice my size slithered and slid in my wake.

Pats on my back from teammates did more damage that afternoon than any opponent. The PE teacher shook my hand at the end.

Even the shower didn't phase me, as I washed the filth from my body in tepid water - a newfound confidence swelling me, as I depicted Sharon's luscious lips wrapped around me.

A skip cockified my walk home - a different route, as the field wasn't attached to the school. I'd get home, wait for dad to head out to the pub, and finish the tape. I'd give it to Sharon at school the next day, and she'd listen to it that night. On the Friday, we could discuss it on our walk home. Perhaps we'd meet up over the weekend.

Valentine's Day was only two weeks away.

Home. Changed out of my uniform. My kit dropped by the back door for mum to wash.

I remember it all so vividly - the layout of the house; the smell of it; the sounds it made.

Dad was at work. Mum wasn't in. It wasn't unusual. With me being early, she was probably at the shops. Perhaps she popped in to see uncle Russ or one of her friends.

Sharon...

Locking the bathroom door, I masturbated into the sink. It was a 'just in case'. I'd stay on top of such things, so I'd have some staying power the next time.

Semen congealed as water met it. I pushed it down the plug with my fingers.

I wrote the inlay card for the tape, drawing a cartoon title on one side - 'Cherry-Picked For Sharon: Episode One'.

Would I get to pick her cherry? Had she 'done it' with anybody else? She must have done. She was seventeen, after all.

Losing track of time once again. Engrossed.

The sun set at ten to five, or thereabouts. That was ages before - not long after I got in. I became aware of my hunger.

The front door opened and closed. That unmistakable rattle it made as a result of all the angry slammings.

"Mum?" I called out, as my socks rode the stairs.

"Where is she?" my dad asked.

A glance at the clock in the hall told me it was just after six.

"I don't know. I haven't seen her."

"What time did you get in?"

"Half four. PE."

"You've not seen her since you got home?"

"No."

"Where is the fucking stupid bitch?"

"I don't know."

"She'll be at Russ's. Lost track of time again, I expect. Dopey cow."

Dad went to the phone and dialled the number, messing it up in his haste, as he impatiently span the next digit before the last one could complete.

"Is Pauline there...? Has she been there...? Then where is she...?"

Springing back, I leapt up two steps.

The phone was suddenly smashing into the wall, the main body breaking as it did, and the receiver bouncing away and stretching the coiled cord. When it reached its maximum, it crawled back along the hallway.

Dad ran from the kitchen to the living room as I stayed out of his way. He pushed by me, and bounded up the stairs.

A door hit a wall.

And then an awful, ominous silence.

The few minutes I stood there waiting were as terrifying as anything I'd experienced in life.

In the end, I went to find him.

He was sat on the bed. The ceiling light was on, and the curtains open.

In his hand was a letter.

I took it as he held it out to me, and I read.

'...gone... cruel... hate... someone else... kind... love... don't try to find me... look after Nicky...'

In the uncovered window, I saw my own reflection. White with shock and fear.

"Now you know what a whore your mother is," dad said, before screwing the letter up and walking to the toilet.

I stood in the hall and listened to him urinate. He washed his hands and face in the sink, violently lathering soap.

Emerging, he asked, "have you eaten?"

I shook my head.

He gave me some loose change. "Go up the chippy and get yourself something."

"Do you want any?" I offered.

"No. I've got some stuff to do."

And he descended the stairs and left the house.

When he got in from the pub a few hours later, I made sure I was in bed. I pretended to be asleep when he stuck his head round my door.

And I never did finish the cassette for Sharon.

As I lie here with the unknown song playing in my head, my wish is not for any of that day to be altered.

After all, I couldn't blame my mum for leaving. Any ruefulness I feel stems from her not taking me with her.

No, my regret is more animalistic and basic in nature. I wish I'd had sex with Sharon on the bus two nights before, as we'd travelled back from Birmingham.

I wish I'd finished the cassette, and that she'd been my girlfriend.

I wish I'd had the confidence.

Had that happened, I don't think I'd have cared so much about everything else.

The thought accompanies me as I drift off to sleep...

10.

...I'm having sex with Sharon on the back seat of the bus, my jeans and undies half way down my thighs - my mouth pressed onto hers as she uses her feet to pull me to her rhythmically.

I'm in situ. This is vivid - this is real.

The scent of sex and her vodka-orange breath in my nostrils. The wetness of her coats my scrotum, and her blue eyes look wildly into mine.

A clash of our teeth as the bus lurches through a lane-change, as we bottle up any sounds so we won't be discovered.

I don't last long.

Sharon clamps her hand over my mouth to hold in my moan, and she begins to giggle before I'm completely spent.

I don't pull away, because I never want to pull away. I want to stay here forever. Just here. Like this.

Nothing in my life is more important than this right now.

I wonder if it ever has been?

We alight in Tredmouth, and walk along the river to the point where two water-worlds collide.

"I've loved you since I first saw you," I tell her, and she shyly turns away and looks over the railing.

"What are you going to do when you leave school?" she asks evasively.

"I'm going to be a Disc Jockey."

"What? On the radio, you mean?"

"Yes," I tell her with absolute certainty. "And I'm going to marry you."

She giggles and bows her head down self-consciously.

"Shit, what do you think the time is?" she asks suddenly
I look up at the moon. "It's gone half eleven. About quarter to midnight."

She looks where I looked. "You can tell the time from the moon?"

I nod.

"How? Isn't it in a different place every night?"

"Yes. It's not exact. But I know roughly from where it is."

"You're clever, aren't you? There's a depth to you," she says, and we walk on picking up the pace.

We part at the end of my road. A brief snog, and on our way; school the next day.

I push through the gate, jog the path, and let myself in.

A raised voice. His, as always, shouting at her. Calling her names. Awful names. I think about heading straight upstairs. I don't think they heard me come in.

No, though. I want to let mum know I'm home safely. She'll worry.

So I walk along the hall, but pause a moment before stepping round the door.

She doubles up as his fist meets her stomach. There's panic in her eyes as she struggles to breathe.

"Leave her!"

It takes a second for it to register, the fact it was me who said it.

It's about me, the fight. I heard my name. More specifically, it's about why I'm out so late. Mum tried to defend me - herself, too - saying how I was fifteen, sixteen in a few months. That I was with an older girl; that she was looking after me.

Dad won't listen. He never listens. It's just an excuse. If it wasn't me being out, it would be something else.

"What did you say?" he snarls.

At the same time, mum wheezes, "get up to bed, Nicky."

"Leave her alone," I repeat.

I'm shaking. Partly with anger, partly with fear.

He pushes her away, and she stumbles and bangs her head on the radiator.

He's coming for me. Fists clenched. Mouth tight. Shoulders hunched.

I see the drink in his narrow eyes - it's in the way they catch the light, and it's in the redness of the whites.

He's not big, but he's solid. Lugging and tugging all day at work. Loading and unloading. Doing what he does to earn enough to keep a roof over our heads, and food in our bellies.

Just about.

Drink comes first, though.

Uncle Russ bails mum out when there's a shortfall. Mum always says she'll pay him back, but I don't think she does. Even if she tries, he won't take it. 'Keep that for yourself. Treat yourself and Nicky,' he tells her.

I think about that as dad's fist connects with my head. I duck and try to cover up, so it's more of a glancing blow. Just enough to make me sink to one knee.

Mum's now telling him to leave me alone.

He turns and swats her away.

As he does, I push up and pile-drive myself into his midriff.

Drunk and unsteady, he almost topples, but uses me to keep himself upright.

He has a hold of me, his fist pummelling the back of my neck and head.

I should have pushed on when he was teetering. He'd have gone down, but it's too late now.

Mum's shouting. I'm trying not to cry. Dad is silent in his assault.

Down I go, mostly in an attempt to escape the blows. It's the only way I can go. Gravity takes me there.

He kicks, then. His shoes are on. Into my ribs. Thwack, thwack, thwack.

Curl up. Roll away. On he goes, bruising my spine and kidneys.

"Had enough, you puny little bastard?" he asks, pausing his barrage.

I won't give him the satisfaction of an answer.

I wish I was a bastard, because then he wouldn't be my dad.

Having no dad would be better than having this dad.

"Let that be a lesson to you," he ends with, and leaves the room.

Mum and I don't speak as I raise myself. She's sat with her back to the radiator. It's cold, despite the winter. He likes to save money for the drink.

We look at each other, mum and I, in the dim light of one bulb beneath a dense lamp shade - once cream, but now yellow with nicotine.

My lower back throbs. I have a stabbing pain in my flank.

Mum reaches for her glasses. They're in one piece as she slides them onto her face with a tremulous hand.

It's only then that she cries. It's as if she needs to hide any tears behind a screen.

"School tomorrow. Bedtime, lovey," she says.

Her voice is normal despite her tears. Her inflection is almost bright and cheery.

I don't know how she does it.

Or maybe I do...

...a jolt passes through me - a white fizzing in my head...

...I'm on the rugby field, wide on the wing. It's hard to tell who's on which side, such is the mud caking thirty boys.

Infield a little I go, into the quaggy mire, looking for the ball.

It's not like me. But I'm not like me. Not any more.

Not since I fucked Sharon on the bus. Everybody fancies Sharon. But I'm the only person to fuck her on a bus.

As far as I know.

Besides, I told her I was going to marry her, and she didn't say no.

And I made a tape for her - a C60. Filled with tunes I like and thought she might like. I stayed up late finishing it. It didn't matter. I wouldn't have slept anyway. Not with the way Sharon felt when I was inside her so fresh in my mind.

And not with the bruises on my body from the beating I took.

Dad was absent. He didn't even come home for his tea last night. He went straight to the pub. Mum and I agreed that was a good thing.

And when he came home, he sat in the dark smoking until he fell asleep in the chair.

Mum got a good night's sleep for once.

Sharon loved the tape when I gave it to her in the corridor after assembly. It didn't matter that there were loads of people around.

She smiled, slipped it in her bag, and kissed me on the mouth with her bulbous, gorgeous lips. In front of anyone caring to look.

I'd seen her other lips. Just as pink. Just as pouty.

Slipping and sliding on the infield, those big lads too stupid to push out wide where the terra firma is firmer.

Me, daring to venture infield, because I am the man. I am different. I stood up to my dad. To save my mum a beating,

I took it for her. I'm growing up, and the day is coming - a day when I'll be bigger than him. Then I'll deal with him. Give him a taste of his own medicine.

I'll put a stop to it. For my mum, I'll do that.

We'd be better off alone than with him. Uncle Russ will help.

The ball sticks in the mud - scooped up - a boy going down - more a man, really. With trunkish legs covered with dark hair.

He manages to release it, a looping ball in my direction that the wind catches and almost carries over my head. But I get my hand behind it and snatch it down to the safety of my belly where my other hand coddles it.

And I'm off, my lightness not bogging me down, heading out wide where a little green remains.

Aching from the beating less than forty-eight hours before, but untouchable because of Sharon and what we did. What we will do again. Every night when we're married. Twice a night. And when we feel like it during the day.

Crunch, as a tackle comes in - the squirmy ball going in to touch. Before I follow it. A man-boy propelling me, eight or nine months older than me, because I was born in the summer.

Landing on clammy earth; the man-boy landing on me. And another, unable to stop himself with all the mud in his studs.

I was a stud. It was less than two days ago, since Sharon and I on the bus!

That glorious Monday night on our way back from Birmingham. T. Rex were brilliant. I'll never forget that night.

My first time. My first time for so many things.

Oh, the pain in my flank and back!

Bruises forming already. On top of bruises formed.

I'm not like this. I'm not like my father.

I'm like my mother. Soft, really. Caring and sensitive.

But I am half him. I see it in my face. In the mirror. The bits of him I inherited.

And I think the thoughts sometimes. They're the thoughts I imagine he has.

Blood in my mouth. I must have bitten the inside of my cheek when the impact came.

A whistle blowing. The teacher coming over.

He reaches out and takes my hand. Helps me to my feet.

Shaky legs. The ground not quite where it should be.

"Go and get cleaned up," he says, so I walk over to the changing room.

A tepid shower. Slightly warmer than usual, because I'm the only one using the water.

I don't rub myself. It hurts too much. Rather, I let the water cleanse me as best it can, the pressure too weak to rid me of it all.

The redness of my spittle lessens with every rinse, until it runs clear into the drain.

In a mirror I see my body. The bit of me that was inside her. It droops limply now, too tired to raise its head.

I look at that and think of her in my narcissism, because it stops me seeing and feeling the bruises.

Oh, I'm tired.

Two late nights are catching up on me.

I'll linger a while - try to catch Sharon leaving school so we can walk home together.

Better still, I'll head home, get changed, then meet up with her.

Her rosebud lips on mine - that's all I need. That'll set me right, and inject a bit of energy.

The quiet suits my mood, as I cut through the allotments. No activity this time of year. Sheds are locked as plots show brown over green.

A lone robin regards me from atop a fence post. I try to whistle, but my lips won't form the shape. A rush of air is all that escapes me - a lungful I replenish with a greedy gulp of frigidness.

Ah, the stabbing pain in my side once more.

Is this how my mum feels all the time?

Home.

Mum's not in. Perhaps she called in at uncle Russ's, or one of her friends. She might be down the shops, getting something for tea.

Dad's at work.

Good. I want to be alone.

I'm never alone. Not really. I have my music and my dreams. And now I have Sharon. They consume me fully. There's no room for anything else.

Last night, mum came into my room and asked me if I'd want to move away from Tredmouth.

Of course I don't. Sharon, Sharon, Sharon!

My whole life is here. That's what I told her, in a roundabout way.

She told me she loved me, my mum. But it isn't her I want to hear those words from.

And no sooner had she left my room, than I got out of bed and finished the tape.

My filthy kit gets dropped by the back door for mum to wash ready for next week.

The calendar catches my eye - one from dad's work depicting a forklift truck. It's Valentine's Day in two weeks.

I'll get a card for Sharon, and make her another radio show. I'll save my dinner money for a new cassette.

Standing at the toilet, I urinate with my head tipped back.

It's so dark, my piss, when I look back down. Was there some cleaning stuff in the water?

Flush it all away.

I undress and lie on my bed, the curtains open, but the scant grey light can barely penetrate the glass in the window.

My eyes close. So tired.

There's no heating on as usual, and I'm cold. Shiveringly cold.

I mummify myself in my bedding, tucking it under me so the air can't creep in - my head down so my warm breaths can be recycled and put to good use.

And I think about Sharon.

Dozing.

Waking.

Dark outside.

Sodden with sweat, yet so gelid. My mouth dry.

A breath leaves me.

It feels like my final breath.

Dozing. Waking. Dozing. Waking.

An explosion of pain in my side!

I moan out loud, but there's nobody present to hear it.

Where's mum? She should be home by now.

Where's dad?

The moon briefly shows its face, and tells me it's gone nine. Nearer half past.

Rolling from my bed, I shuffle through to their bedroom - tiny steps with the bedding swaddling me.

I use my shoulder to flick the switch. The stark bulb hanging from the ceiling illuminates, scarring my vision.

On the bedside unit on his side I spy an envelope.

I tear it open, my eyes having trouble focusing.

'...gone... cruel... hate... someone else... kind... love... don't try to find me... look after Nicky...'

Dad must have gone straight to the pub again.

The phone. The phone becomes my focus.

It's in the hallway downstairs. I'll call uncle Russ.

Crawling. My naked body exposed as the bedding falls away from me.

Reaching the top of the stairs and closing my eyes.

So tired.

So terribly cold.

Sharon...

- *you've been listening to the Nicky Cherry Show. Thanks for tuning in! That's all we have time for. Bye!*

...a jolt and a fizzy white flash across my brain...

Sucking in a breath my body desperately needs - the force of it sitting me upright.

And I wake up a millisecond before the moment of my own death.

11.

"Morning, Nick."

"Morning, Dave."

"You look like shit," he points out.

"Do I?" I ask, knowing full-well that I do, but still checking my reflection in the monitor on the desk. "Just tired, I think. I didn't get much sleep. Or I got too much sleep. I'm not sure which."

"It's all in the mind, tiredness. See, I've conditioned my body over many years."

I look at his body through the glass. It doesn't seem very conditioned. He's waiting for me to ask.

"Conditioned it to do what, Dave?"

"To go without sleep. I can function perfectly well on three hours a day."

"What do you do with the other twenty-one hours?"

"Not much. Too fucking knackered. Right, we have the oldies from March 1976, which are shit. Fortunately, it'll blend well with the current chart music shitness!"

"Try not to attribute every song to Ed Sheeran. Chuck in Taylor Swift every once in a while. Or Lady Gaga and Coldplay. Particularly if it sounds like a woman.

"We have a while. Name five songs with the word sleep in the title."

Dave does this. I don't know why. It's just something he does.

"The Lion Sleeps Tonight."

"By?"

"Oh, erm, give me a sec. Tight Fit, was it? But that was a cover. A doo-wop group…"

"The Tokens. You're shit. I'll give it you, though. Next one?"

"Cheer Up Sleepy Jean."

"Nope. That's a lyric. I said title."

"Okay. 'I Dream To Sleep' by H2O."

"Yep. Try to get out the eighties. Same goes for your dress sense."

"'Sleepy Maurice'. Marc Bolan and T. Rex."

"Oooh, obscure. Very good. You and your Bolan!"

"Pretenders, 'I Go To Sleep'. And before you ask, Ray Davies."

"Ker-chung! Yes. That's four. One more..."

"Beatles. 'I'm Only Sleeping'."

"Get in. Good man."

"I had this weird dream yesterday," I tell him, as I fiddle with the setting on my chair. "Whoever's using this studio before me must have a very odd posture."

"I have weird dreams sometimes."

"In the three hours you sleep every day?"

"No. They come when I'm awake."

"They're not really dreams, are they? They're just things you imagine," I point out.

"Same thing."

Is he right? Is that all they were - imaginings prompted by yesterday's thoughts?

It felt like more. It felt real. As though I was allowed an insight into how life would had panned out, had that one element been altered - had I had more confidence stemming from sex with Sharon.

Someone once told me - if you dream you die, you will die.

It felt close.

Dave interrupts. "One minute to name five song titles with the word 'dream' in. Go."

"H2O, 'I Dream To Sleep'."

"You had that for 'sleep'. Doesn't count."

"Depeche Mode, 'Dreaming Of Me'. The Jam, 'Dreams Of Children'. Small Faces, 'I'm Only Dreaming'. Roy Orbison, 'Dream Baby (How Long Must I Dream?)'."

"One more."

"No. Roy Orbison has it twice."

"Only counts as one."

"Okay, how long?"

"Fifteen seconds."

"Erm... Ha! Marc Bolan And T. Rex, 'Teenage Dream'."

"It's always Bolan with you. Unbelievable! Five seconds. Four... Three..."

- *Morning. Thanks for being here. This is Nick Cherry, on Tred FM. No, this is not a dream, and you are not asleep. We're live on the air, with Dave in the chair getting it all out there.*

- *Send us your texts and emails, and tell us what you're doing on this mild, but damp early morning.*

- *Here's some tunage to ruffle your plumage!*

"Fucking hell! Are you alright, Nick?"

"Yes, Dave. Why?"

"Well, that was a bit... Keen, I suppose."

"I've decided it's time we injected a bit of personality into this show."

"Juxtaposed with the music we play?"

I ignore him and say, "as a kid, this is all I wanted to do with my life - to be on the radio playing music. At least I still get to do that."

"You're living your dream," he says flatly.

"I'm serious..."

"I know," he interrupts. "I wasn't having a pop. You're doing what you always wanted to do, since as far back as you can remember. That's great."

"It is, isn't it?"

"Yes. What's brought all this on?" he asks.

"I'm not sure. Turning sixty in three months is probably playing on my mind."

"Don't believe what you hear about that. Nothing changes. It's just another day," he informs me sagely.

Then he adds, "you'll still wake up with a hard-on, and that's all that truly matters in life.

"Right, I'll bring you in over the end of this song, so we don't have to listen to it all. Back on in five. A quid for every time you slip in the word 'cock'!"

- *That one's riding high on this week's chart, which I'm sure they'll be cock-a-hoop about.*

- *Speaking of the chart, later this morning we'll be taking you back, back, back in time - sponsored by Knight & Day antique timepieces - as we run through the chart from this very week in 1976, which producer Dave is cockily predicting will be a good one.*

- *he's pretty cock-sure you'll enjoy it!*

- *where were you, what were you doing? Drop us a line and let us know, what was going on forty-two years ago!*

"Nicely done!"

"Thank you. Oh, I actually quite like this song!"

"Wonders will never cease!"

"Who is it again?"

"Portugal The Man. It's on the screen in front of you."

Time was, I'd dance around the studio. It was energising. Now I rely on Dave to whip me in to shape with his daft questions. I think he does it to get my brain ticking - get the blood pumping.

He's a good Producer. As good as I've known. He should be on a better show than this one, really.

And he stays informed. He's far more current than me.

But you wouldn't know any of that to look at him. That's his trouble. The newbies won't touch him on their primetime shows. They blank him in the corridor.

Yet, when it comes to music and the technical side of things, he could wipe the floor with all of us.

Despite seemingly complaining all the time, he never actually complains. He's happy with his lot in life.

If I were to lend him the unknown record, and it invited him to reflect in the way it has me, I honestly don't believe he could think of anything he'd change in his life.

Change: Make different, alter or modify. Convert from one state, form or substance into another. Replace something with something else.

Sharon changed me. But not too much, I now see.

Mum leaving changed me. But I cannot sit here and wish she hadn't gone. I would have feared for her, had she remained.

My confidence took a knock after she left. There's no doubt about that. I went into my shell, and gave up on Sharon.

It highlighted issues I have with abandonment. Thus, I feigned disinterest, because I could see that she was too good for me, and would meet someone better one day, and leave me.

Just as mum had.

12.

- *1976, a year synonymous with punk! That was Barry White with the biggest climber, up to fifteen from forty-three with 'You See The Trouble With Me?'*
- *Yes I do.*
- *Highest new entry, straight in at number fourteen - Brotherhood Of Man and 'Save Your Kisses For Me'.*

"Shouldn't Barry be a new entry, Dave, if it was outside the top forty?"

"It's what came up on the computer."

"I might go to the toilet," I say.

"Can I come?"

I don't go to the toilet. Rather, I stride down the corridor, off which sit the three broadcasting studios. There's not a soul around. My steps are silent on the carpet-tiled floor.

The live broadcast isn't piped through the building as it once was. Nobody cares to listen.

In reception, I startle a lone nightwatchman.

"Can I help you?" he asks.

"No, back in a tick," I tell him, and leave him to the television show re-run he's watching on his phone.

Pushing through the door, I emerge into the night, a drizzle hanging in the air. I'm in a light jumper, but not cold.

A milkman fizzes by in his electric cart. You don't see many milkmen these days. He pulls up at the building next door, the radio playing in his cab.

"Morning," I say.

"Morning," he replies, a crate rising in his hands with a rattle.

"I'm Nick Cherry. The DJ," I volunteer, and point at the studio next door.

He looks nonplussed as he stands with the crate at waist height.

"What are you listening to?" I go with next.

"An audiobook. On CD. I don't bother much with the radio this time of night."

"Ha!" I snicker, and watch him press a button by way of gaining access. "Won't you miss the story?" I ask, the CD still playing away.

"No, I've read the book. It's just a bit of company," he chuckles, and pushes his shoulder against the door when it buzzes.

Walking on a few yards, I pass along three cars on the taxi rank. No music drifts out from them. One of the drivers sits staring at his phone. Another talks into his. The third stands outside smoking a cigarette.

He drops it and twists his foot, before bending and picking it up in his hand. Discarding it in a bin, he walks the few yards back to his car. The door opens, and no music reaches my ears.

Nobody listens to the radio anymore.

I rush back to the building, the nightwatchman pressing pause on his screen, before rising to let me in.

A short dash along the corridor, the breeze caused by my speed playing on the moisture coating my face.

A glow on my ears in the heat of the studio - left for love, right for spite - both aglow!

My ears, the best of my senses; the thing in which I've always had faith.

I'm a listener.

Listening to Dave through my luminous lugs. "You cut it fine. Why are you all wet and breathless? Pissing upside down again? Tell me in a minute. Ten seconds till you're on air. Fatback Band just finishing, then link straight into number nine, Guys'n'Dolls, 'You Don't Have To Say You Love Me'. I bet you're glad you rushed."

"A computer could present this show," I say following my minimal fuss spiel. "A pre-programmed robot could do all that we do."

"This sounds dangerous."

"We're making ourselves redundant, Dave. Where's the personality? Where's the freshness?"

"I don't like the sound of this..."

"What's the back-in-time chart for tomorrow?"

"Erm, 1977."

"Actually, that might be a good one," I concede.

Dave raises his eyebrows at me through the window.

His expression is explained by, "biggest climber - Cliff, 'My Kinda Life'. Highest new entry, Boney M."

"In 1977?"

He nods his head. He looks like he wants to cry.

"At least Showaddywaddy were up to number six from nineteen, helping to push Leo Sayer's 'When I Need You' down to number seven," he adds considerably more brightly.

"I was eighteen in March '77, soon to be nineteen, and I didn't buy any of those singles! Why are they doing this?"

"Do you really want to know?" Dave asks.

"Yes!" I reply against my better judgement.

He fortifies himself with a shoulder-shuffle and a deep breath, which he uses to say, "because it's where the money is, or so they think. It's all based on spending power tied to advertising, and the fact that some tit in an office has worked out on a computer that our average listener is between fifty and sixty-five, mostly still earning and with disposable cash sitting in the bank. So they look at that age-range, born in the fifties and sixties, and play to them by picking charts from their teenage years.

"But here's where it all falls down. We're in that range. We are the people they're trying to appeal to. Where they get it wrong is that we didn't buy those records - our parents did, and they're mostly in the ground, or not spending much because they don't see any point.

"They almost certainly wouldn't listen to this show at three in the fucking morning, because they're not awake even if they happen to still be alive.

"The people who would potentially listen to this show are just like you and me, and, as you correctly state, we were hardly buying any of the shit in the charts, and we wouldn't have done even if we'd had some fucking money back then.

"Their algorithm is all fucked up. You have to get to the eighties, or very late seventies, or go back to the sixties, before the chart becomes relevant in those terms, but, far more importantly, how did you manage to piss on yourself? You're back on in ten seconds..."

13.

- 'Manuel & The Music of the Mountains' by Rodrigo's Guitar Concerto de Aranjuez, sliding down the slippery slope one place to number five this week in 1976.
- We'll be back in a few minutes, as we go from the mountains to the Ocean, before C W comes McCalling!

"So, what do you want to do?" Dave asks as an advert for a local carpet cleaning service runs. Followed by one for absorbent underwear.

"Theme it!"

"Come again?"

"A dozen songs that are somehow linked. Come on, we do it all the time. Pick a topical subject. You heard the news."

"They reckon Toys'R'Us is going to close down."

"That was the main news story?" I ask dubiously.

"It was the one I paid attention to."

"There you go! In honour of Toys'R'Us, we give you songs about toys! Visage, 'Mind Of A Toy'. Your turn."

"Boomtown Rats, 'Like Clockwork'."

"Write them down, Dave. Write them down."

"We might get into trouble, Nick."

"Nobody's listening. It doesn't matter. I'm as sure as I can be that nobody will even notice! And, if they do, so what? We apologise, make some excuse, and go back to the music we were playing before."

He's not sure. He needs this job. As do I.

By way of reassurance, I tell him, "I'll say I made you do it. Okay?"

He nods. "Small Faces, 'Tin Soldier'."

"Donovan, 'Little Tin Soldier'."

"He only had one leg."

"It's true. It was tragic. John's Children, 'Come And Play With Me In The Garden'."

"Hey, what about Carl Perkins, 'Matchbox'?" he throws in.

"Oooh, I like it! Lateral thinking. Elvis, 'Teddy Bear'."

"Genesis, 'The Musical Box'. It'll give you time to go to the toilet."

"We could just play all of Family's 'Music In A Doll's House'."

We grin at one another through the glass screen.

It'll never happen, any of it. Tomorrow morning, we'll play the chart from March of 1977 as programmed.

1977.

"What were you doing in '77, Dave?"

"That was the year I settled down."

"How come?"

"I turned twenty-two and met the missus."

"As simple as that?"

"Oh yes. Forty-one years we've been together, and I love her today as much as I did the day I met her."

"But yesterday you were saying about making it in the music business, touring the world and shagging loads of women," I remind him.

"In the context of music and 1974 and 1976, yes. But now we're talking '77. The world had changed. My world changed at least, the instant I met my Tina."

"She was a dancer, wasn't she?"

"Yep. She did a few of the music shows back in the day. She was the best dancer out of all of them, but they'd always hide her away at the back."

"How come?"

"She had terrible teeth and couldn't afford to get them fixed. And she was no classic beauty, I must concede.

They'd tell her not to smile, but she couldn't help herself. She's always been such a happy person. And she had a body to die for!"

He's lucky, Dave. I've never had any doubt that he loves his wife. And that Tina loves him.

"You're lucky, you are," I decide to tell him.

"It's nothing to do with luck," he says seriously.

"Well, it..."

"I made smart decisions, and I knew a good thing when I saw it. That's not luck. I knew what I wanted in life, and I went for it."

That, I reason, is where we differ. Other than being a DJ, I've never really known what I've wanted from life.

I've always been consumed by the belief there were opportunities I failed to grasp.

But what if it's the other way round? What if there's something I actually did that I'd have been better off not doing?

"What do you wish you hadn't done in life, Dave?"

"Nothing."

"Nothing?"

"No. It's all a journey, see. It all leads you to where you are."

"So, no regrets?" I push on.

"Walker Brothers! Tom Rush wrote it. No, to answer your question. No regrets."

1976 was the year I left school, almost exactly on my eighteenth birthday. It had been hellish living with dad, but I'd got through it. An impending sense of freedom came with it.

That day - the day I turned eighteen - it was gloriously hot. A Saturday was spent celebrating and bidding farewell to my A-Level classmates at a pub by the river in Tredmouth.

It was also the day I had sex with my soon-to-be stepmother.

Yes, I'd undo that if I could.

14.

Mum got in touch a few months after leaving, but I was a resentful teenager. She was miles away in Somerset, living with her new bloke. I figured, if she wanted me with her, she'd have taken me with her.

A court hearing was held, whereat custody and visitation rights would be decided. Mum quite correctly highlighted dad's abuse.

When it came to my turn to speak, sat there with my dad brooding at my side, I muttered, "if he was as bad as you say, why did you leave me with him?"

That shut them up. Nobody had an answer to that one.

As a result, dad got custody, such as it was required since I'd turned sixteen. And I chose not to see mum in the school holidays. Life was simpler that way. Simpler for me, I mean. A week with her would cost me a month of resentment from him.

Somehow, I survived the two years between that and leaving home to attend Technical College near Oakburn.

A few months before I did, dad informed me that a woman was moving in with us. She had three kids, all quite a bit younger than me, and she was a drinker - a nasty drunk. Though it was verbal more than physical.

She didn't like me, and I didn't like her. She didn't want me there, and I didn't want to be there. We actually had a lot in common, looking back.

I partied that Saturday night in late-June of 1976 - that glorious summer of my escape.

God, it was hot. The hottest I'd ever known it. It was nearly a hundred degrees - June 26th - and it went on for weeks.

I drank beer because I wanted to, and because it cooled me down. And I drank beer because everyone else was drinking beer, as we sat on the bank of the river Tred with our feet in the water.

They're dangerous, those waters, but I only dipped a toe.

I sauntered home from one of the best of all days, and didn't even care about dad, and what I'd encounter. I'd soon be free of it all.

He wasn't in. He was away, tempted by a cash-in-hand side-job, and a weekend pissing it up the wall with the usual gang in a different town.

She was there, though, his new woman. Elaine.

No kids milled around. It was their weekend with their father.

No different to any other weekend, as she handed them off so she could enjoy the good life.

"Hot," she said, because she was economical with words.

I nodded in agreement that it indeed was.

"Been out?" came next.

Of course I'd fucking been out. All day. Till then. I'd just come in.

"Yeah," I said instead of all that.

"Drink?" she offered.

It was twenty past eleven, a glance at the clock informed me as I sank down on the sofa.

"Okay," I was surprised to find myself saying. The walk home had induced a thirst and somewhat sobered me up.

She rose from the chair and returned toting a wine bottle and an extra glass.

Pausing to pour, I saw the slight tremble in her hand as she did. She was thirty-seven, but the drink had a hold of her.

Handing me one, she retook her seat in the chair almost facing me. The television was off for a change.

"Happy birthday," she said, and actually fucking smiled at me as she raised her glass in a toast.

Oh, that wine was nice on my lips and tongue - so cold and fresh after the warm beer and intense heat. It was, to my mouth, what the river water had been to my feet.

"Thanks," I said to her.

That was as civil as we'd ever been to one another.

"So hot!" she reiterated, and unpicked the button on her blouse.

I stared at the domey top-flesh of her breasts, heaving as she sucked in breaths of sticky air that didn't seem to contain enough oxygen.

She was an uncouth woman, devoid of any nicety. She made no real effort with herself - her ill-fitting attire always emitting a dirty, sweaty odour.

Her lips were tight and narrow, and her eyes characterless and passionless, framed by her dark brown naturally curly-wurly hair.

The mottled skin on her legs was revealed as she flapped her rancid nylon skirt, the putrid air wafting over to me.

"So hot!" she said again, and flashed me a still-frame snapshot of her densely-darkly-haired nethers.

I did it.

Not for her. She meant nothing to me. And not for myself.

I did it because it was taking something that belonged to my father.

There was no intimacy. I kept my face as far away from her as possible, and slammed into her, each sloppy-slappy insertion bringing a whinnying sound from her mouth as she knelt before me on the sofa with her face rammed down the side of a cushion.

When I was done, I made her suck her filthy self off me, her curled hair held firmly in my grasp.

No sooner was I clean, than I laid her face up on the coffee table, and did it all again, a rabid white froth whipped up.

I did it because I was eighteen, and I could. I did it because she was there. And I did it for all he'd put me through, and for driving my mum away from me.

Again, she cleaned me with her mouth, and I finished my wine in one draught before heading up to bed.

In which I lay and reflected and felt such an awful shame.

15.

I'd scraped a B in A-Level physics, coupled with a C in Maths and another B in English. It was just enough to get me into Oakburn Technical College.

There were no qualifications open to me in Radio Broadcasting or similar, so I went for Electrical Engineering. At least I'd know how to wire a radio.

Very little remained for me in Tredmouth. Not at that time.

Sharon had left school the year before me, and had moved away to pastures new. Nothing further had happened between us.

Oakburn lies thirty-something miles from Tredmouth, and rather than commute on the train, I moved out.

Into digs close to the college, and a four-room flat shared with a lad approximately my age called Harry.

All I took were my clothes, a table, my tape recorder, record player and records, books and a few personal bits and bobs.

Luckily, the kitchen came with the basics.

Money was my problem. The government gave me a bit, but it wasn't enough. And there was no support from home.

Still, it all led to me becoming a DJ at the gigs. I'd get free admission, free drink, free food, and a small share of the ticket revenue.

And, thankfully, Harry had a twin-deck set-up that was sitting idle.

Once I was gone, I contacted mum, and we picked up a relationship. She came up to Oakburn, and stayed close by.

And, for Christmas and New Year, I went down to Somerset and stayed with her and her new fellow, Merv.

Uncle Russ was there, too, and it was great to see them all - to have a family again.

On the way back up, I had to change trains at Tredmouth. Being a holiday Monday, there was time to waste before my train to Oakburn. On a whim, I walked to my former home.

I watched them through the window, the lights on early that time of year. They seemed fine. Dad was playing a game with the kids, the board laid out on the same coffee table I'd laid Elaine on.

It satisfied me to see them like that - the five of them - Elaine plump with child. I had no urge to knock the door.

Just before I'd left home, Elaine had announced that she was pregnant.

Did it cross my mind that I might have been the father?

Yes. As disgusting as that thought was to me, I couldn't help but think about it.

Dad never twigged. I guess she never told him. Had she blabbed, I feel sure he'd have had something to say about it.

As it was, having a young child somewhat altered him. He stopped going to the pub, and drank at home with Elaine. He didn't care one jot about me. I was from another time and place, as far as he was concerned.

But, if I could turn back the clock to my eighteenth birthday, I'd not do what I did. If only for the sake of my own conscience, I wish I could undo that gross act.

The unknown song accompanies me to bed, earworming its way in, and lulling me into a false sense of sleep...

...I'm happy, smiling as I walk home from a grand day out, drinking with a group of people I've known for six years - some longer. Yet, a melancholia lingers beneath my happy veneer, knowing that life is changing and I shall probably never see most of them again.

It's my birthday - eighteen - and with it comes a sense that freedom lies just over there within touching distance.

It emboldens me, to an extent that I'm not worried about dad and the extreme likelihood of him being up for a row when I get in.

He didn't even get me a card. A plastic key with eighteen written on it was tossed at me.

A key to the door.

Yes, so I can lock it behind me on my way out.

Mum sent a card - a childish one - because, in her mind, I'm as I was when she left. I'll stay like that for ever in her eyes.

Inside the card was a tenner. I spent nearly every penny of it on beer with my mates.

Uncle Russ sent a twenty, which I've hidden in my room. It's good of him, as I haven't seen him since mum left.

I hope the thieving tart my dad's with doesn't nick it. At least her bratty kids are away for the night - they're always poking around my cupboard and taking my stuff, the sly little fuckers.

They took all my comics and ripped them up to make papier-mâché out of - flour and fucking water caking everything in the kitchen.

I'd looked after my comics. One a week I got, from mum on a Saturday, ordered at the local newsagent and held behind the counter for me with my name written on the top edge.

She gave me the money for a comic even when she knew she didn't have enough for the week ahead.

I guess it explains why I valued them, and took such good care of them.

It also explains why I was pissed off at them being taken and torn to shreds.

I grabbed the eldest one. He was about twelve.

And I told him, "leave my fucking stuff alone."

She went mad, his mother. Elaine, her name is. Sneering at me, calling me a fucking baby for reading comics.

"At least I can read! Unlike your thick-as-shit sprogs!"

That was when dad punched me in the mouth and rattled my brain.

It took me by surprise, the punch. I didn't see it coming.

When they'd taken his old toy Dinky cars and ruined them in the garden, it had been a different fucking story. There were rules laid down about touching other people's stuff.

The rules only applied to his stuff, as it transpired.

After the comics, it was open season on my belongings.

I pause at the path leading to the only front door I've ever known. A glance up at the moon tells me it's about a quarter past eleven.

It's too late to walk over to uncle Russ's, to thank him for the money and card. He'll be in bed, sweltering in the heat. It wouldn't be fair to disturb him and his wife. My gratitude can wait.

Stalling. Lingering. Prolonging the day.

Busting for a piss, I let myself in.

It's quiet. She's here, sat on a chair with the telly off, her tawdry offspring away at their father's, like every weekend.

"Where's dad?"

"Work. Side-job. Till tomorrow." She rarely uses more than two words in a sentence.

Her mankiness is exacerbated by the heat - a mouldy, staleness pulsing from her. Filthy, ugly woman.

I use the loo, an almost clear stream of processed lager crashing into the pool of water at the base of the crusty-brown-ringed porcelain.

"Hot," she observes when I return and stand in the doorway before heading up to bed.

I nod in agreement.

"Been out?" she asks.

Fuck me. I've just come in. I've been out since late-morning.

"Yeah," I say, because I don't want a fight. Not tonight. Not on my birthday.

"Drink?" she offers.

I glance at the clock as I sink down on the sofa. I'm tired. The heat is draining. Still, the walk home has sobered me up. It's only twenty past eleven.

"Okay," I surprise myself by saying.

She returns after half a minute, gripping a screw-top bottle of cheap wine and an extra glass.

I watch her pour it, a shake in her hand as she does. She's only thirty-seven, but could pass for ten years older.

She hands me a glass before retaking her seat in the armchair opposite.

"Happy birthday," she toasts me, and actually smiles.

"Thanks," I say, trying to hide the surprise at her attempted pleasantness from my voice.

The wine's probably crap, but its crispy-coldness is beautiful in my mouth.

It's as civil as we've ever been with one another.

"So hot," she mumbles again, and unpicks the button on her nylon blouse, sweat patches showing at the armpits.

Her mounded flesh heaves as she sucks in soupy air.

She repulses me. Her shifty eyes and narrow-lipped, meanly-mouth. Her curly wiggish hair covering a scalp she picks and scratches.

My breaths become shallower, as she wafts her nylon skirt, billowing rancid air in my direction.

"So hot," she says again, and I look at her as she flashes me a snapshot of her darkly hirsute vulva.

"I wouldn't touch you if you were the last woman on this earth," I tell her, and place my wine on the table.

"What? Filthy bastard!" she says, letting her skirt drop. "Just hot. That's all."

"Right," I say, and rise from the sofa...

...I'm in class, pretending I care about the conductivity and resistivity of a multitude of different materials.

The door opens, and a policeman comes into the room. He approaches the teacher, as we all sit in silence and wonder what's going on.

A whispered exchange takes place at the front of the room, before they both turn and face the class. A quick scan by the tutor, and his eyes settle on me. His finger points, the policeman nods, and I wonder what I'm supposed to have done.

A nervy knot tightens in my stomach as I walk from the classroom, the copper close by.

Outside is another - this one plain-clothed.

A detective.

"What's going on?"

I keep asking, but they won't say anything until we're in a room and seated.

"Have you seen your father?"

"No. Not in..." I have to think about it and count back. "Seven months. Why?"

"Is there anywhere he might have gone that you can think of?"

"No. You could try Elaine Jarvis. They were together, the last I knew. She and her three kids were living with him."

"When did you last see Miss Jarvis?"

"Around the same time. Seven months ago."

"So, last September?"

"Yes. When I left to move up here."

Another policeman jogs over. I see him crossing the grass. He enters the room we're in.

"The flat's all clear. No sign of him having been there."

"My flat?" I ask.

Nobody answers me.

Instead, the detective orders, "go talk to his teachers. And find his flatmate. I want to know if he's left here recently."

"Me?" I ask.

"Yes."

"Try asking me," I snap at him.

He smirks and scoffs.

"Why haven't you seen your family in all that time?"

"I... Because my dad's a drinker. He can be quite aggressive. And since he met her, he seems to have got worse."

"So you blame her for you not having a relationship with your father?"

"What? No. Kind of. No. He was always bad. That's why my mum left him," I stammer. "What's going on?"

"Your mother left in..." he lifts a page on his notebook. "Three years ago. Is that right?"

"Erm, yes. A little longer. It was in the January of '74."

"In the custody hearing later that year, you said that your father wasn't a violent man."

"No I didn't! I said... I was making the point that my mum had left me with him. That was all."

"Do you hold a grudge against Miss Jarvis for taking the place of your mother?"

"No! Don't be ridiculous."

"You have a temper, don't you?"

"Not really, no," I reply, trying to remain calm. "Look, please, just tell me what's going on."

"Why don't you tell me what's going on?" he responds, and leans back in his chair.

"I have no idea," I say, and adopt his posture.

I have a sense that I'm being set up. Or, at least, that they believe I know more than they do - more than I do.

Silent stares. Who'll blink first?

He does. He has the urgent need. Me? I don't care much.

"Miss Jarvis is in hospital," he reveals, and watches for my reaction. "She's unconscious. Someone viciously beat her."

I shrug.

"You don't care?" he asks.

"Not really."

"You're not surprised?"

"I watched my father beat the crap out of my mother most days for fifteen years. No, I'm not surprised."

Yet another policeman asks the detective if he can have a word. Outside.

For the two minutes he's absent, I feel my pulse throbbing through my body.

It seems dad's gone too far. It was always likely to happen one day. But why are they so interested in me? I suppose they need to be sure that he did it. Or, more vitally, that I didn't. What do they call it - minimising the list of possible suspects?

A DIFFERENT MIX

Well, I've been nowhere. It must have happened recently, and I've been here all of today, and was in the area over the weekend. Harry, my flatmate, will vouch for me.

"Okay," the detective says on his return. He looks jaded all of a sudden - a little defeated.

He offers me a cigarette, but I shake my head.

"Okay," he begins again once he's lit his smoke, "Nicholas, right?"

"Nick," I inform him.

"Nick," he repeats. "I'm sorry to have to tell you this. I've just heard that your mother has also been attacked. Your father was arrested near the scene."

I can't quite comprehend the information.

"No... My mum lives in Somerset. The woman in hospital isn't my mother."

"No, pal, you don't understand. We now know your father assaulted Miss Jarvis. After which, he drove down to Somerset. He's confessed to both crimes."

"No, no. My mum and dad haven't seen each other in three years. You're thinking of her. Elaine."

"I'm not, Nick. It's definitely your mum. Pauline, right? Is there anybody I can get for you? Is there somewhere you can go? A family member, perhaps?"

I shake my head. "Is my mum going to be okay?"

He licks his lips and picks a fragment of tobacco off his tongue.

"Your mother didn't make it, Nick."

"Didn't make what?"

"She didn't survive the attack, Nick."

I sit in stunned disbelief. My thumb and index finger pinch my lips closed - literally holding it in.

"I have to go," the detective says. "Down to Somerset. One of my men will stay with you. For as long as you like. Okay?"

"I don't need anyone staying with me."

"It might be for the best..."

"I'm fine," I cut him off.

"Even so..."

"I'm eighteen. Nearly nineteen. I don't need a babysitter. Am I free to go?"

He nods.

He looks at me for a long time before sighing and rising. He holds out his hand. Numbly taking it, I pump my arm up and down without standing...

...back in the flat. Keeping busy - keeping my mind occupied.

Rewiring the DJ equipment. Copper wire for the speaker cables.

I choose copper for its single valence electron, making it a highly conductive metal. It also offers good resistance to corrosion.

One way to find out, as I cut a length and take it through to the bathroom.

I strip off,

Splish-splash the water runs into the sink.

I don't wait for it to run hot. It makes no difference. Cold is fine by me. Better, in fact, as I splash my entire body with it.

Goosebumps.

Feeding the copper wire into the plug socket.

Flicking the switch...

...and I flinch to wakefulness, and think about my mum being in her early-eighties, and living a happy, healthy life down in Somerset with Merv.

And my dad, who died about ten years ago, over in Jemford Bridge where he settled with Elaine, and they raised their daughter - my half-sister, I think - or possibly my daughter.

It didn't matter.

She looked like my dad, because she looked like me and I looked enough like him.

It settled him down, having a little girl.

When she was a couple of months old, she cowered away from him one day, and it broke his heart.

So he got help. Stopped drinking. Took pills that calmed him down. Decided that she was worth it, whereas me and mum weren't.

Not that he wanted anything to do with me. No, I was the past. And he couldn't deal with that. It was enough of a struggle for him dealing with the present.

I snuck into his funeral and stood at the back, leaving before the service was complete.

His body slid into the flames, and I walked outside and didn't even bother to look back at the smoke exiting the chimney.

16.

- *Mary Macgregor with 'Torn Between Two Lovers', down four places to number eight this very week in 1977, back when summers were golden and Jubilees were silver.*
- *Leo Sayer up next, after a short commercial break.*

"I don't even remember that song," I say to Dave.

"Nor me, and it only just finished."

"No, I mean, from back in the day."

"All that matters is, it's one step closer to Showaddywaddy," he says, and grins like a madman.

"You're serious," I realise.

"Oh yes. Deadly fucking serious."

"Why?"

"No, 'When'."

"What?"

"No! They did 'When'. Top Of The Pops, early-March, 1977."

"And?"

"And that was the best night of my life. It was when I met my Tina."

"Because of Showaddywaddy?"

"Yes. I managed to get a ticket through Ally Mac and Baz Baxter. If you go on the internet and look at the footage from Showaddywaddy's performance broadcast March 3rd 1977, you can see the backs of our heads as the camera pans across. And before it cuts to Jimmy Savile at the end, you can just make out my profile. Now, the reason you get treated to my profile, is due to me looking sideways, rather than at the stage, because my eyes had alighted on Miss

Tina Wrestleboughton, and once they had, I had great difficulty removing them.

"It was at that precise moment that her eyes met mine, as she smiled her goofy smile and blushed ever so slightly, and we both felt our stomachs take a tumble like we'd driven over a whole great long line of humpbacked bridges.

"We got chatting, I called Jimmy Savile a wanker, and was asked to leave, so we headed out to a quiet little pub tucked away in a London side-street, wherein she explained how she happened to be there auditioning for Legs & Co, but had been rejected for not being quite what they were looking for, the cheeky fuckers. As I said to her that very day, 'I can assure you it wasn't on account of your legs and co not being up to standard.'

"Anyway, to save it being a wasted trip for her, they threw in a free ticket to Top Of The Pops, which was fucking fortuitous for me, because it was where I met her.

"Legs & Co's loss was most certainly my gain, which became very apparent that night back at her place when she did the splits. Whilst performing a handstand.

"Within two months, she was up in Brakeshire dancing at Baz Baxter's clubs, and living with me, and by the end of May we were engaged to be married, a betrothing that didn't last long seeing how we got hitched less than six weeks after that.

"All thanks to Top Of The Pops and Legs & Co.

"See, here's the thing. Had she passed that audition, she'd have been backstage or up dancing, or not even present as she wouldn't have required any consolatory ticket.

"As she's always maintained, not getting in Legs & Co was the best thing that ever happened to her.

"So, to answer your question, 'When' by Showaddywaddy has always held a special place in our hearts, as it was the very song playing when we first saw one another."

"When you smile at me, our love will always be, you see?"

"Good grief," I say, and mean it.

"See, that's the point," Dave continues, "we judge the songs we play, but it's all about time and place. One person's shit is another's treasure. I doubt that many would have Showaddywaddy's 'When' in their top five singles of all time. I doubt they'd even plum for The Kalin Twins' original. But, for me personally, it makes the cut, purely for the memories it evokes and the moment in my life that it captures.

"It's an integral part of the music mix that tells the story of my life. Everybody's mix is different, because every life is different.

"You're back on in five seconds."

- *Leo Sayer, dropping down five places to number seven in seventy-seven.*

- *A special song now, for Dave and Tina, who met that March, forty-one years ago. 'When' by Showaddywaddy, climbing from number eighteen to number six.*

- *Enjoy it, Dave. This is for you two.*

"Thanks," Dave says, and we remain silent as the track plays.

I watch him through the glass, miles away, no doubt depicting the very moment they met. A tight-lipped smile accompanies his thoughts, and I find myself matching his expression, until a noiseless guffaw escapes me when I get to Tina doing the handstand-splits.

Dave would have been twenty-two, Tina eighteen. She's around the same age as me. I attended her fiftieth - a surprise party Dave arranged for her. It was a small gathering at an Italian restaurant in Tredmouth. I was surprised to get an invite, as I'd only met Tina a couple of times.

I didn't invite them to my fiftieth. Probably as a result of me not having one. A party, I mean. Reaching fifty wasn't anything I wanted to observe. The occasion passed uncelebrated and unremarkably.

A few days before that landmark, I'd sat in a meeting at the station HQ, and half-listened to a presentation about the financial crisis, and its effect on investments and the US market. I didn't see that it had any impact on a radio station in Brakeshire, three and a half thousand miles away. Or, if it did, how could it possibly hinder me, a humble presenter of the DriveTime Show?

They revealed the new schedule at the end, and I double-took the projected chart looking for my name.

I found it after a time - lurking in the dead of night, four times a week. Dave kicked me under the table.

"Can I have a quick chat, Nick?" the CEO asked as we all rose to leave.

"Of course."

It was spelt out to me - how I would go from eighteen hours of prime airtime a week to eight. My salary would have to reflect that.

And so my fiftieth birthday was spent sitting and working out how on earth I would cope on the reduced income, and fretting about the future.

I felt old and one scoop of a grabber away from the scrapheap.

For nigh on ten years since, I've been dreading it - that release from the clutches of a crane that will deposit me in the tangled mess of former somethings.

Nick Cherry, former DJ.

It's why we do as we're told, Dave and I, and we play the tracks as pre-selected for us without fuss. It's why we're playing the songs from 1977, rather than the playlist about toys we dared to dream up.

And now, sitting watching Dave nod his head in time with Showaddywaddy's 'When', I'm glad we did.

The show is considerably more tolerable when I think of it in that way. We sail through the next twenty-five minutes - or fifteen-hundred seconds - as Bowie, Mr. Big, Heatwave and ABBA, plus a few emails and a lot of adverts, take us up to 'Chanson D'Amour' by The Manhattan Transfer - ra-da-da-da-da!

Song of love, I translate in my head.

I've never known love. Not really. Not equal, reciprocated love, of the type Dave and Tina have. I never met my soulmate.

Sharon was my first love. At least, from my perspective, if not hers.

Gilly, I think, was the only woman I truly loved. And I believe that she loved me. But not enough.

And Amanda, I suppose, for a time. Right up until I actually got to know her.

There were others, but I didn't have the courage or will to pursue them fully. I preferred to keep my options open.

Besides which, if I didn't get too involved, I couldn't be too badly hurt when the inevitable breakdown came.

Still, the year 1977, and the French sentiment in the song make me think of Henrietta, and what might have been.

17.

A detour on my way home, and a stop off at the baker's for a fresh loaf. Spoiling myself. It's still warm, the bread, as it dangles in a bag from the handlebar of my Vespa.

The smell rising up from it sets my stomach off in delightful tumbly-rumbly anticipation.

It's a perk of the graveyard shift, being up at such an hour to take advantage of the loaves coming out of the ovens.

It ties in to my scooter, and the attempt at Italian cafe culture - it's what I've always aspired to. Milan or Rome were the places I saw myself, prompted by some film I'd seen during my time with Harry.

He was a rich kid, whose family lavished on him everything except the love he really desired. Still, it was why he had a television, in addition to the disco equipment, so it wasn't all bad.

The first thing I had to do with both the television and the turntables, was rebuild them. Harry had a habit of taking things apart in a futile bid to understand them. I learnt as much from that as I did any lessons I attended at college. Plus, I had access to all the tools and wiring required.

Why was Harry there? Because it was thought learning some kind of skill might be for the best, even though he'd never actually require it.

He was tall, about six-four, and as skinny as a rake. His cheeks were concave and his eyes sunken. There was something of the cadaver about him. In keeping with that, he had an interest in the occult when I first arrived.

As with most of his interests, it didn't last long.

His only enduring love was for Dungeons & Dragons. A wizard was how he saw himself, with his long straight hair and old-before-his-time demeanour. There was no old soul in Harry, though, despite his belief to the contrary.

I relish slicing the end off the bread, just as I always do. And another slice, the loaf flattening down before springing back up, the crust not yet dry enough to maintain the shape. I butter my slices as my coffee cools. Nothing else. Why would I want to detract from the taste?

Oh, and I devour them and smile at nothing as I do. It's one of the undoubted highlights of my week.

"This is Henrietta," Harry introduced her. "My sister."

I nodded a greeting and rolled the multi-sided die.

"Aren't you going to offer me tea, Harry?" she asked in her plummy voice.

He didn't offer. Rather, he rose and put the kettle on. She reached down and took up one of the metal characters.

"Is this you?" she asked me as she turned it over in her hand.

"Yes. That's my character."

"What is it?"

"A Fighter."

"Oh, how ghastly. I was hoping you might be something rather different. Do you know, the word die can mean orgasm?"

"Erm, no."

"Well it can. Rather archaic these days, of course."

"Right."

"Nicholas, correct?"

"Yes. Nick."

"What do you do, Nick?" she said, emphasising the K-sound at the end of my name, and leaving her mouth open after she had.

"Electrical Engineering. What about you?"

But she tossed me the model, turned her back, and took the few paces to the kitchen area, where Harry looked in the fridge for milk we didn't have.

Strangely, I found my eyes following her as she did.

She wasn't my type. My type was Sharon - the bubbly blonde.

Henrietta - for she was always to be called Henrietta with no abbreviation or truncation - wasn't dissimilar to her brother. There was enough commonality to instantly recognise them as siblings.

She had more flesh on her bones, though. She appeared to be more recently deceased.

It resulted in her eyes being dark and mysterious, and her cheekbones being pronounced. Her form was elegantly slim, and her bearing superior and staunchly upright.

Yet, she wasn't an attractive woman at first sight. Augmenting her coldness, was something slightly reptilian.

I sniffed an opportunity to slip away and escape.

"We ran out of milk. I'll pop down the shop and get some," I offered, already pulling on my jacket.

"I'll come with you," she informed me in a manner that wasn't to be countered.

"Where's your car?" she asked once we were outside.

"I don't have a car."

"Oh god. Right, well, I suppose you'll have to drive mine, then."

"I haven't passed my driving test."

"How old are you, about fourteen?"

"No. I'm eighteen. I wouldn't be at Technical College if I was fourteen, would I?"

"Say University. It sounds better. With a capital U."

"The shop's only a three minute walk away," I pointed out.

"Grotty little place," she countered. "I thought we'd drive into town and get milk and fresh bread."

"What about Harry?"

"Oh, I think he'll survive."

She had a white Triumph TR7, into which I lowered myself. No sooner had I done so, than the car coughed to life, and she took off, revving the engine to a screaming pitch before every gear change.

"Is he seeing anybody? Harry, I mean," she wailed over the din.

"Not that I know of."

"We were rather hoping he'd grow up in this place. Throw him in the deep end - sink or swim, if you follow?"

"Not really," I confessed.

"God! Can't you fix him up with a friend of yours? A girl, I mean."

"I don't have any female friends," I volunteered, and instantly regretted the comment.

"Are you one of those?" she asked.

"One of what?"

"Oh, I knew it was a mistake sending him here. After all, as I said to mummy and daddy, a Technical College sounds like the type of place predominantly frequented by young men. And some of them shall undoubtedly be males of a sensitive nature."

"I like girls," I blurted out defensively.

She stared at me sceptically for several seconds. In the end, I had to point at the road ahead as she drifted over towards the on-coming traffic.

"I had a sense you were bent as soon as I saw you," she said dismissively, and violently pulled into a parking space.

"I'm not!"

"Don't worry, darling, I've dabbled in a bit of that myself."

"But, I..."

"Still, at least I can feel safe around you. Now, this door sticks. Will you come round and open it for me, please? If you're man enough!"

I did as bidden, having quickly realised that to contradict her in any way was utterly pointless.

The door was indeed stiff, and appeared to have dropped on the hinge a little. As Henrietta emerged from the car, she took my hand. Once clear, she slipped her arm through mine and steered me to the shops.

"See, with you being the way you are, nobody shall have any problems with us being friends!" she trilled, and waited for me to open the bakery door for her.

18.

She bought a rustic loaf, unsliced. Unsalted butter and a pint of creamy Jersey milk came from the shop two doors up. I'd never had any of those things before.

I carried the bags as she glided along with her arm threaded through mine.

"Where do you live?" I asked her.

"Surrey, darling."

"How long are you visiting for?"

"I'll head back tomorrow evening. Why do you ask?"

"Just curious. What made you visit?"

"To see Harry, of course. It's been absolutely yonks since we saw one another."

"Where are you staying tonight?"

"Oh, how kind and thoughtful you are! See, this is why I like homosexual men!"

"No, I just wondered where you were..."

"It'll be so much simpler if I stay with you at the flat. Super! And you don't mind giving up your bed?"

"I..."

"We can go to the concert tonight! I really want to sample this punk thing - see what all the hullaballoo is about. What should I wear? Are you going?"

"Er, yes. It's a gig, not a concert. You should wear what you normally wear. Punk is about individuality."

"Is it? Oh, I thought it was about spiky hair, ridiculous clothes and angry-angry people. Grrr! Angry!" she said, pulling an angry face and growling at me.

"You're quite oikish, aren't you?" she said next.

"Not really."

"Don't be embarrassed. I quite like it," she stated as I dropped the bags in the footwell before opening her door for her.

Once we were seated, she further sought, "how short should my skirt be for 'punk'?"

"It doesn't matter."

"About here?" she asked, tugging her knee-length up to her mid thigh.

"Whatever you're comfortable with."

"Well, how about here then?" Her skirt rose another six inches or so.

"Honestly, I don't really know much about punk. I'm not even sure the bands playing tonight are punk," I admitted, and averted my eyes.

"Oh! The poster looked like it was punk," she said sulkily.

She started the engine with her skirt so high I could see the cotton of her undies. With every aggressive gear change, her knee rose and descended at a splayed angle that flashed white in my peripheral vision.

Did I believe she was flirting with me? I wasn't entirely sure. Had it been anyone else, there would have been no question. But the fact she believed I was gay made me doubt it all.

Besides which, I didn't actually fancy her.

Physically, I kind of did. But her personality and class were off-putting. I found her incredibly intimidating, and pompous. I felt she was constantly inwardly laughing at me.

"Harry thinks he might be queer. But he isn't. He's not the real deal like you," she commented, apropos of nothing.

"I wouldn't know."

"I thought you might be able to tell one of your own?"

I sighed and shook my head.

"How do you know your way around," I asked by way of changing the topic, "have you been here before?"

"Yes, when Harry moved up. It's a shabby little place, but the baker is rather good. Always find a good local baker, darling, and make it a priority."

Back at the flat, the three of us sat eating buttered bread, washed down with creamy tea. It was all so rich. Bread for me had always been white sliced; tea dark and watery; milk more white than yellow.

Then, at the age of eighteen, a certain taste for something was established - a luxury that, to this day, I still cherish and luxuriate in.

It feels indulgent even now, as I rinse my plate and wipe it with a bubbly sponge before standing it in the rack to drippily dry.

It's the unknowns that haunt me. Just as they appeal to me.

The unknown record gets placed gently on the felt mat on the deck. A velvety brush sweeps the surface before rotations begin.

Harry and I spoke in hushed tones as Henrietta soaked in the bath.

"It's very complicated," he whispered.

"In what way?"

"She is my sister, but she isn't."

I glanced confusedly at him. "You certainly look alike."

"I was born in '57. Son and heir, and all that," he told me, and winked meaningfully.

"When was she born?" I asked.

"Same year."

I thought about it. "So... Are you twins?"

"No, no, no. She's a couple of months older than I."

I looked at him uncomprehendingly.

"My father," he explained, "he was mastering two dungeons at once, if you follow."

"Oh, I see. So you have different mothers?"

"Yes. Although, in fairness, they were sisters."

"Really?"

"Yes. As a result, we are kind of as close to brother and sister as you can get without being brother and sister. It's all a bit of a mess, to be honest. We're half sibling and half cousin. Not much of a difference in the mix, when you think about it."

"No."

"But it all worked out rather well in the end. My mother died - oh, let me think - seven years ago now, and the Old Man had a readymade substitute standing by."

"God, I'm sorry Harry."

"No need, no need. It's how things go sometimes. Luck of the draw, and all that."

"My mum left when I was fifteen, and my dad..."

"Nicholas!" came a call from the bathroom, "I seem to have slopped water all over the floor."

"You'd better go," Harry suggested.

She was wrapped in a towel. Another was turbaned around her head.

Evidently, she'd overfilled the tub and her body had displaced water over the sides.

"I'll fetch a towel," I decided.

"Use this one. I'm done with it," she replied, and whipped away the one encompassing her body.

Taking it, I mopped up the spillage. She turned away, unabashed, and patted her straight hair dry between her hands.

Her prominent cheekbones were matched by her razor-edged hips. There was certainly something skeletal about her form.

I thought of Jason And The Argonauts, and the skeletons doing battle. Unlike their mechanical movements, Henrietta had a fluidity about her.

"What shall you wear this evening?" she asked into the mirror.

"Jeans and t-shirt as usual."

"Is that what punks wear?"

"It's what I wear."

"Do you have anything I can borrow?"

"Not really, no. Look, some people pick up stuff from Army Surplus or secondhand places in town."

"How exciting! Let's go!"

And that was that decided. Five minutes later, we were back in the TR7, her hair still damp and her clothing back in place.

19.

Henrietta prattled on as we sped back into town.

"I have seen them, you know? Punks, I mean. Up in Town. A gaggle of them came slouching down Regent Street the other week.

"Mummy was appalled. Daddy was ogling the girls. Some of them had safety pins shoved through their faces!

"Anyway, when they noticed daddy staring, one of the girls lifted her top and jiggled her breasts at him!

"Daddy agreed that it was disgusting behaviour, but I saw him smile.

"I suppose she was an anarchist. Nihilism might be a better word for it, don't you think?"

"I don't know," I admitted, unsure what nihilism meant, as I struggled to see any difference between the girl in London and Henrietta's conduct that very day.

Harry and his 'sister' were, it occurred to me, polar opposites. Where Harry was all dreamy fantastical whimsy, and, as a result, completely unsuited to a Technical College, so Henrietta was devoid of any imagination whatsoever.

Her flirting was crude and unsubtle. It lost any allure as a result. In the shops we visited, she had no vision; no ability to see any potential transformation. To her eyes, things could only ever be what they already were.

"It's just a t-shirt, Nicholas. I want punk."

"It will be. You can cut the sleeves off and tear it up a bit. It's also very slim and long in the body. Look," I pointed out, holding it to her.

She looked blankly back at me.

"It's long enough to wear as a dress," I further explained.

"Gosh, I would never have thought of that."

In the Army Surplus her long boney feet enabled me to pick out a pair of black paratrooper boots. She had a pair of woolly tights with her.

Back at the flat, Harry was out. I set to work as Henrietta sat by and observed.

The white t-shirt sleeves were crudely snipped off at an angle with scissors. A blade opened up a few slits. Tiny tins of paint Harry used to paint his D&D models were gathered.

With brush in hand, I asked her, "what would you like on the front?"

She shrugged.

"Come on, Think of a word."

"It needs to be angry, right, the word?"

"It can be anything."

"Tuer," she eventually said.

"Tuer?" I asked, the lack of understanding now mine.

"French, darling. For 'kill'."

Thus, in bright red enamel paint, I wrote the word across the front.

As it dried, she asked, "will you cut my hair?"

"No, I'll make a right mess of it."

"Isn't that the point?"

And so I used the same scissors to crudely lop off her long tresses. They glided off her near-naked form and floated to the floor in sheeny sheets.

"Shorter!" she ordered.

I did it in increments, afraid of incurring her wrath. After each snip, she'd look appraisingly in the mirror and insist on shorter.

"So itchy!" she wriggled her shoulders and complained when I reached a level she was happy with.

I'd butchered her hair.

"Brush me off," came her next demand.

Her bra fell down her arms; and she stood before me in just her briefs.

My hands went to work, rubbing every inch of her in an attempt to remove the stubborn irksome hair.

Once done, she made no effort to cover herself. I swept up as much of the clippings as I could, then ran the vacuum cleaner round. All the while, she sat on the toilet with the lid down, raising her feet when necessary.

She pulled on the t-shirt I'd adapted, the paint on which was still tacky.

"How should one spike one's hair?" she asked when I was done.

"Use soap," I proposed.

"Will you do it for me?" came the predictable request.

I did. I don't know why. It was as if I couldn't say no to her.

A rich lather went from my hands to her uneven hacked locks as I lifted her hair away from her scalp.

It was most odd, but as she transformed, so I found myself more attracted to her physically. As she morphed from the rigidly straight aloof madam she was, into a more accessible lower-grade young woman, so I desired her.

Was that why she was doing it?

Any urge on my part, though, remained in check.

She ham-fistedly applied black eyeliner in a deliberately clumsy way. A red lipstick was similarly thrashed around her mouth, making it fuller and sexier - making her look more like Sharon, I realised.

"Well, what do you think?" she asked me.

I smiled and nodded. She did look punk, there was no denying it.

Turning, I saw Harry standing watching us, and I wondered how long he'd been there.

"Dad will go absolutely mad when he sees you," Harry informed her.

17.

A shriek had me running from my bedroom to the bathroom.

Henrietta had pierced her cheek with a safety pin.

"Jesus!" I sibilated.

"Fasten it for me, Nicholas."

With trembling hands, I did. "You'll get an infection," I told her.

She shrugged her shoulders.

I got a sense of her there in the bathroom with my face close to hers. No matter what she had in life, it could never be enough, because it wasn't everything.

Henrietta wanted it all, and she wanted it now.

That ambitious attitude appealed to me. Probably because I came from a place and society where to have ideas above your station was seen as an arrogantly awful trait to possess.

We went to the gig, her and I, Harry opting to stay at home and design a new dungeon.

Standing near the bar, we watched the headliners go through their soundcheck.

The music hinted at punk, but was in actuality a blending of sixties covers and self-penned songs about love and life. They were the songs the band would have played more sedately a year before, but by then churned out at double-speed and twice the volume.

By the same token, rewind a year and the band - a bunch of blokes in their late-twenties or early-thirties who had been doing the local circuit for years - would have been wearing flared denim and nice shirts ironed by their wives.

By March of '77, scruffy t-shirts covered their uppers, and the jeans had been taken in by the same wives.

Their significant others, I also sensed, had cut their hair for them.

The exception was the keyboard player, who was firmly entrenched in 1971, and, going by the look on his face, really didn't like the direction music was headed.

By some distance, Henrietta was the most punk looking person in attendance. The rest were students at the college, along with people from Oakburn, Millby or Jemford who had made the trip.

It was close to capacity, though, the air thick with smoke and sweatily moist. There was a buzz of change, and an equal, opposite energy emanating from a resistance to that shift.

Even in sleepy old small-town Brakeshire, there was something going on.

And that night it felt as if we were in the midst of it.

The support band were local - from Oakburn - and brought a small clutch of fans with them. Dress-wise they looked like me, but there was a snarling attitude about them as they drank warm lager and scowled at any member of the audience who represented the past.

They were called 'Burn Oak Burn!', and they were angry, hence the exclamation mark. I was unsure what they were angry about, but they were definitely angry.

Their rage, I gathered from the occasional lyric discerned, was at their parents and the government and teachers and the town and anybody who wasn't just like them or, confusingly, was like everybody else. And any town that wasn't their town.

Bang-bang-bang-bang-bang they went on - grrr, angry!

They were rubbish.

But it was fantastic, every earsplittingly brutal moment of it, at eight on a Saturday night in the hall at Oakburn Technical College, with a hundred and fifty people struggling to breathe.

Henrietta dragged me to the front where the sound from maxed-out Vox amps rippled my t-shirt.

The spitting began. Heavy globs of mucusy gob arced over our heads and shrapnelled the four skinny angry lads who scowled back at the crowd and gave as good as they got.

We jostled and shoved and Henrietta forgot about the pain in her cheek, every swig of lager leaking a drop from each hole in her face.

I glanced sideways at her to witness a bullet of spittle leave her clown-painted lips. She was wild and... Nihilistic!

Life is meaningless, I grasped in the moment.

Only the moment mattered.

Tomorrow, we could all be dead.

We didn't know!

I didn't know, at least, that it would be the best part of the night.

She turned to me - unrecognisable from the young lady I'd met for the first time just a few hours before. We stared and grinned insanely at one another - suspended in time as the mob pulsed all around us.

We both went for it at the same moment, the violent clash of our mouths as we lipily chomped on one another's faces as if we were attempting to gain purchase on an apple bobbing in a barrel of water.

She ground her crotch into mine as we remained locked together, forced against the stage by pressure from behind.

I reached my hand down and rubbed her through her woolly tights, and she screamed something into my face that I couldn't hear, so I nodded furiously to simply let her know that I had heard something.

Without warning it was over, the band walking off with their instruments, soaked in spit and sweat. Twenty-five minutes was how long they were on, but it felt like a lot less. My ears rang metallically as the press of people eased off us.

"Was that punk?" she asked me.

"I think so," I replied with honesty.

"Imagine what the main act will be like!"

But the main act wasn't anything like that.

The main act wasn't punk, despite upping their game. I'd seen them a few months before when they'd been a band for all the family.

The keyboard player loved Family.

Henrietta and I drank and talked excitedly between the two, an age taken over cleaning all the gob from the stage and equipment.

"Do you wish to be an Electrical Engineer?" she asked.

"No. I want to be a DJ," I reported, so certain that I one day would be.

"A what?"

"A DJ. You know, playing music."

"DId I hear you say you're a DJ?" a man asked, overhearing me as he passed by.

"That's right," I said cockily.

It was bullshit. I'd done nothing since those days of recording my own daft radio shows in my bedroom a couple or three years before.

I was different that night. Henrietta made me different. I don't know why. But she made me more like her; less risk averse - more straight line in my thinking, rather than the meandering way my mind naturally had a tendency to go.

Having her by my side emboldened me. She looked the part, and despite me being no different to the majority in the room, I was perceived as something by association.

It was all fake. Every single bit of it was a sham.

I didn't mind punk, and quite liked the energy of it. The truth was, though, I was a huge ELO fan. With a bit of Supertramp thrown in.

'Telephone Line' from 'A New World Record' was my favourite song.

Oh, and Marc Bolan. I still had a liking for Marc and all he represented in my life to that time.

"We need a DJ," the man said to me. "I'm Kev, the Social Secretary on the Student Union."

"I'm Nick. This is Henrietta."

"I've seen you around. You're a student here, right?" Kev asked in his farmer's accent.

"That's right. First year, Electrical Engineering."

"We used to have a DJ, but he can't do it any more. Darren, his name is. Darren Smith. Do you know him?"

"Yes," I replied, "I knew him back in Tredmouth." It was true, I'd seen him at the college a couple of times. But I also knew of him from years before. For a brief time I'd attended a Youth Club he oversaw.

"Through the DJing?" Kev asked.

"Yes," I fibbed.

"Ace. So, do you fancy it?" he asked, and looked at Henrietta for some reason.

"Yeah," I answered coolly, my stomach kicking both with nerves and excitement. "When do you need me?"

"Every time there's a gig on. Before, middle and after. Fill the gaps."

"How much?" Henrietta interjected.

Kev smiled at her. "You get free drinks and free nosh. And you won't need to pay to get in, will you? Either of you."

"But he'll need to buy records. And the equipment needs maintaining," she pointed out.

"Three percent of the door," Kev suggested.

"Five percent," she demanded, and held out her hand to him.

"Go on, then," he reluctantly agreed, and shook both our hands.

That was how I became a DJ.

The headline band opened up with Del Shannon's 'Little Town Flirt', played at a canter rather than a gallop.

Everything about it was wrong. The wrong choice of song, played in the wrong way, by five blokes who looked wrong and played their instruments wrong.

When the hippy on keys went into a drawn out solo, the first boos rang out.

Some of the crowd drifted away, headed to a local pub to hang out with the opening band.

"Are you coming?" we were asked.

I looked to Henrietta. She gave nothing away.

"No, I'm going to hang around here," I decided.

"I'll come," she announced, and broke away from me.

I watched her walk away, and I stood at the bar and suffered the out-of-step band, as they laboured through their set, their hearts not really in it. I nursed another couple of lagers, and thought about being a DJ.

But my mind kept wandering on to Henrietta, and what she might be getting up to.

She didn't come back to the flat that night.

She showed up briefly in the afternoon, packed her things, and bade farewell to Harry.

I carried her bag to the car.

"Did you have a good time last night?" I asked her, acting like I didn't care.

"It was good fun," she replied airily, the safety pin gone, leaving two awful purply-red marks on her cheek. Only her hair betrayed what she'd briefly been. Except it was flat and straight once more.

"Great," I mumbled.

"What's wrong with you?" she asked.

"Nothing."

"You should have come."

"It wasn't my kind of scene."

"No, well, so I gathered," she said, shrugging.

"What do you mean?"

"There's one thing I don't understand, darling," she said.

"What's that?"

"Last night, when we kissed, and you touched me?"

"Yes," I encouraged, as I levered and lifted the door for her.

"Was it because I looked like a boy with my short hair?"

"No! Why would you think that?"

"Because of what I asked you when the punk band played," she further said as she took her seat.

"What did you ask me?" I implored her.

"I asked if you were sure that you were gay, and you nodded and smiled."

The engine growled to life. Grrr, angry!

"Ah," was all I had a chance to say.

"I think I may have converted you a little bit!" she beamed.

And she roared away in her TR7.

In my room, I found the paratrooper boots left standing behind the door. In the bin was the t-shirt I'd cut and painted for her.

I never saw her again. By the end of '77, Harry was gone. Back to Surrey or somewhere.

He did leave me the decks, though, as a parting gift.

He also left me homeless.

20.

I play the record again. I can't seem to stop myself.

It always felt like one of those pivotal moments in my life, that night. If things had been just slightly different, what course might my life have taken?

Henrietta is the reason I became a DJ, and got to follow my dream. It all began in earnest at the gig, and meeting Kev.

I wonder what other doors she might have opened for me?

She wasn't my type, but there was something about her. An energy. A bloodymindedness. A nihilism.

She was, I think, a bit punk after all.

I wish I'd heard her question that night.

The morning sun blankets me as it radiantly pours through the window. It shows burntly-orange on my lids as they close, and the more I look into them, so purples and reds wash in and mingle on the otherwise black backdrop that isn't black at all when you really study it.

And I drift into the land of nod...

...we're at a gig - drinking lager and watching the main act perform a soundcheck. I'd seen them before, the headliners, when I'd first enrolled at Oakburn Technical College.

I'd quite enjoyed them, as they'd reinterpreted some of the songs I knew from uncle Russ's records. They did a very good extended take on Wayne Fontana & The Mindbenders' 'Game Of Love', with an organ solo that went on for at least two minutes.

Since then, they've changed their image. Well, most of them have. The keyboard player retains the old look.

"They don't look very punk," Henrietta observes.

"No," I agree.

A snarling, sneering gang around our age loiter near the stage, staring daggers at the band as they go through the motions. They nod a greeting to us.

I try not to smile as Henrietta takes a swig of beer, and has to wipe away the drops that leak through the holes from the safety pin piercing her cheek.

I'm aware that I do fancy her, and that my desire increased as I transformed her.

Just as importantly, I think she fancies me. I've seen her naked. I've brushed hairs off her perky little breasts and run the spans of my hands down the length of her antelopey legs.

But she thinks I'm gay...

The support band slouch on stage - no soundcheck for them. They're supposed to play at the levels set for the main attraction.

They don't, though. They strut toward the Vox amps and crank everything up to maximum, much to the chagrin of the sound guy.

One of them tells him to fuck off.

I see him mouth the words.

The gang from Oakburn town close in, and I'm joining them, led there by my t-shirt as Henrietta drags me forward. I don't go willingly, but neither am I kicking and screaming.

A screech and a roar - four clickety taps, a snap on a drum that makes me physically jump.

There's an energy...

They're rubbish, the first song over in under two minutes - less time than a solo on 'Game Of Love' - and the second song is almost identical to the first, but with different sounds shouted from the 'singer's' gob.

Gob flying through the air, catching the light as it travels, the bass player approaching the front of the stage on the side we're on, and discharging a ball of mucusy snot into the hair of an urchin who jumps up and down seemingly oblivious.

Or wearing it as a badge of honour.

I turn to Henrietta, her cheeks drawn in, her mouth opening and her tongue turtle-heading as a globby mouthful of spit leaves her.

I don't see where it lands, as I continue looking at her, wild and animalistic - nihilistic and... Sexy!

She turns to me, and we grin at one another, our eyes locked, rammed against the stage by the throng of life behind us.

We want the same thing.

Our pelvises twist to buy a little room, and our mouths clash violently. We gnaw greedily at each other, our lips bruising, such is the ferocity. But any pain is dismissed in favour of lust and energy.

Her, grinding her crotch into mine. Me, reaching down and rubbing her through her woolly tights. Her mouth opening and staying ajar, just as it did when she first said my name - Nick!

She shouts something, but I can't hear her amidst the awfully brilliant din.

"What?" I scream back.

"Are you really gay?"

"No!" I tell her, and she smiles and runs her tongue over her bottom lip.

Only this matters!

Here and now.

Tomorrow, we could be dead.

Bang-bang-bang-bang-bang - grrr, angry!

Bang a gong, get it on!

She laughs, her head tipped back, mouth wide, spit flying over her.

I laugh too.

I laugh like I've never really laughed before. There was nothing much to laugh at when I was at home. With mum and dad.

Not mum.

It lasts less than half an hour. An abrupt end, and off they pop, making wanker signs to the audience as they do.

"Was that punk?" Henrietta asks me as the crowd dissipates.

"I believe it was," I inform her, even though she already knows it was.

"Gosh, that was exciting!"

"The main band are a bit different. They're not punk."

"Come on, let's go."

"Go where?"

"We'll get a drink somewhere."

"We can get a drink here. It's cheap," I point out.

"No. I want to go. And then, darling, I want you to fuck me."

"Oh. Okay."

We walk out into the night hand in hand, glad for the cold freshness. She smokes a cigarette - and another - one after the other, using one to light the next.

I don't know why, but when she offers me the packet, I take one. I tried a couple when I was younger, but don't smoke.

Smoking reminds me of him - my father. It's also why I don't generally have more than a few pints. Rarely anything any stronger.

I fear I'm inherently similar, deep in my depths, so avoid things I associate with him.

Not tonight, though. Tonight I'm letting my hair down and having a good time with a posh girl from Surrey - a girl everybody looks at.

Step right up see the main attraction!

We push through a door and into a pub, Rod Stewart playing on an Ally Mac jukebox.

They look at her because of how she looks, and I made her look the way she does. Without me, she wouldn't have had a clue.

The old school look at her curiously and with distaste. The new wave look at her with admiration and respect. And something else.

And that admiration and respect from our peers - it spills over and I get it, too, because I'm with her and she's with me, sucking my tongue as we wait for drinks at the bar.

I'm in. Practically home and hosed. She's already made clear what's going to happen later. I've seen her naked. I know precisely where I'm going.

There have been a handful. A girl I knew from school. She was the first. It happened that summer I turned sixteen - a few months after mum left. A few months after Sharon.

We bumped into each other outside the Co-Op, and got chatting. A walk through a park, a sudden summer shower and a run to my house. Dad was at work. Mum was long gone. So we had sex. No frills, no spills. Clumsy, awkwardly shy intercourse on my bed.

That was it.

Nick Cherry popped his cherry!

And hers.

She thanked me afterwards. She actually thanked me! That was weird. I think she'd been trying to lose her virginity for a while. She said as much, but she wanted it to be with someone who was nice.

I was nice. Nice Nick.

We repeated it a few times afterwards, usually when we both had nothing better to do. We didn't even bother becoming boyfriend-girlfriend. After a few weeks, she got a job at a shop in town, and started seeing someone else.

I wasn't bothered. I had no regrets about that one. It was time and place, and was what we both wanted, for just as long as it lasted.

It was never going to be the rest of our lives.

Then, of course, there was Elaine.

How much more experienced is Henrietta than I?

How many have been there before me?

Burn Oak Burn! and their band of mates fill the pub a few minutes after we arrive. We're still at the bar, and they get chatting to us, asking us what we thought.

"It was brilliant," I tell them, because, in a way, it was.

The whole night has been brilliant, and it's not even ten o'clock.

But they aren't really interested in what I think. It's Henrietta's opinion they covet; more so when they find out she's from London - Surrey being close enough.

Jabber-jabber-jabber they go on, asking her questions she doesn't know the answers to. Christ, she doesn't even understand the questions! But she deftly handles them all with vagueries and bullshit. At the end of the day, how are they going to fucking know?

Another lager. Yes, please!

Go on then, I'll have a vodka if you're offering. And a smoke. Bring it on! The more the merrier.

Because I'm alright, Jack, stood at the bar with her pressed against me, the pair of us surrounded by a crowd.

Burn Oak Burn!, still the support, and their audience now our audience.

"Attitude," I find myself saying, "it's all about attitude. It's how you look, how you sound, and what you have to say."

A flock of heads nod at that. Baaah-baaaah! I know a thing or two!

I know more than this mob. At least I'm from Tredmouth. It's a fucking city, not some small market town full of know-nothing yokels.

Sheep in wolverine garb!

The last time I got drunk? My eighteenth nine months before.

And here, at the bar, in a pub surrounded by fledgling punks, I'm not like I was then. I've grown up, and escaped my father and all that he was. I only took what I wanted from him, and it wasn't much.

Her back's to my front, and my hand massages the cheek of her skinny arse, pulling it apart and opening her up, unseen by anyone as they stare at the pin in her face and the mess around her lips and her nipples clawing at the t-shirt dress I made for her, the paint on which has long since impressed itself on her body...

...a fizzy white light as I flinch in my slumber...

...See you, I'm off!

Down to Surrey to embark on my life. No more Technical College for me. It was a waste of time, anyway. I'm going to be a DJ. On the radio. And London is the place to achieve that.

Henrietta has her own flat, and I'm moving in, my clothes and a few bits and bobs flung in the back of the TR7. My boxes of records are left behind. They're outmoded and stuck in the past. Punk is the new thing, and I'm at the sharp end of that.

Window down - a wind blowing in and whipping the ciggie smoke away.

She wears a scarf, Henrietta, the punkiness and safety pin gone, so I lean over and kiss the purply-red marks in her face, beginning to yellow where the blood leaked.

I'm knackered, but I won't doze. I'm too excited and pumped up. We didn't get to sleep until about four in the morning as we shagged each other senseless.

It wasn't difficult. A couple of pills we scored from the lads in the pub kept us on our toes - kept my pecker up!

She was wild - like nothing I'd ever experienced before. Everything to the limit, just like her gear changes.

Poor Harry, lying in the next room having to listen to it all. It must have been bad, especially with it being his almost-sister.

They had a fight when we finally emerged around midday. I heard him say how she always had to take what was his. I think it stemmed from their father and his involvement with Henrietta's mother.

Harry stormed out.

Two hours later and we were hitting the road, following a quick 'one for the road' in the kitchen as she hopped up on the countertop with her arse in the crumbs of bread nobody had cleaned up.

All I wanted was sleep after that, but no! Pop a pill and away we go.

We might be dead tomorrow!

Life is short, I've come to understand. One bite at the Cherry!

Nick Cherry, Disc Jockey. I was most certainly a jockey last night, the way I was riding her.

Revving to the max, just as she does - foot to the floor, always wanting more.

Now.

Wanting it all now...

...we're in her place - crap everywhere, because tidying up and cleaning anything is beneath her.

Just as I'm beneath her, flat on my back with her astride me, her knees raised as she slams up and down on me, my hand reaching up and grabbing her throat, squeezing.

She likes it.

She loves not being able to breathe when she climaxes - it adds to the intensity and thrill. Henrietta always wants more from everything.

And who can blame her?

To stop myself ejaculating, I close my eyes and think of other things. Anything else.

I need a job. She has money, but it isn't enough. Not with the life we live. Fresh bread, unsalted butter and creamy milk are the least of it.

The drink and drugs - the lines of coke - and the way she flits from one whim to the next are where most of it goes.

Up the nose!

More and more clutter to add to the ram-jammed place we call home.

But fuck it. That can wait till tomorrow.

If we're even still alive.

La, la, la, la, la, live for today!

Up I go, lifting her with me, still inside her, and standing, her antelopey legs wrapped around me.

Bang-bang-bang-bang-bang - grrr, angry!
But not really. It's all an act.
I'm nice.
Nice Nick.
The kind of boy a girl would like to lose her cherry to.
Reaching out and grabbing the scarf from where it lies discarded on top of a pile of clothes on a chair.
She wears a scarf to hide the marks on her neck sometimes.
Dropping her down on the bed, flipping her over, and pistoning into her from behind, the scarf reining her in.
Jockey!
On we go, because the drugs give me energy and she can't get enough of me.
She can't get enough of anything.
There simply isn't enough in the world for Henrietta - she'd take it all if she could.
There isn't even enough oxygen for her...
...And I'm panicking because she won't wake up.
Her lips are blue - her skin as white as the milk I had as a kid.
Tuer! French for kill, darling!
I blow into her mouth and recall the time she pierced her cheek with a safety pin. I can still see the marks, but nothing leaks from the holes now.
To run is my instinct. But I can't think of anywhere to run to. I have nowhere to go.
The radio speaks to me. I wasn't aware it was even on.
A packet of white powder becomes my focus - that'll make me think more clearly.
Swiping the countertop clear of debris, I pour out a third of the contents. Too much, thanks to my shaky hand, but I'm not in any state to put it back.

Chopping it crudely with the blunt edge of a butter knife, and lining it out. A rolled up page torn from a book allows me to snort the whole fat lot of it.

I slump into a chair and close my eyes - all my worries drifting away, because it's all a dream and when I wake up, everything will be as it was.

The sun comforts me like a blanket, as it dances over my eyelids and swirlily lullifies me to sleep - my breathing becoming slower and slower, but not as slow as hers...

...A huge relieving breath, and I take stock of the room I sit in, in a house I bought fifteen years ago after Amanda and I split.

An unknown record bumpety-bumps on the deck.

How long has it been?

Looking at my watch, I have trouble working out which hand is which.

I stare at it as the second hand ticks on. It reveals that it's five to six in the evening, not half past eleven in the morning, as I'd first thought.

It is the evening, because it's getting dark outside.

For seven and a half hours, I've been sleeping in this chair.

A ready-meal needs preparing, before I head in to work at the radio station.

21.

"Morning, Dave."

"Alright?"

"Fantastic as always! What did you get up to yesterday?" I ask, as I try to set the chair to something in which a human being can actually sit.

"Nothing exciting. You?"

"You know me - always something going on!" I brightly tell him.

"You don't look like you've slept a wink," Dave observes.

I smile and check the bags under my eyes in the screen. God, I look awful. It must have been a fitful sleep in the chair, and I woke up stiff as a board. My lower back took the brunt of it.

"Ah, living the life," I inform him, and widen my tired eyes to show him just how lively a life I live.

Life: The period between the birth and death of a living thing. Vitality, vigour, or energy.

Isn't something alive before it's born?

I lack vitality, vigour and energy, but I am alive. Aren't I?

My life is being laid out before me - those major forks on the path that have led me to where I currently am.

Of the few things I've regretted, the dreams have very clearly shown me that they needed to be the way they were. One deviation, it seems, leads to something else and, ultimately, my own demise.

The irony of it! That having sex with Sharon and Henrietta would have ruined me. Yet, not having sex with Elaine would have done similarly.

But there must be a wrong turn; a choice I made that sent me off-track; another way to go which I failed to see at the time

I can't believe I was always destined to end up here and now, exactly as I am - that this is as good as I can reasonably expect my life to have ever been.

There must be a moment when...

"1975 today, Nick. Do I need to say that it's a bit shit?" Dave intrudes on my musings.

"Not for everyone, remember," I remind him.

"No. This one really is appallingly shit."

"Highest top forty new entry?" I dare to ask, and find myself biting down quite hard on my bottom lip.

"Moments And Whatnauts. 'Girls'."

"I've never heard of it," I confess after releasing my teeth. "I've been on the radio for three and a half decades, and I've never heard of it!"

"It's why we do this! The learning!" Dave beams at me. "So, a lesson for you - it was ten weeks in the chart, peaking at number three, and you actually played it three years ago as part of this very show!"

"Did I?"

He downturns his mouth and nods at me quite severely. "It's never too late to learn shit in life, Nick. As soon as you think you know all the shit there is to know, that's the day to hang up your headphones and step away from this shit."

"Right."

"Hey, it's not all bad - Steve Harley & Cockney Rebel at number three."

"Come up and see me sometime?" I ask.

"The very one!"

"It's been a very seventies week," I point out.

"Random on the computer. Next week might be eighties!"

"Or sixties," I say optimistically.//
"There you go."
"Anything planned for the weekend, Dave?"
"Just the usual. You?"
"A few things going on."

There's nothing going on at all. Why do I do that - paint my life to be something so much more colourful and vivacious than it actually is?

"Are you doing a bit of charity bingo calling on Saturday, mate?" I ask with a grin.

"Ah, you remembered that." Is that the slightest blush playing on his cheeks?

"Oh yes," I reply, with what I hope is an evil glint in my eye.

"You're on in forty seconds. Five songs with numbers one to ninety in the title. Go!"

"Route 66, Rolling Stones. And before you ask, Nat King Cole. 68 Guns, The Alarm. Twenty Flight Rock, Eddie Cochran. Nineteen, Paul Hardcastle."

"One more."

"One Inch Rock, Tyrannosaurus Rex."

"Bingo!"

- A very good morning to you, this is Nick Cherry, picking the best tunes for you on this Thursday morning. It's great to be here, and even greater to have you with us.

- If you're up and about, take care. If you're lying in bed, stay there! Either way, here's a bit of Ed Sheeran to keep you company.

"Did you ever want to be famous, Dave?"

"Not really, no. I dreamed of being a pop star, as you know, but I was never a very comfortable front man. I've always preferred being in the background.

"You take Tina and her dancing, for example. I got a bigger thrill out of watching her perform, than I ever felt when I was up on stage myself. That's the truth of it."

"It's the same with you and me. I'm happier being on this side of the window."

"Did you never have a problem with other men ogling her when she was dancing?" I ask him.

"No, I saw it as a compliment. After all, she'd leave with me at the end. And I've always trusted Tina."

It makes me smile, to hear that.

"Even when she was stripping," he adds, and my smile withers.

22.

- Johnny Mathis kicking off the top ten from 1975, with 'I'm Stone In Love With You'.

- Let's check out the weather, and we'll be back with Guys & Dolls. And Dana! Was it all really only forty-three years ago this very week? It feels like a lot longer.

We plod our way down to number one - Telly Savalas. 'If'.

"I'll see you on Monday, Dave. Have a good weekend."

"You too."

"Enjoy your bingo."

"Look, erm," he begins tentatively, "I know how busy you are. But if you wanted to come and see what I do... The bingo and whatnot, I mean. The charity thing."

"Where and when?" I ask.

"Well, the main event is on a Saturday lunchtime. It starts at midday."

"Where?" I ask again.

"At the hospital. Tredmouth General."

"I'll have to check my diary. I'll call you," I say, knowing there's absolutely fuck all in my diary.

I don't even have a diary.

'If' stays with me as I scoot home, much as a spoonful of cod-liver oil might.

If only...

If only I'd met 'my Tina' - my soulmate. Or found my niche in life, just as Dave has. He's so comfortable in his support role to his wife, to me, and to others.

It's where he belongs.

Belong: Be rightly placed in a specified position. Fit in a place or environment. To be happy or comfortable in a situation.

Where do I belong?

A flatness comes as the Vespa is silenced, and my key scrapes around the lock to the door before finding the slot into which it fits.

Bespoke and made to measure.

Thursday is the worst day. It'll be Sunday night before I can once again think about the radio station, and feel a small sense of purpose.

My routine is largely maintained even when it doesn't need to be. I sleep my day away as always, but not too long or the night shall feel never-ending.

The bread, so fresh a day ago, is now past its prime. Still, I cut and butter a few slices. The remainder will be toasted tomorrow.

It could be rejuvenated - sprinkled with water, wrapped in foil and popped in the oven. If I did that, it would be almost as good as it was yesterday. But I simply can't be bothered.

It's not worth the effort.

I'm not worth the effort to myself.

No music this morning. I don't even turn on the computer. I'm too tired. My bed is all I want.

For six hours I sleep in a dreamless world of nothing, and wake feeling refreshed and more positive.

So much so, that shortly before five-thirty in the evening I head out for a walk. Despite being the middle of March, it's chilly but dry. The new moon at the ides of March once signalled a new year, and with it a chance to reset and begin again.

Pushing through the trees, I pick up the river bank and cross it at a bridge not far north. A footpath leads out into the wedge of countryside between the railway to the west, and the river Tred to the east.

Life's not so bad, I consider, as I head in the direction of Wrenbrook.

I used to live there. With Amanda. It's the place to live, if you like that kind of thing. Large detached properties with swathes of land behind tall hedges. It was Amanda's dream. Well, mine too, once she'd sown the seed.

I acted as though it was pretentious and a betrayal of my class. But I loved it, if I'm honest. It spoke of success and being amidst the elite.

A fork appears, and whereas I normally bear left, sticking to the route I know in the direction of Wrenbrook, this evening I take the Millby path to the right.

The sun shows her face. It'll be a sunset worth witnessing.

And sure enough, when the time comes, the rays kick up onto the partly cloudy canvas to show as gilt-edged orange cushions on which I could so easily rest my head.

Over a neglected field with darkly beryl trees as a backdrop, a starling murmuration dances against the sky, as I stand transfixed and lost in marvel.

They move as a single entity, creating depth and texture, as if smoke blown by a wind unfelt.

There are many hundreds of them. Possibly many thousands! Too many for my eye to take in and hazard a guess, as they shift again and swoop over and through one another.

How do they know which way to go and when?

How can they possibly know when to turn and rise and fall in such coordinated play?

Is it play?

What's the purpose, other than to demonstrate happiness at being alive?

Or is it some kind of mating ritual - a dance to attract a partner - a dance they reenact over the winter months in readiness for now, as spring approaches and procreation must begin anew?

Do they hear music that I cannot? For this is so choreographed, they must!

Can they pick up radio waves and hear the music DJs play?

Is it the music I have on the unknown record back home? Back home...

It'll be dark soon. I should start heading back.

- *Back, back, back in time, with me, Nick 'Cherry Picker' Cherry!*

They asked me to stop using the name 'Cherry Picker' a few years ago. Someone took offence at the slang connotation.

I was sad to let it go, having used it in innocence since I was a kid in my bedroom making shows on my old tape recorder.

But one person complained, and that was that.

It was on my flyers, back in the late-seventies, plastered to any noticeboard or door at the college I felt I could get away with. I'd pop into Oakburn a few days before a gig, and hand some out at supportive pubs and record shops.

As well as pulling a few people in, they led to me getting DJ work at other places. I had a good reputation.

Following the offer from Kev, I popped over to Palmerton Chase a few weeks later, and hooked up with Darren Smith.

He was generous and supportive, and never saw me as a rival or a threat. When would that have been? May of '77, perhaps.

In addition to giving me a handful of reggae singles to spin, his main advice was to get suitable transport. I smiled. After all, he was in Palmerton for driving lessons with his friend, Bill. Bill was also fixing up Darren's pride and joy - a wreck of a Fiat 500.

It didn't strike me as being suitable transportation for a DJ.

Every penny I earned went back into the business, such as it was. Punk singles were finally hitting the shops, which, when coupled with a few choice oldies, plus reggae and ska, gave me enough to fill a few hours.

Also, I bought my own lighting set-up, again through Darren. I relied on favours for a few months, before passing my driving test in the summer.

Darren's mate, Bill Goods, found me a van come the autumn of that same year. Ford launched the new-look Transit van in the August, I think. A few months on, and the old style were hitting the second-hand market.

I don't recall what it cost me, but it served the purpose for the next seven years. Bill did a smashing job of fixing it up. It was red, with windows along the sides which I curtained off.

When Harry moved away, I dropped a mattress in the back and slept in there with all my worldly goods.

Come Christmas, and I thought about heading down to Somerset. I had so many bookings over the break, that I couldn't. I'd have been letting down an awful lot of people.

So, I remained and slept in my Transit, wrapped in a sleeping bag, with a couple of coats piled on top of me. Despite being young, I felt the chill. Every couple of hours, I'd wake up with cramps, start the engine, and sit waiting for the heater to get warm enough to thaw me out.

By mid-January, I found another flat-share above a hairdressers in Oakburn. My bedroom was tiny, with a shared kitchen and bathroom that were bloody awful. Still, it was better than the Ford Transit.

And I got free haircuts. From a girl a year or so younger than me. Her name was Mandy. Amanda, as she'd rebrand herself. But in 1978, she was Mandy.

A few years would pass before we'd get together, but it was the moment we first met.

Prior to it all, came September the 16th, 1977.

It was the day Marc Bolan died.

23.

It's dark by the time I return from my walk. I should have left a light on.

The unknown record calls me. I haven't played it today.

I was nineteen and cocky, a popular local DJ with a bit of a following. For probably the first time in my life, I felt respected and in demand. I had a sense I was heading somewhere.

And so it proved, as I borrowed uncle Russ's car, and headed over to Canterwood for an interview at the city's independent radio station.

Someone connected to the station had seen me DJing, and gave me a number to call. I did, and was invited down for a meeting. By September '77, everyone was clambering blindly aboard the punk train. It was big business all of a sudden.

Those ninety miles between Brakeshire and Canterwood constituted the longest trip I'd taken since I'd passed my driving test a few weeks before.

I drove there imagining my new life in a new city far away from the baggage I carried in Brakeshire. It was a chance to reinvent myself. No, not reinvent. Rather, to be true to myself.

Technical College would be a thing of the past. I was wasting my time there, anyway, my primary focus being on the music scene. I was often too tired after a late night to attend classes the following morning.

Yes, there was definitely a good feeling as I bore southeast across Brakeshire and crossed the county boundary that early morning.

As my confidence grew, I switched on the radio and wound down the window. As soon as I was in range, I decided, I'd retune and pick up the station I was heading towards.

It felt preordained, as whatever station uncle Russ had opted for, enhanced my optimism by playing 'Metal Guru' by T. Rex.

I sang along with the window lowered, winding my way to a rosy future - breaking away from Brakeshire!

Beginning again.

A half-heard voice came from the speakers.

Did he say what I think he just said?

I wound up the window to stop the noise rushing in.

Too late, as the next song played. Elvis.

Did I hear it right?

Retuning, turning the knob, stopping every time a signal was picked up.

Did he really just say that Marc Bolan was dead?

No, he was probably referring to Elvis. After all, it had only been a few weeks since he'd died.

Another station played T. Rex. It must be true.

I looked up from the radio. I was already on top of the next bend, but too inexperienced a driver to hit my brakes, as I tried to steer through it.

Understeering, forcing an approaching car to veer onto the verge to avoid me.

The sound of a horn.

Then oversteering.

A horse and a dog - the horse rearing up - the dog running out in front of me.

Still, I didn't think to hit my brakes.

I felt and heard the impact.

It was over in a second.

And I drove on, taking the next bend in sequence, everything disappearing from my mirror.

There was nothing I could have done. I couldn't have stopped in time.

But I should have stopped.

It's haunted me ever since. What became of the lady on the horse? Did the dog survive?

I drove on because I was afraid. And because I had an important meeting that very day at ten o'clock. And because, well, what in all honesty could I have done?

There were other cars. Somebody would have stopped and made sure everything was okay.

And the radio confirmed it - Marc Bolan was dead.

The more distance I put between myself and the scene, so my regret ratcheted up.

At some point, I pulled over and checked the car. There was no sign of the incident. It was just a small dog. It may even have been a cat or some other creature, so not a dog at all. And anyway, it was probably just a glancing blow that did no lasting damage.

As for the woman on the horse, I didn't actually see her fall. The horse reared up, but she was still on its back the last I saw.

I assured myself that it wasn't as bad as I'd first thought.

Despite that, the guilt wouldn't go away.

The closer I got to Canterwood, so the weather went from the sunniness I'd set out in, to a dingy oppressiveness that mirrored my mood exactly.

As for the interview, I at least attended.

I mumbled my way through, bullshitting answers to questions I didn't understand. I tried to steer the conversation to punk, because I knew about that, but the man didn't want to talk about punk.

My heart wasn't in it, and my head was distracted. None of that made any difference. I wasn't what they were looking for. I was too young and inexperienced.

I recall the advice I was given. "Get yourself some know-how by volunteering at a local station. There's a lot more to it than playing records and saying a few words. And broaden your horizons. Punk will be a thing of the past in a few months."

My perfect day had disintegrated to dust fine enough to slip through my fingers. I drove back deflated, taking a different, more circuitous route home to avoid the scene of my crime.

Nervously I waited. For hours. Then days and weeks. I kept expecting the police to track me down and reveal the extent of what I'd been responsible for that day.

But nobody came.

There was no stern knock on uncle Russ's door from uniformed officers of the law. No questions were ever asked of me about a dent in the bumper, or something macabre discovered in the wheel arch.

There was no mention on the national or local news.

As time moved on, I came to terms with it. I never forgot, though.

In the forty years since, I've hit a handful of other creatures whilst driving. A cat and a couple of rabbits spring to mind. On each occasion, I pulled over and checked.

And now, with modern technology all around, I never ever use my phone or allow myself to become otherwise distracted when I'm behind the wheel.

I learned a valuable lesson that day.

Even so, as my eyes close and sleep ushers me in, I wish I'd pulled over to check on the lady on the horse, and the dog I hit...

24.

...I'm on the move, moving up in the world, away from Electrical Engineering at a Technical College, and heading to the bright lights of Canterwood, the next stage in my journey.

A steppingstone to bigger, even better things!

I'll have a car like this soon enough, as I cruise along in uncle Russ's blue Rover SD1. It has a couple of thousand miles on the clock. It still smells new.

Everything feels new this sumptuously sunny day, as I set off early - my interview at ten - allowing plenty of time to cover the ninety miles. I want to savour it, and enjoy every moment, because it feels important.

Even my clothes are new - from black t-shirt to black leather jacket and dark blue bondage-type trousers, down to the boots that pinch my feet on the pedals. They cost me a pretty penny at Brake Up! in Tredmouth, but it's an investment.

Feeling more comfortable as the miles tick by, winding down the window so I might taste the fresh air that ruffles my hair, brushed and pasted to match a style I saw on Paul Simonon.

I turn the radio on - loud enough to offset the sound of the car bouncing back in through the window off the trees and walls I carve my way between.

Oh, and all the stars align, as T. Rex come on the radio.

Metal guru, is it you?

Yeah, yeah, yeah!

I sing it, nothing behind me and nothing in front of me - a clear path ahead. I know where I'm going, because there's only one way to go.

Onwards and upwards!

Yeah, yeah, yeah!

What was that? As I was singing the last line on repeat, the DJ said something.

Did he say Marc was dead?

No, I must have misheard - he was probably referring to Elvis, as 'Way Down' begins. Yes, that makes sense. Elvis has only been dead for a few weeks.

Still, something about it nags at me. I'm sure he said Marc Bolan was dead.

I twiddle the tuning knob, looking for another station. Perhaps I'll catch the news.

Another T. Rex song. 'Ride A White Swan'. Sharon loved this one.

It must be true, or it's a hell of a coincidence.

I wonder if Sharon has heard.

Looking up, and the next bend is on me, so I turn the wheel and round it, my speed drifting me wide as I cross over the solid white line.

A car veers to avoid me, the driver punching the horn, my hands pulling harder on the steering-wheel to regain the correct side.

Oversteering, as I crunch gravel and bounce a little on the rough ground.

Why am I still pressing the accelerator? My booted foot rises, but I don't have the wherewithal to dab the brake.

A horse rears up alongside me, a woman leaning forward and hanging on, as a dog runs out into the road.

There's nothing I can do to avoid it. Not without hitting the horse.

Thrump, ba-bump, and a slight judder through my hands.

And I hit my brakes and pull over, just as the radio confirms Marc Bolan is dead.

"Are you alright?" I call as I jog back along the verge.

The woman is down off her mount, holding the reins in one hand as she tries to get to the dog lying on the side of the road.

"I'm fine," she replies, but she's as pale as a ghost.

I go to the dog, primarily so she doesn't have to.

It lies on its side, its tongue hanging limply from its snout.

"I'm sorry. I'm so sorry," I gush, as I kneel down by it, looking to see if it's breathing.

"What the hell have you done to my dog?" an angry voice shouts from the other side of the road.

"It's not your dog?" I ask the horsewoman.

"No. It always barks at me when I ride past. It looks like the gate's broken, and he got free," she points out, and nods in the direction of the house opposite.

"What the bloody hell have you done?" the angry voice repeats.

I notice she's not putting her weight on her left ankle, the woman.

The dog emits a soft whine.

"I think I startled your horse," I say.

"It wasn't you. The dog did that. She's fine with traffic. It's being on a farm, I expect, and all the heavy machinery. But she does hate things running around her feet."

The man is with us, leaning down to inspect the stricken Jack Russell.

"Did your bloody horse kick him?" he rages.

"No," I answer for her, "he ran out in front of my car. There was nothing I could do."

"Your gate's open," the young woman adds.

Without so much as another word, he scoops the dog up and carries it back to his house.

"Have you hurt your leg?"

"Oh, yes, a sprain, I think. When I jumped down, I found a rut, and it turned my ankle."

"Do you need an ambulance?"

"No, I can move it. I'm sure it isn't broken. It was good of you to stop."

"Well, where do you live? Can I give you a lift?"

"Do you think she'll fit in the back seat?" she asks, and smiles at me.

"Ah."

She's around my age, and pretty, with light-brown hair swept back and sticking out the rear of her riding cap. Her jodhpurs show her trim fitness.

The horse bends its neck and tugs on a tuft of dry grass.

"There has to be something I can do to help," I further say.

"I'm pretty sure I can ride, if you can help me get back in the saddle."

"Yes! You'll have to tell me what to do, though. I've no idea how. I don't know much about horses."

"Really?"

"Really. The closest I've ever been was DJing a party at Tredmouth Racecourse."

"Are you from Brakeshire?" she asks as a lorry blasts by.

"I am. You?"

"From here. But we do go to the races at Tredmouth a couple of times a year. And there's an agricultural show at Drescombe once a year. We usually show up there."

"We?" I fish.

"My parents. Siblings."

"And you."

"And me." That smile again.

"I'm Nick. Nick Cherry."

"Deborah. Debbie Harrison."

"Almost Debbie Harry," I point out.

"Who?"

"Nobody. Okay, what do you need me to do?" I ask.

"I'll mount from this side, so my weight is on my right foot in the stirrup. If you can offer me a shoulder so I don't have to stand on my left, and then sort of push me up and over."

It's only when we're in position that I realise I'll need to push with my hands on her bottom.

She balances, her right foot in the stirrup, her left floating as she effectively sits on my shoulder. I can smell the horse, my face close to its flank.

"On three," I call up to her. "One, two, and three!"

Up and over she goes, as my hands cradle her buttocks. She winces when her foot snags a little, but she's in position.

"How far is it?" I call.

"Half a mile or so. On the left."

"Will you be okay?"

"I'll be fine. Blondie knows the way home."

"Blondie?" I wonder if she knows who Debbie Harry is after all.

"Yes. She has the flaxen gene. See how light her mane and tail are?"

I nod that I do.

"I'll follow you," I propose.

"No. I've kept you long enough. Where are you heading?" she asks as we make our way towards the car.

"Canterwood."

"Oh, what for?"

"An interview. Oh god, what's the time?" I suddenly think.

"A quarter to nine."

"I'd better go. You're sure you'll be fine?"

"Yes. What's the interview for?"

"At a radio station. I'm a DJ, as I said."

"Well, best of luck."

"You too."

"Bye."

Back on the road again, the traffic heavier as I near Canterwood, crawling into the city and getting lost on the one-way system around the bus station.

Eventually, I park up a couple of minutes after my interview time. I jog to where I think I need to be, my feet blistering in my new boots, only to discover it's the wrong building. Another five minutes lost as I get directions and agonisingly run the few hundred yards.

Sweating and out of breath, I blurt an apology for my lateness. It's okay. It's all okay.

I'm ushered straight through, into a room where a man behind a desk rises to shake my hand.

"Sorry I'm late," I say for the tenth time. "I set off with plenty of time in hand, but a dog ran out in front of me, and a woman hurt her ankle when her horse reared up on her."

"My goodness! Are you okay?"

"Oh, I'm absolutely fine. But I couldn't just drive on and leave her."

"No, no, absolutely right. You're sweating. Would you like a drink?"

"Please. Anything cold."

"Water?"

"Perfect."

I was expecting it out of a tap, perhaps in a mug. But no. It arrives in a glass bottle with ice and crystal tumblers.

"Thank you."

"Was the dog hurt?" Geoff Moses, the Managing Director of Canterwood Media Ltd asks me.

"Unfortunately, yes," I reply. "I'm not sure how badly. The owner carried him away. A Jack Russell."

"Oh, poor little sod! And the lady on horseback?"

"She twisted her ankle. I had to help her remount. It all took time."

"Yes, I'm sure. Well, can't be helped. You're here now, and in one piece. No harm done."

"Thanks for understanding."

"Dogs and horses are my thing, along with my work. What's your thing, Nick?"

"DJing. It's all I've ever wanted to do. I realise I don't have any experience of broadcasting, Mr Moses."

"Please, call me Geoff."

"Geoff," I echo, because it's what I do.

"How old are you?"

"Nineteen."

"Then you won't have experience, will you? I'll be honest, I have concerns, Nick. If I take a chance on you, it's an investment. You'll need training. You have to learn your trade, so you'll be bottom rung. What do you make of this punk thing?"

"It's a thing. For now, at least."

He smiles, his eyes regarding me over the top of his glasses. "I've been in this lark for a long time. Through the fifties, and sixties. I've seen a lot of things come and go. Punk's the latest fad. It'll all blow over before you know it."

"You're probably right, but some of it will stick. I heard on the way over that Marc Bolan died. Last month it was Elvis. They're still relevant. They still have an influence."

"Not according to punk. My understanding is that Elvis is the enemy."

"It can't be erased," I throw in.

"I'm worried, Nick. I'm worried about taking you on, investing a lot of time and effort, and that you're one-dimensional. Take away punk - and it will go away - and what's left?"

I smile and nod. "I like the energy of punk, and the scene. To be honest, though, some of the actual music doesn't do much for me. Reggae influence will factor into it, I think. And technology will play more of a role. I've studied Electrical Engineering, and synthesisers are set to come in."

"They've been around for years," Geoff slips in, and shrugs.

"Single note models. But polyphonics are coming, with microprocessors."

"Meaning?"

"Meaning a fuller sound, and the ability to pre-programme and store data. In the not too distant future, music will become more electronic - more synthesised. A singer won't even need a band with him or her."

He considers me for ten seconds or so. I sip my water as an excuse to remove my eyes from his.

Nervous. For the first time since the horse and dog incident, I have time to think. And what I think is that I have a chance here. But it isn't done and dusted.

"Do you have to be anywhere today?" he eventually asks.

"No." It isn't true. I'm supposed to be DJing a gig at the college tonight. The afternoon was set aside for set-up. I thought I'd be away from Canterwood by midday, and back by two. Plenty of time.

But I know this is more important.

"Good. Stick around. I'll give you a tour, and we'll get lunch. Introduce you to some people..."

...I'm thrillfully tingling, driving uncle Russ's Rover, retracing my route back west to Brakeshire, my head full of plannings about relocating and giving up college and having my own show on Canterwood City Radio, spinning the latest sounds and having emerging bands come in for live sessions, all going out on a Thursday and Friday night between nine and eleven.

If it goes well, there was talk of London and even national radio through the parent company.

Marc Bolan's dead. Long live Nick Cherry.

I'm nineteen, and realising my dream!

The signal from the station I shall soon be working for fades and dies, but rather than retune, I silence the radio and lower the window to let the cool dusky air keep me focused.

If I get a move on I can still make the gig. I'll miss the start, but I can be set up and ready for the break after the support band. I don't want to let them down. After all, Kev has been good to me.

I had food - top nosh - which soaked up the liberally flowing wine and the after-dinner alcohol-laced coffees. I'm not a drinker - just a few beers for me - but I was celebrating, and everyone else was drinking.

I look for her - Deborah - Debbie Harrison. At least, I look for her home as I approach the scene of our earlier encounter. She said it was only half a mile on.

My head turns to the right, my eyes searching for a light.

I'll call in and check on her - make sure she's okay. There was something there - a connection between us. I'll tell her my Big News. For some reason, I'd like her to be the first person I tell.

Before I know it, I'm approaching the bend where I encountered her, and the chance is gone. It's okay. I'll go to the Agricultural Show at Drescombe. And the races at Tredmouth. We'll see each other once again, if it's meant to be.

It feels as if everything is meant to be!

A grin parts my lips as I regard the precise location where I helped her back into the saddle.

Shit! An old broken gate slides off the back of a small truck into my path.

Pure instinct as I steer round it, on to the wrong side of the road.

Where the red paint and silver bumper of a much larger truck fill my screen before the devastating head-on impact...

...and I wake up in my bed, alone and with a sense that I am damned if I do and damned if I don't.

Marc Bolan, I recall, died that day.

25.

It's merely supposition. It's me subconsciously conjecturing. I can't know that any of my dreams would actually have come to pass.

But it feels so real.

The message I'm getting is that things needed to be the way they were. There were reasons why everything happened just as it did. Yet, I've never subscribed to preordination.

Okay, so I never quite made it. But I'm alive. I'm okay. I'm still on the radio four days a week, albeit with a small listenership. I'm still doing it.

I'm still living my dream.

Rather than constantly looking for what I don't have, I need to see all I have.

It was 1979 all of a sudden. I was twenty, and things had moved on musically. Even if I hadn't.

Somehow, I saw my time at college through, and left with a scraped-through fairly low-grade qualification in Electrical Engineering.

I spent a week typing letters to every radio station the local library had an address for. It was soul-destroying, waiting in vain for replies.

The advice from the interview in Canterwood had remained with me - get some know-how by volunteering at a local station.

A visit to the very local small operation in Oakburn, as well as similarly sized broadcasters throughout the county, proved fruitless. And I spent a miserable day in a drizzly Tredmouth, calling in at the two main county stations based there.

Feeling despondent, I went to leave my last hope, following a brief chat with the Programme Director.

"Hey?" he called to my back.

"Yes?" I asked, turning and shuffling backwards towards the exit.

"Are you prepared to move away?"

"Depends where," I shrugged and stopped moving.

"Tinbury Head."

I knew where it was, down on the coast, but had never been there.

"Sure," I replied, and felt a tiny green shoot of hope emerge on an otherwise barren plantation.

"Wait a minute. Let me make a call," the man said.

So I did. I took a seat and waited, my leg jigging anxiously.

People came and went, the local station playing out in reception. For all I knew, a man I nodded a greeting to could have been someone I listened to every day. They were largely faceless in those days, the DJs on local radio.

The Programme Director, Tim, bustled back in.

"Come on through," he invited me.

We sat in an empty studio - my first ever time in one. Instinctively, I took the chair at the desk, an old-style microphone a few inches in front of my face. I touched and repositioned it - such a wonderful feeling.

"My CV," I said, as I offered him an envelope containing two sheets of paper outlining my education and working life to date.

He waved a hand, but took it anyway.

"Electrical Engineer?" he observed.

"Yes."

"That's useful to know."

"Is it?" Again, I touched the mic.

"You've been running a mobile disco for... How long?"
"Three years. I average three a week."
"So you know how to set up broadcasting equipment?"
"It's what I do," I blagged.
"Interesting. What are you looking to get out of this?" Tim asked me.
"I want to be a DJ," I replied cockily, before adding, "but I know I need to get some experience of radio. So, anything, really."
"Okay. Sounds good. I spoke with my colleague at a sister station down at Tinbury Sound. His name's Mark Canham. They're looking to set up a roadshow on the beaches down there.
"If it takes off, it may be expanded. The way we see it working is, stations such as ours will go down there with guest presenters, and play to crowds over the summer holidays. That will then be beamed back to the local area for live broadcast. Make sense?"
"Yes. Perfectly."
"I'll be honest with you; they have the expertise on the more technical side. That said, your electrical know-how will be useful, as will your live set-up experience.
"You'll be a bit of a dog's-body, and the money won't be great, but is it something you might be interested in?"
"Definitely," was my instant reply. "When do they want me to start?"
"Yesterday! Mark's got to get everything up and running in a few weeks ready for the holiday season. And he's struggling."
"I can be there on Monday morning."
Shit, it was Thursday. I had three days to move to a town I'd never visited in a county god-only-knew how many miles away.

"Super. Here are Mark's details. I'll call him and tell him you'll be there on Monday. Okay?"

"Yes. Thank you."

And that was it. I gave notice on the flat above the hairdressers, packed all of my gear in the Transit van, and readied myself to move.

I had no contract and nowhere to live. I didn't even know how much I'd be earning. It was forty quid a week, I discovered following my chat with Mark Canham.

As things transpired, that, right there, was one of the smartest decisions I ever made in my life.

The trouble is, no sooner have I thought that, than I begin to wonder what my life would be like had I not taken that offer on the spot.

No, I don't want that to change. I think what immediately followed was the happiest time of my life.

If only I'd hung on to it.

26.

My feet barely touched the ground. I liked Mark Canham right away, and he seemed to take to me.

For the first couple of nights, I slept in the Transit on the mattress, my disco equipment and records towering over me.

The weather was warm, with it being June, not that I got much time to enjoy it. We were working towards a late-July deadline, and the pressure was on.

Despite that, it was a glorious few weeks. I may not have been on the airwaves, but I was a part of the scene, and the radio was a constant companion.

I'd always loved music, and had a predictable fondness for the soundtrack to my early-teen years, as so many do. But if I have a favourite era for music, it is the post-punk soundtrack that accompanied the toil of summer '79.

Sparks, 'Beat The Clock' became our anthem, as we were always chasing time on deadlines. 'I Don't Like Mondays' was another. But it was phony. I didn't mind Mondays at all.

It was an honour for me, and a sign of acceptance, when Pete The Supervisor bestowed on me a nickname. I became Tubeway Cherry because I was an electric friend.

Without being fully aware of it, I'd absorbed a great deal from my time at college. I was useful! And as time passed, I was often consulted on best approaches. Being fresh out of tech, I was bang up to date on practices and safety aspects.

Further, I had more experience than anyone else on how to operate and run a mobile sound-system.

My time sleeping in the van was short-lived. Canham spotted me emerging one morning.

"No, no, this won't do," he muttered. "I have a small cottage a mile or two out of town, in Wishaven-Next-The-Sea. It needs rewiring and sprucing up a touch. Painting inside and whitewashing outside - that kind of thing. Do that, and you can have it for the next twelve months. I want it ready for rental by next summer."

"No problem!"

And it wasn't.

Here comes the summer!

I kept a diary. For the first time in my life, I had something worth mentioning in its pages. Horace Wimp inspired me. My ELO love endured. I was electric and light and part of an orchestra of industry.

An industrial orchestra!

In a new place, my past was irrelevant. My family were distant. Once a week, I'd ring mum, and that was it. We got on okay, but I was too busy living.

I didn't quite trust her after she'd left the way she did. And, if I'm honest, there was a bit of me that wanted to punish her for leaving.

Such energy we possess when we're that age! If only I could have kept some in reserve for now.

Work was frantic, but I still found time to toil on the cottage. Not to mention socialise. The town was lively enough on arrival. The population, I was informed, would quadruple once the holiday season began.

The weather wasn't great, that summer of '79. The risk of rain led to me suggesting we house the whole set-up in a caravan. It would also make relocating a lot simpler, and save having to break everything down and reassemble as we moved it from beach to beach. Indeed, we could potentially take it anywhere in the country. Prior to that, they were looking at a flat-bed trailer with a curtain round three sides.

The caravan was the presenting unit, with the desk in the back of the van that towed it. The DJ and Producer could see each other through the front and rear windows.

A simple hook up of cables on arrival, and it worked. It actually worked!

The side of the caravan dropped down to make a stage for when the weather was conducive. Pete, as well as being supervisor, was also a carpenter and general handyman. There wasn't much he couldn't make.

We had a back-up generator for when we couldn't connect to mains power. It was noisy, though, so wasn't ideal.

The radio played along through everything. One DJ in particular, Ray Nuno, who hosted 'Nuno At Noon' would become a huge influence and mentor to me.

He was on for three hours every weekday, and as I listened to him, it dawned on me that there was more to presenting than merely announcing a song title and artist. Behind the decks in the discos, that was all I'd been doing.

It took me days to work out why he appealed so. And then it clicked - I could hear his smile.

Without ever opining verbally, I knew what records and bands he liked and didn't like so much. I knew when he was teasing or being lighthearted, and when he was being serious. Yes, it was in the tone of voice and inflections, but it was also the fact I could hear his facial expression.

When I got to meet him, I already knew what he was like, and, surprisingly, what he looked like. In fact, I recognised him before I was introduced.

Charisma. Personality. Empathy. Wry humour. They were all things I learnt to subtly transmit because of Ray Nuno.

He was late-forties, and had been in radio for twenty years. The first record he ever played over the air was 'Somethin' Else' by Eddie Cochran. He was adamant that it was the first punk single. The fact The Sex Pistols recorded it was proof enough in his eyes.

My birthday fell on a Tuesday. My twenty-first.

Pete The Supervisor knew, despite my attempts to keep it quiet. At about five o'clock, tools were downed. I was seized, given twenty-one unceremonious bumps on the beach, and tossed in the sea. Not too far - just into the shallow waves near the shore. They knew I couldn't swim.

Canham had the foresight to go to my cottage and get me a change of clothes - my best clothes. And, once changed, I was taken on the town where I didn't buy a drink all night long.

Was that the best summer of my life? I can't think of a superior one.

And it kept getting better.

27.

It was my first time on the airwaves.

Pete proposed I do the interview - a five-minute segment on 'Nuno At Noon' to talk about and promote the upcoming roadshows, and the caravan that was ready to roll.

"Be more natural," Ray Nuno advised me afterwards. "Leave a few ers and ahs in there. It makes you sound human, rather than reading from a sheet of paper, or reciting something you've memorised. Watch out for repetition. Every answer you gave started with 'well Ray...'. And slow it down a touch. Let your character come across."

I was a little crestfallen, as we sat celebrating in a pub that evening, the hard work behind us.

"Hey, you did well," Ray further informed me, seeing I was down. "But you need to do better than that if you want a career in broadcasting.

"Look," he continued, "anyone can introduce a song on the radio. Pretty much anybody can read out a script. What do you bring to it? That's what determines whether you get to host your own show or not. Yes, a knowledge of music is useful, but you need to stand out from the crowd. Do you know what I do?" he asked me.

I shook my head.

"I imagine I'm sat comfortably on one side of a table, just as I am now, and that I'm talking to one person. Again, just as I currently am. It's as if I'm chatting to an individual, not thousands of people doing whatever it is they're doing. It's just you and me, having a drink, and catching up. Go on, try it."

"What should I say?"

"Anything. Introduce a record. The record playing on the jukebox now. Tell me about the weather. Something."

I cleared my throat. "Well, that was Skids..."

His raised eyebrows cut me off.

I reset as the song ended. "The saints are coming, and so is the Tinbury Sound Roadshow - this Friday at noon with Ray Nuno. Er," I faltered as the next song came on the jukebox.

Ray rotated his hand; keep going. "The weather's set to be glorious, so come and join us on the main beach. Blondie, 'Sunday Girl', taking us up to the news, and the main news is, it's Ray's round!"

He smiled. I smiled. I heard my lips part, and imagined the microphone picking up that tiny click as they did. Perhaps, even, the almost inaudible crinkling of my eyes and the skin around my mouth and jaw.

"There you go!" Ray said approvingly. He placed his hand on my shoulder as he rose to get the drinks.

I cast Ray, I now see, in the role of father figure. He was, I think, the father I wish I'd had. Patient and kind, he showed me a guiding hand, rather than a closed fist.

Later that evening a group of us were chatting. I was emboldened by the day's events.

"Will he make it as a DJ, Ray?" Pete asked Nuno of me.

"I think he has every chance," Ray replied.

"Careful, he'll be after your show!"

"If you need me to stand in, Ray..." I quipped.

He smiled. "They'll farm me off to a late-night slot soon enough. Who knows? Perhaps you could take over the noon till three show. A few years from now, I mean."

"Really?" I asked, trying to read if he was joking or not.

"Why not? In another five or six years, it could happen. Learn your trade, young Nick."

A DIFFERENT MIX

"I always planned on being on national radio before I was thirty," I said.

An awkward silence greeted that. I hadn't meant it disparagingly, or even boastfully. I certainly hadn't intended to demean Ray Nuno. It was my silly little dream - my target in life.

"Sorry, I didn't mean..." I began.

"No!" Ray cut me off. It was the first time I'd seen him show any sternness.

My face burnt, the redness apparent to my lowered eyes.

"Never apologise for that, Nick. You hang on to that ambition. I hope you are. I hope you're hosting The Breakfast Show on BBC Radio One. I'll be proud of you when that day comes."

"It's not too late for you, Ray. You're the best I know," I said, and meant it.

He chuckled. "I'm pushing fifty, Nick. If it was going to happen, it would have happened by now. But don't let people strip that away from you," he added in a quiet voice. "They'll try. But you keep sight of your dream. Understand?"

"Yes."

"You promise?"

"Yes, I promise," I assured him.

"I'm serious," he continued seriously as he swilled the last of his whisky. "See, I've lowered my expectations to match where I am in life. Every day I con myself into thinking this is all I ever wanted - the extent of my ambition. Don't be like me. Right, I'm off home. I'll see you on Monday for the Roadshow."

"See you Monday. Thanks, Ray. For everything."

In that moment, all I wanted was to be just like Ray Nuno.

His words that day have remained with me for all of the intervening years.

Whereas Ray had given up on his dream before he was fifty, I still cling on to it despite being almost sixty. Not least, I do it because of the promise I made Ray Nuno that Friday evening in a pub in Tinbury Head.

It's also why I make an effort to appear younger than my years, by dying my hair and whitening my teeth, and why I look every day for the next-big-thing. And why I'm drawn to the unknown acetates I see in shops and on the internet.

If I could just find it, I could use it to hop up the ladder a few rungs.

How different my life would be! I could keep the house up here to retreat to, and have a little flat in London - in some exclusive part where the stars live. They'd be my friends and neighbours, those celebrities, courting me for my notoriety and ability to get them the exposure they covet.

The up-and-coming, too, would be keen to rub shoulders, their chances of success being greatly enhanced by my simple endorsement.

A taste-maker. A trend-setter. A talent-spotter. A respected voice in the industry. A cutting-edge purveyor of good taste.

Invitations to recording sessions would swamp me. Lend them my ear!

Advance promotional copies would once again overwhelm me, because my opinion could make or break it.

I log-on, the buzz of optimism daring to peer round the edge of the door that is nudged ever so slightly ajar, as the computer whirrs and purrs and does whatever it is computers do.

A password is entered as soon as the keyboard and mouse are operational, and a wait while a scan performs to see if updates are required.

No! I'm all up to date.

In I go, hitting send and receive on the email - that beautiful blue line indicating I've been sought out and targeted for my relevance.

My relevance, it becomes apparent, is as a consumer, as a long list of emails that have no connection to me unfurl themselves on the screen.

Why would I want a new boat engine? I don't own a boat. I've never owned a boat. I have no intention of ever owning a boat.

I can't even fucking swim.

Oh, and because I've bought vinyl records in the past, I must - I simply must! - be craving expensive reissues of shit albums I could buy in a second-hand shop for a tenth of the price. Albeit, not on coloured vinyl.

There's nothing. Absolutely nothing is of any actual interest to me. They know me so little, despite seeing everything I do on-line.

And so I return to the unknown - the record that has occupied my turntable for days on end.

Backward is the only way I can see to go.

- Back, back, back in time, with me, Nick Cherry, DJ.

28.

A Bank Holiday weekend - Monday August 27th, 1979.

Tinbury Head was packed. In addition to the regular holiday makers, there were mods on scooters and a gang of leather-clad bikers. Skinheads wore braces over short-sleeved t-shirts, and a new breed of more androgynous looking New Romantics peacocked about the place. The post-punks had shed their studded leather for the day, the heat too intense. As a result, white limbs dangled from sloganed t-shirts.

It was all very tribal.

Ray played The Who, because they all liked The Who, didn't they? A bit mod, a bit rocker with their 'Summertime Blues', and Keith Moon liked the whole punk thing.

Who are you?

Weather-wise, it hadn't been the greatest August ever, but that Bank Holiday weekend was stickily hot.

She came up to the side of the stage to get Ray Nuno's autograph. I was there, checking the cables and making sure nobody messed about with the equipment.

"Can I help you?" I asked.

"Maybe."

She was dark beyond a tan. It was a natural pigment she carried, showing in the hue of her eyebrows, and the chestnut of her irises. Her hair, though, was lightened by streaks of gold. She was petite, an inch over five feet tall. I didn't appreciate how small she was until I stood and approached her. From even a short distance she seemed taller.

I was instantly struck by her attractiveness.

A DIFFERENT MIX

Despite my nerves, I handled it well, that first encounter. As she told me later, I appeared really cool. She assumed I was a DJ on the radio. Or, at least, very comfortable in that environment - perhaps I was in a band.

Another assumption on her part, was to think me older than I was. She, after all, was nine years my senior.

"Well?" I asked her, and smiled.

"I was hoping to get a signature."

"I'll sign anything you want," I said to her with seriousness.

There was a reluctance to dismiss me and potentially hurt my feelings, as well as embarrass herself.

"I suppose that would be okay," she eventually agreed.

"I'm joking. I'll get Ray to sign something for you."

I held my hand out, and she handed me a pen and a sheet of paper.

"Shan't be a minute," I chimed to her happily.

As I turned away, I could still see her - her hourglass figure imprinted on my mind's eye.

I hadn't been looking for anything during my time at the seaside. I'd been active, seeing a couple of girls staying in the area, but they'd gone back home after a week. Two at the most.

"Ray!" I called out as a record began playing.

"What's up, Nick?"

"Need your autograph."

"No problem, bring it up," he said, so I stepped up on the stage.

I looked out on a sea of people - two thousand plus - and the actual sea beyond them. It was glorious!

"There you go. Can you show Gilly where to set up?"

"Gilly?"

"That young lady there," he explained, and waved at the autograph seeker. "I'll pop round tomorrow - thank you!" he shouted to her.

It dawned on me, then. Ray had said he was getting the team lunch that day as a thank you.

And what a lunch it was!

Gilly's family owned a restaurant just east of Tinbury. I'd heard of it, but had never been there. She was from Iran, but wasn't Iranian. It just happened to be where she was born. Until her family had moved to England a decade or more before.

A feast of flavours, textures and colours was laid out in the marquee we used as a base. Ray wound up the show and joined us, as we tucked in to rice, lamb cutlets, and dish after dish of vegetables and fruit. There were olives, and other things wrapped in leaves. And pastries that Ray told us originated in Russia, and large flat breads we used to mop up every morsel.

Wine and beer was handed round, kept cool in a tub filled with ice.

It was a struggle, working after that banquet. But there was no hurry. It was the end of the season - the final Roadshow that year. The pressure was off, and we packed everything into the caravan, and away it went to storage until the following year.

A flatness came with it; a sense of finality as the caravan was towed away - the crowds having long-since drifted back to the town. What would become of me now the job was done?

The marquee was the final thing to be dismantled. Gilly came to collect the empty bowls and plates.

"Thank you," I said to her. "The food was fantastic."

"I'm glad you liked it."

"I'll give you a hand," I offered, and picked up a box to be loaded on the small van she arrived in.

"Thanks. If I get done, I might get to enjoy the last few hours of the Bank Holiday." She had a very slight accent, but spoke perfect English.

"Any plans?" I asked as we walked back to the marquee together, the sides of which had already been removed.

"A quiet drink somewhere, I think. I've had enough of crowds this weekend."

"Sounds perfect."

"And it would be nice to sit outside, and enjoy the weather," she added. "I think finding somewhere quiet might be difficult, though."

"Oh, I don't know - a lot of people are heading out of town this evening. They were only down for the weekend."

I slid the last box into the van. "Look, erm, I live out near Wishaven. I know a place just west of there that never gets too busy. And they have a garden. It's where I'm going later, if you want to join me."

She regarded me, a neutral expression hinting at nothing.

"I could get the bus," she mused. "I don't want to drive."

"What time will you be finished?" I asked her, having trouble containing my utter delight.

"In about an hour."

"Me too. Why don't I meet you right here, on that bench, and we can get the bus together?"

"Okay," she decided. "Six o'clock?"

"Perfect."

She was.

29.

We didn't drink much, content to sippily let the time drip by.

"I'm not sure I want to be in the restaurant trade for the rest of my life," she volunteered. "I'll be thirty next year, so I suppose I ought to work out what I do want."

It shocked me, that information, but I hid it. I think we'd each presumed the other to be mid-twenties.

"I'm going to be a DJ on the radio."

"Good for you. I thought you already might be."

"Not yet. Why aren't you married?" I clumsily asked.

"I am."

If her age surprised me, that one floored me. I didn't know what to say.

After a time, I mumbled, "then why are you here with me?"

"Why am I having an innocent drink with a friend of a friend?"

"Erm, yes. I suppose."

"Why shouldn't I?"

"Won't your husband mind?"

"I doubt it. I doubt he'd even notice."

"I'd notice. I'd definitely notice that you weren't there."

She demurely played with her wine glass.

"No ring," I said, pointing at her left hand.

"I don't wear it to work."

That made sense. We continued chatting. It was easy, talking to Gilly. Music, books, dreams and life - past, present and future - made up the bulk of our dialogue.

"Do you want another drink?" she asked me after a time.

"It depends."

"On?"

"On whether you want to see the cottage where I live. If you do, we should probably skip the drink and get to that, or we'll run out of time."

Again, her non-committal smile.

Secret Affair, 'Time For Action' played in my head.

"Where does your husband think you are?"

"Working. With a friend. Who knows?"

"What does he do? Your husband, I mean. For a living."

"Wine. Imports."

"Do you want to go, then? My place is a ten minute walk away."

The smallest of nods. She was too bashful to say the word 'yes' out-loud. It was, I think, less incriminating for her not to verbally accept.

As we walked back, we didn't touch one another. There was no physical contact between us prior to entering the cottage I called home.

Even then, we clumsily danced around each other, as I offered her a drink.

Gilly stood in the kitchen, her back leaning against the countertop above the washing machine. The uncovered west-facing window let the last of the light in. She appeared as if glowing golden in those rays.

Again, I think she did that self-consciously; silhouetting herself as if a shadow - as though none of it were real.

I went to her, compelled, and our very first physical contact was mouth on mouth. God, the taste, smell and feel of her!

My hands ran up the inside of her skirt, lifting it to the narrowest point of her hourglass, before sliding back down, taking her underwear with them.

She raised one foot, then the other, to enable their full removal. A dark triangle of soft hair showed in the scant twilight.

Lifting her, I set her down gently on the countertop.

There was something extra to be had from her being an older woman. And, yes, a married woman - another man's woman.

It wasn't the first time. Elaine flashed into my mind, but I nudged that thought away, before pushing forward and slipping perfectly into Gilly with far more ease than I'd anticipated.

She didn't touch me that first time. Beyond our locked lips and genitals, we barely connected.

However, we connected like I'd never connected with anyone before or since.

She made hardly a sound, other than more rapid, deeper breaths, and a couple of unstemmable sigh-like exhalations that sent a shiver down my spine.

"No!" was the only whispered word she uttered as I went to withdraw.

It was dark by then, the sun having dropped and extinguished so suddenly, as it tends to near the coast. I don't know why sunsets are so brief at the beach. Is it because of the flatness of the sea, so it has nothing to hide behind?

No lights were on, and I remember thinking how strange it was - the darkness, the near-silence, the majority of clothing still in place, the lack of contact when observed, and the fact she'd hidden herself in front of the last of the light.

Yet, paradoxically, we'd just fornicated in front of an uncovered kitchen window a few yards from the street.

We were still fornicating. I was still inside her.

She was exotic fruit, like the food I'd eaten that very day.

Unlike lunch, it was forbidden, the fruit I gorged that evening.

I knew I wanted to do it again and again and again. All the time. For ever.

I was, I suddenly realised, in love.

Just like that! Without warning. From meeting her some eight hours before, and spending a couple of hours in her company, I was absolutely, undeniably in love with Gilly.

30.

One man's loss is another's gain.

"Are you ready?" Mark Canham asked me one Friday in January of 1980. I'd been summoned to his office at eight, and had feared the worst.

Since the summer last, I'd been drifting, playing a regular disco at the Haven Bay Caravan Park to a tiny out-of-season crowd.

Tinbury Sound had kept me on, on sixty-percent of my summer earnings. I still had the cottage, and I was still seeing Gilly at least one night a week.

"Ready for what?"

"Ready to go on the air."

"What? Yes! When?" I stammered.

"Today. In four hours. You're taking 'Nuno At Noon'. Ray's laid up with the flu. So is the person who would normally step in. Can you do it? Ray says you can."

"Yes! I won't let you down."

I was shitting myself. Ray had kept me close, encouraging me to sit in the control room during his shows. We'd go for a drink, on the nights I didn't see Gilly or have a DJ booking, and he'd pass on those fatherly pearls of wisdom of his.

The playlist was already set. It was predominantly current chart music, a dozen oldies, and a couple of free-choice oddities Ray had thrown in.

My hands were damp with sweat as I sat in the chair with a couple of minutes to go. I couldn't think straight, and my heart was going at fifty to the dozen.

"Three, two, and one..."

- *This is Nick...*

Shit! I'd spoken all over the jingle. My face flushed furiously. The Producer smiled and splayed his fingers to tell me to calm down.

- *This is still Nick Cherry, standing in for Ray Nuno. Get well soon, Ray. This one's for you.*

It was 'On My Radio' by Selecter, the first song on the first show I presented.

You don't forget that. You don't forget your first one.

Despite it not being my choice, it was a track I liked and may have chosen - a regular selection on the discos. Its aptness wasn't lost on me. It was almost as if Ray knew.

Equally as fitting, was the fact it was a new decade - a new wave, and I was determined to be at the forefront of whatever was coming.

I had a sense, as I found a rhythm and settled down after twenty minutes or so - a sense that things were changing. The ska boom was red hot, but a more electronic synth driven sound was set to elbow it aside.

Gary Numan, OMD and Japan had all emerged. I witnessed the shift at the caravan site, and clocked the songs that got the New Romantics up and moving.

A keen eye was also kept on the music press, particularly the underground magazines. I'd even written and had a few articles published in them. Again, it was Ray who encouraged me. "Get your name known, Nick."

Ray's list that day was a mixed bag, just as you'd expect for daytime radio.

The Inmates, 'The Walk', was the second song played, for example, with Tourists 'I Only Want To Be With You' and Joe Jackson's 'Different For Girls' filling the first fifteen minutes.

I loved every second of it. Sitting in the chair or pacing the studio, I had it confirmed - there was nothing else I wanted to do in life, other than be a DJ. It was where I belonged.

The time flew by - three hours feeling like an hour. I cryptically dedicated a track to 'G' in Tinbury Head - Queen's 'Crazy Little Thing Called Love'. And when I signed off before the last track, 'London Calling' by The Clash, I had no doubt that London would come calling.

The Producer gave me a nod of approval, which was high praise indeed, and Mark Canham shook my hand and thanked me.

"Looks like we found a back-up presenter," he commented and winked.

Ray told me how well I'd done over a drink a few days after.

He enjoyed a drink, but, unlike with my father and others, it softened him.

As he said to me one night, "it's my way of unwinding. Alcohol is a mood enhancer, rather than a mood alterer. My advice, for what it's worth? Only drink when you're happy, and you'll simply get happier."

I could never imagine him being anything other than jovial. His hair showed grey on light brown - proper salt and pepper. A smile naturally curled his lips beneath a broad nose and forehead, to match his broad but softly-rounded shoulders. There was something very honest about his face.

He had no flashiness, content to sit in a quiet corner and shy away from the limelight, in his jacket over an open-neck shirt. I never saw him wear a tie, or even a suit. And I never once heard him raise his voice.

He was, I believe, the most decent man I ever met in my life.

Gilly heard the show, and visited me that same evening. She drove over to the cottage in the restaurant's delivery van. It was a risk. She ordinarily caught the bus and snuck in furtively on a weeknight.

We'd been carrying on for five months, always meeting at my place. Since that first time, we'd never been out together.

It was a Friday night, though, and I had a rare night off. I wanted to celebrate.

"I don't suppose it matters. I think he knows, anyway," Gilly informed me.

"Your husband?" I asked, even though it was obvious.

"Yes."

"What makes you think that?" I felt a twinge in my tummy, as a tangled twine tightened to a knot.

"Something he said. I don't think he minds. In fact, I think it makes his life easier. He can drink and be with his business friends."

"Will he do anything?"

"To you?" she asked.

I nodded. "And you."

"Probably not. If you want to give it a rest for a while, I..."

"No!" I adamantly stated.

She smiled at that, raised herself on her tiptoes, and kissed me.

"Let's go out. Just down to the pub. If he knows, it doesn't matter, does it?" I proposed.

"I still have to think of my family. I don't want to bring shame on them."

"Nobody will see us. It's January, and the weather's miserable."

She thought about it. "Okay."

I didn't see. I was oblivious to the fact things were escalating. She was the one with everything to lose. And in that moment, there were no consequences to anything I could think of; there was nothing I wasn't prepared to take on.

We went to the pub. It was quiet. We canoodled in a dark corner and drank more than we normally would.

She rang her husband from the pub phone. I didn't hear the call, but she told me she claimed she was with a friend, had too much to drink, and didn't want to risk driving back.

She'd stay the night.

"Did he believe you?" I asked her.

"I don't know. Besides which, it's kind of the truth."

"We're more than friends, though. Doesn't he care?"

She considered her reply. "Only as far as his reputation goes. I think, as long as it isn't public, and he isn't embarrassed by it, he ignores it."

"But if he knows you're with another man... Look, if it was me, I wouldn't want to share you with anyone."

She squeezed my leg appreciatively. "Sex isn't important to him."

"Really?" I asked disbelievingly.

"It never has been. In eight years of marriage, he made a bit of effort at the start, but not for long. He's the kind of man who will turn the television over if anything sexy comes on. For years, I thought perhaps it was me..."

"It isn't," I assured her.

"No. I don't believe it is. But I was young, and you doubt yourself. He's seven years older than me. Even when we did have sex, it was in the dark with the lights out, and there was no build up. It was perfunctory. An obligation he had to fulfill as part of his duty almost. Like washing-up or taking the bins out. I got a feeling he derived no pleasure from it."

"God!" I said, because I couldn't think what else to say. "When did you last have sex with him?"

"About six years ago. It dwindled until it stopped. We often share a bed, but there's no intimacy. We don't argue, and we live together harmoniously enough. But it isn't what I envisaged from a marriage."

"Until last August, you hadn't had sex in five and a half years?" I further enquired.

"I had an affair a couple of years ago."

"What happened?"

"The man I saw wanted an affair. I wanted something more. I do, I mean. I want more. I want children. I want a normal life."

It was my turn to gently massage her leg.

"Does the age difference between us bother you?" she asked me.

"I haven't even thought about it," I answered honestly.

I did, though, as we sat there drinking, my hand stroking her. I thought about how, when I was her age, she'd be nearly forty. And that seemed so old.

"Didn't you spot there was something wrong when you were going out with him? Before you were married, I mean."

"Because of my family, we didn't really know each other. Besides, I was so young. I was married at twenty-one."

She'd been my age.

Okay, when I was eleven, and she twenty, that wouldn't have worked. But as we got older, so the gap reduced. I'd gone from half her age, to two-thirds her age in those ten years. And when she's eighty and I'm seventy-one, it will be nothing, that age disparity - it won't matter a damn.

Oh, and she was so beautiful and sexy, it made no difference to anything whatsoever.

"Are you hungry?" I asked her to move things on.

"I fancy some chips," she replied, and smiled.

Gilly always fancied chips when she visited me. It was different to what she was used to - something not available in Iran, or at the restaurant she worked in.

It was an indulgence - a naughty little treat - drizzled with vinegar and sprinkled with salt. A different flavour to what she was accustomed to. Just as the food I'd eaten that Bank Holiday back in August was hitherto alien to me.

Yes, Gilly loved chips.

And I loved Gilly.

I'm as sure as I can be that she also loved me.

31.

We carried on, Gilly and I. For years, we carried on just as we had been. Albeit, in a different cottage - one further from Tinbury Head, and within my means.

The disco work kept me solvent. The Roadshow ran each summer, and I stood in for Ray a handful of times as he took holidays, etcetera. But nothing much changed.

I was impatient. Twenty-two, twenty-three, twenty-four. Ray and Gilly advised me - learn my trade, and my chance would come.

Why rock the boat? That was what Gilly and I decided. Her husband knew. He'd mentioned it to her. He was okay with it all, her seeing me discreetly. It grew, our relationship, from one night a week, to two, then three. Sometimes she'd show up on a Tuesday evening, and not leave until the Friday morning, when she was required in the restaurant.

Biding my time. Treading water. Going nowhere.

We had it all planned and mapped out. I'd get my break on the radio. With that, a decent guaranteed weekly wage. Gilly would leave, and move in with me. We'd buy a little place. She was reluctant to act without that security. Her family would never understand.

Oh, but I think she would have come to me, if only I'd pulled.

Why didn't I pull?

Why didn't she push?

We drifted, but didn't go anywhere. Round and round we went, like the records I played three or four nights a week to holiday makers and just-married couples and birthday boys and girls.

The thing was, there was no real incentive to change anything. I was happy. I genuinely was. And the no-commitment liaisons with Gilly didn't exactly appall me. In an unacknowledged way, I think they perhaps suited us both.

Not that I cheated on her through that time. There was no urge to look elsewhere. Gilly was enough for me.

It was the summer of '82 and the Roadshow was in full-swing. I was taken on as Assistant Producer for the guest DJs who visited the town. At least I got to look into the studio and wear a pair of headphones.

I was getting closer.

Eddie Noakes was the main DJ in Tredmouth. I remembered him from my teenage years. He hosted 'Morning Brake', the breakfast show on Brakeshire County Radio, before it became Tred FM. He'd been around since the mid-fifties, and traded on having 'been there' through the sixties.

Coach-loads of people made the day-trip down from Tredmouth. I watched them disembark, and saw no familiar faces.

It felt like a lifetime ago, those three years since I'd upped sticks and relocated down to Tinbury. In all that time, I'd felt no compulsion to return.

"Can you go and find Eddie, Nick? Tell him we need him to pop over and do a soundcheck - make sure we get the levels set. And he needs to know how this rig works," someone asked me.

"No problem."

Off I went, skippety-skip, not at all perturbed at the prospect of meeting a minor celebrity. After all, he was no bigger than Ray, and not nearly as good. He was never going to be anything other than on local county radio.

"Eddie," I called out, opening the door and poking my head into the mobile home he'd travelled down in.

I saw his piggy eyes looking at me in the mirror he faced. A young woman was in the process of fitting a wig on his bald pate, and teasing out strands to make it look as if it permanently resided there.

"Shut the fucking door!" he snapped.

I stepped inside and closed it behind me.

"We need you to do a soundcheck," I informed him.

"I told you what fucking levels I want."

"I know, but with it being an outside broadcast, it needs setting up right. And some elements might be different to a normal studio."

"I've been doing this for nearly thirty fucking years! You think there's going to be something I haven't seen before?"

"I'm just the messenger," I pleaded, and raised my palms in surrender.

What a wanker.

He huffed and puffed, the lady brushing a little more foundation around his newly-fitted hair, lest a white line should betray him.

"All done?" he asked.

The young woman nodded. He regarded himself in the mirror, turning his head from side to side before raising his chins. A couple of them stayed glued to his neck.

"Excellent!" he said to her approvingly, and slid his chair back before standing. He was about five-six in height, but grew at least two inches when he stepped into his lifted shoes.

A playful slap on the makeup woman's backside was her bonus for a job well done. With his back turned as he slipped his arms through his jacket sleeves, I smiled at her with sympathy.

Good god! I knew her. And she evidently recognised me. A shake of her head stopped me from saying her name. Mandy.

She'd been a hairdresser in a salon I'd lived above for a while, when I was at Oakburn Technical College.

"Right," Eddie Noakes boomed, "let's go and waste my precious fucking time."

Every member of the team detested Eddie Noakes. The thing was, he simply didn't care. As long as he had celebrity and an audience, he treated people with disdain. To those beneath him, it was open contemptuousness.

But stick him in front of a mic or crowd, and he became Noakesy; a man with time for everyone and everything, replete with a voice that spoke of care and love for all, beamed forth by his ultra-white teeth.

He was flashy to Ray Nuno's cosy. He was glib where Ray was sincere. He was playing Star next to Ray's Everyman.

And the thing was, at the age of twenty-four, and even though I couldn't abide the man, I wanted to be more like Eddie Noakes.

Gilly dropped by in the afternoon.

"What time should I come over later?" she furtively asked me.

"Not sure. It depends what time this lot leave," I whispered.

"There's something I need to tell you."

"Eddie Noakes is a big deal, Gilly. This could be a chance for me."

"Oh. Okay. Perhaps we should give it a miss tonight," she suggested.

"It might be for the best."

Why? Why did I say that? Because I was angling for an invite to the party arranged for Eddie Noakes and his team.

Mandy had said she'd get me in. I wanted to catch up with her, and learn the latest on Brakeshire. I wanted to catch up with her in every sense.

"Very nice!" Noakes sneered to me as he watched Gilly walk away.

"She is," I confirmed.

"Does she work for the radio station?"

"Kind of. She does some catering."

"She could cater for me."

I kept quiet and smiled over at Mandy.

"Too much of the tar-brush, though. I don't think my listeners would approve," Noakes added. "Still, they're all pink when you open them up."

I bit my lip and smiled more broadly at Mandy.

Noakes strutted away, and I looked over to see Gilly watching me from her van.

It was the first time in three years I'd not wanted to see Gilly.

Mandy had reverted her name back to its root, Amanda, so she'd be taken more seriously. Altered, too, was her look - from the spiky, edgy teenage girl who'd cut my hair four years before, to the slick, professional young woman who styled the stars.

32.

Nothing happened between Amanda and I that evening. Through her, though, Noakes took a liking to me. I told him about my aspirations, that I'd stood in on shows a few times, and ran a mobile disco.

He had shares in Brakeshire Radio Ltd., and a lot of clout as a consequence. Had it not been for that level of boardroom influence, I'd come to learn that they would have farmed him off years before I met him.

It was, I heard it said, the reason he bought the shares - so that he might hang on to his position.

Amanda and I exchanged contact details, and promised to stay in touch, and get together when I was back in Brakeshire.

It was the following day before I saw Gilly.

"He's had an offer from a company in America," she reported to me.

"Your husband?"

"Yes. California, to be precise."

"What will you do?"

She looked at me dully. We were in bed. We were always in bed, either having sex or recovering from having had sex. What else was there to do? It wasn't as if we could go out.

"He said it would be good for his image if I was with him. After all, he's supposed to be a settled, dependable married man."

"Oh."

"Oh?" she echoed.

"Well, what do you want?"

"Wow, someone actually asked me what I want!"

"What's wrong, Gilly?"

"I don't know. Being thirty-three soon. This! Us, I mean. Where are we going?"

"Are you saying that you want to move to California?"

"To tick a box and fill a quota," she muttered miserably.

"Then what do you want? I've been waiting for three years for you to decide what you want. God forbid you should upset your bloody family."

"That's not fair! I would have left. It was you who kept saying about landing a radio presenter job, and being more... I don't know what."

"I just thought your family would be more accepting if I was more successful," I countered. "I was thinking of you."

"Who was the girl you were smiling at yesterday?" she asked suddenly.

"Which one?" I replied, knowing perfectly well who she was referring to.

"The tall, slim one with the long straight fair hair."

"Oh, she's just Eddie's Stylist."

"Were you with her last night?"

"What? No, of course not. What are you talking about?"

"She looked more your age."

"She probably is. But I don't care about age. Look," I began, and seriously thought about stopping, "I knew her vaguely, from back in Brakeshire. When I was at College in Oakburn. She was a part of the scene at the time. But nothing happened then, and nothing happened now."

"She's very pretty."

"She's not a patch on you." That was true. "Hey, Eddie Noakes asked me who you were. He took a shine to you, I think," I added teasingly, shifting the focus from me to her.

"Probably a good job I wasn't out with him yesterday evening, then," she acerbically replied.

Long gone was any bashfulness in her. She slipped from the bed, and stood looking out the window through the net curtain.

"Do you want to go to America?" I said quietly.

"No, Nick. I don't want to go to bloody America. I mean, god! Yes, I'd like to live in California, on a huge hillside vineyard, with an income far in excess of anything I've ever dreamed of. But I don't want to do that with my husband."

That was it - that, as far as I can fathom things, was the moment.

Had I said that I wanted her to be with me, and to not go abroad, I know she would have stayed. We would have moved in together. She'd have got a divorce. Gilly and I would have been a couple.

Why didn't I? For a number of reasons. Ambition, was the main one. Selfish ambition would inform all the life-choices I took around that time.

I tell myself that it was a noble option, to not deprive her of the opportunity to better her life. But that's largely bollocks.

Appallingly, I even considered that she might move there, miss me terribly, and that I would go and join her. Where better to find the celebrity I coveted than California? Oh, yes, they'd love me over there, with my British accent and general way. I knew all about the emerging scene back across the pond. How could they refuse me?

And Amanda. She popped in my mind as I admired Gilly's curves and olive skin and exoticism.

Comments peppered my thoughts. Eddie Noakes with his 'tar-brush' slur. Other ignorant things said mostly in jest, but lodging nonetheless.

So I depicted Amanda in her place, with her long pale legs and comparatively shapeless form. Her flat chest and backside and general straight up-and-downness. More English like that. More the kind of woman I could see myself with. More in line with who others would expect me to be with.

I did nothing and said nothing. I opted to let her decide what she wanted, and I'd deal with whatever that was.

And no sooner was she on a plane to California with her husband - to check the place out and have a bit of a holiday - than I was heading back to Brakeshire for the first time since I'd left over three years before.

Amanda was the first person I called when I got there.

We met for drinks and a natter, and were friendly with one another. A little more than friendly. I kissed her when we parted, but only on the side of her mouth, and made my way to uncle Russ's and a bed for the night.

Gilly returned from her 'vacation', and said very little beyond how scenic it was.

There was no argument - no scene - no falling out.

Two months on, and she moved there permanently.

I never heard from her again.

I've regretted it ever since. Thousands of times, spanning decades, I've rued that moment.

A hollow sonsy-shaped nook exists within me that, I believe, only Gilly could ever have filled.

My only effort to find out about her welfare, came from a visit to her family's restaurant perhaps six months on. They weren't her family any more. The business had been sold, and they, like her, had flown away to begin again. It was enabled by her husband, through his job in California.

It is my firm belief, that all I had to do that night as she leant on the windowsill bearing all, was to tell her that I loved her.

Had I done that, and left her in no doubt that I wanted her, she wouldn't have got dressed and left a few minutes on.

From the moment she had, things were different between us.

I wish I could go back and put that right, is my thought as I silence the record, and make my way to bed...

33.

...she's so beautiful and exotic - orchidaceous next to the daisies and buttercups and English roses.

She leans on my window-ledge and radiates pure gold as the setting sun is filtered through her.

"I love you. Don't go," I say from the bed I lie in, and she twists her neck and smiles at me.

"Say it again," she asks in the perfect classical English she learned in a bid to be more accepted.

"I love you, Gilly. From the moment I first saw you."

Her hips rise and fall sexily as she sashays towards me, her bounteous breasts hanging invitingly as she kneels on the mattress. I gently bite her pinky-brown nipples.

She likes it like this, with a cushion under her bottom to change the angle. And for the first time since the first time, we don't take precaution. Because there is, from this moment, no caution required. There are no unwelcome consequences to anything now.

"Don't go," I beg her when the time to leave beckons.

She shrugs. "Okay. But I need to ring him. Or he'll worry. He might ring the police."

"Yes. of course. Call him. Use my phone."

"No. I'll use the pay phone. Let's go for a walk, Nick."

"Good idea." It's the first time she's suggested we be seen in public together. A couple of furtive nights at the local are all she's ever permitted, lest her family should find out.

We amble along the narrow, winding lane that echoes the coast. Arms proprietorially envelop, for she is mine and I am hers.

It's still light. People are out strolling. Normal people, just as we are - couples and families and a few on their own. We smile. They smile. Everyone's happy because the weather's nice - perfect for an evening saunter with the warm fresh breeze carrying the scent of oceanic life to our noses. So much so, that we can taste it on the air.

I listen to her call, the phone box door ajar. She tells him she'll be away for the night. Before she informs him she's been thinking, and won't be going to California with him. Not even for a couple of weeks to look at the place.

I hear him say "okay." It's the first time I've heard his voice. It's the closest she's ever allowed me to get.

"Fish and chips?" I suggest, because she loves her chips.

"Hmmm! Good idea. I might have a saveloy."

"He's not a bad man," she explains as we walk to the chip shop.

"I hope you won't hate me for this," I say.

"For what?"

"For your not going to live in California."

"Never! Anyway, perhaps I will go. With you. Or somewhere else. When you're a famous DJ, I imagine we'll get to go to a lot of places."

"Ha!" I scoff dismissively. But it isn't ridiculous when I'm with Gilly. Anything and everything seems possible.

On we walk, eating our supper as we do, her shoulder gently bumping my arm because we stay so close...

...She's quiet. This is what we do several nights a week - set up the disco at the caravan park and play to the crowd. We have to make as much money as we can during the summer to see us through the winter.

"What's wrong with you?" I ask her.

"I'm fine. I'm just tired."

She's always tired, and always moaning. Yes, she works long hours at the cafe, up on her feet all day. And with her being pregnant, it must take its toll. Still, I have to stand here for hours playing records.

Gilly comes home stinking of cooking fat. It gets in her clothes and hair. I taste it on her skin. All that fried food she can't bear to eat any longer. The smell alone is repulsive to her. Time was, she loved a bag of chips.

Her family ostracised her when she left her husband to be with me. In actuality, he was the one who left. Still, she was the one who didn't dutifully follow.

They were stressful days. They still are. Every day feels like a struggle. Particularly since the radio station let me go just before Christmas. Ray Nuno spoke up for me, but the others judged me for stealing another man's wife. A threat by Gilly's family of no more catering, and pulling any advertising were the final nails in that particular coffin.

I learnt my value to the station through that - a few hundred pounds a year.

Ray and I fell out because of it. He could have fucking stood up and fought for me. All he did was advise me to let the dust settle a bit.

The room fills up now the sun's lowered her lids.

"Can you get me a cold beer?" I ask Gilly.

She wearily nods and forces a smile. Some of the spark is gone from her. It's as if a bulb has blown. It's probably the baby parasitically draining her. I see it all, carried in the bags beneath her eyes.

"Wouldn't you rather have some water?" she asks me.

"No, I want a beer."

I watch her waddle away, and keep an eye on her as she orders the drinks. The barman, Jez, is always trying it on with her. He used to, at least. Not so much now.

No, he's more interested in a stunning fair-haired girl in a white dress. He barely even looks at Gilly as he hands over my gratis drink. Six months ago, and he'd have been all flirty pouts and innuendo.

Gilly sits on a stool behind the decks and stares at seemingly nothing. The cold beer's welcome, as I look out on the crowd, the fair girl dancing with her boyfriend. They're so young.

I play songs that I think will keep her on her feet - going from OMD to Wham! to Frankie Goes To Hollywood. A request for Neil's 'Hole In My Shoe' might ruin it all, but, thankfully, she stays on the floor - a floor that's full with gyrating bodies of all shapes and ages - on holiday, inhibitions left at home.

With the white light strobing, I can almost pick out her figure beneath her white dress. Is she naked under there?

A clutch of oldies keep the interest and energy levels up - The Beatles twisting and shouting, The Animals getting out of this place, and Yardbirds.

For your love.

They were all tracks I once put on a cassette tape for a girl called Sharon. A cassette tape I never finished. That was more than ten years ago, when I was not much younger than the girl in the white dress.

These are the same records, given to me by my uncle Russ one day when I was just a kid. And I spin them on the same turntables I was given by Harry, when I was at Oakburn Technical College.

It all happened back in Brakeshire.

Amanda's there. Immaculately made-up and successful, working as a Stylist for the radio and television people, making the stars look so much better than they actually are. Even Eddie Noakes.

Her suggestion we remain in touch has always bothered me. I didn't. I never called or visited. I let her go because of Gilly.

Perhaps we both missed an opportunity in life, Gilly and I, because we chose one another.

Was it the wrong choice?

No! This is a difficult time, that's all. We'll get through it. Something will happen - a break, and a slot on the radio. Tinbury Sound said they'll be in touch if anything comes along - best to let the dust settle. Perhaps Ray was right about that.

- Slowing things down now, with Howard Jones. This is 'Hide And Seek', and I'm Nick Cherry. It's a pleasure being with you this evening.

I speak to the beautiful fair girl, and only her - one-on-one, just as Ray Nuno taught me. And I smile. Did she hear it?

Still they dance, her and her boyfriend. She rests her head on his chest as they sway in time. I put myself in his position, and feel my thumb move as his strokes her hair and face on one side.

He says something to her, and she melts into him.

Gilly startles me, appearing by my side. Her eyes look where mine were pointed.

"I might go. I don't feel great, Nick," she says.

"Okay. I'll pack up here. There's only another half hour to go, and I'll leave the gear for tomorrow night."

She smiles her gratitude. It shocks me to see how old and haggard she appears.

"On your way out, can you pick me up another pint? It's so hot in here."

"You've had your limit on free drinks."

"Tell Jez I'll settle up with him later."

The next record comes in - Tears For Fears 'Pale Shelter' - and my eyes search for the beautiful girl amidst the crowd. She's gone. To the bar, perhaps. It makes me wish I'd fetched my own drink, that chance of being close to her...

..."Another drink?" Jez offers when I'm done, and everybody's gone home for the night.

"Yeah. They owe me a few for what they pay me."

"Busy tonight," he says, as he pours us both one. He adds, "I'm leaving at the end of the summer."

"Oh, why?"

"I want to give the band I'm in one more go. To be honest," he says, joining me on the punter side of the bar and taking a stool, "I'm going to be twenty-five early next year. I don't know why, but it feels significant. If you haven't made it by then, you're probably not going to, you know?"

I think of myself - already past that mark at twenty-six. Shit.

"Who was the girl in the white dress?" I say, by way of changing the topic.

He smiles. "Juliet, her name is. She was in the other day. Tidy, eh?"

I nod.

"Loved up with the boyfriend, though," he adds, and I hear the same tone of missed opportunity I heard when he spoke of his band.

"Is Gilly alright?" he follows on with.

"She's just tired. The heat's hard with her being pregnant."

"Will you stay here? Long-term, I mean."

"Not long-term. But I can't think where we'd go at the moment."

"You have each other," Jez states, as if it explains everything in the world.

"What do you mean?"

"The trouble with a seaside town is all the people you meet are from somewhere else. This isn't really them. This is a version of them they put on for their holiday. Take that Juliet girl."

"What about her?"

"She's from Canterwood. I know the place. If she asked me, I'd follow her there in a heartbeat."

"Really?"

"Oh yes. My plan is, I'm going to push the band thing for a year. Whatever happens, I owe it to myself to give it a proper go. If it works out, great. If it doesn't, I'm going to settle down with someone like her."

"Assuming she'll have you," I point out a little sarcastically.

He flashes me his cheeky grin, and drags his shoulder along his jawline in a James-Dean-shy kind of way.

"Got to aim high," he says, "we only live once."

Jez pours us both a whisky, and we idly chatter. He does most of the talking, as I sit and think of Amanda, Amanda, Amanda - a year younger than me, yet miles ahead, with her job in the media and the parties with the stars, I imagine, and her fashion sense and being back in Brakeshire.

Her energy and youth, in stark contrast to Gilly's defeated lack of effort with herself - her lack of effort with me since she fell pregnant - always complaining or moodily quiet, which is even worse.

I can't help but think I'd be freeing Gilly by leaving.

She'd get her family back, if I was gone from her life, and she could revert to what she was, not that long ago, working in the family restaurant, or over in California with her husband.

He'll be a better father than me, I'll wager. After all, look at my family history. A mother who walked out, and a father who always saw me as an inconvenience - a resented presence that stopped him, to some degree, doing what he wanted in life; being what he wanted to be in life.

That was why he drank. To block it all out, and lose himself in a fog of alcoholic dreams; to shut down his mind and stop him thinking of all the opportunities missed and lost. A fantasy world existed for him in a bottle - an escape!

The drink softens my world and furs the edges - it allows me to slip into a place where everything seems possible again, and my confidence is restored.

As I dance with Amanda, Amanda, Amanda, wearing a white dress and nothing beneath, before we walk out of the discotheque and into the fresh air, where doors symbolically open for us.

Until I remember that I have to go home to Gilly, and a baby on the way, and I wonder if this is what it was like for my father every time the pub closed, and he had to walk home to his disappointing life.

It's in my genes, like cancer and high cholesterol.

Walking through the caravans, looking for her, the girl in the white dress, but all the doors are closed.

Not rushing - prolonging the moment of arrival home.

Home.

Home is Brakeshire, and always shall be, whether I like it or not. This, Tinbury Head, is a fake life where I can pretend to be something I'm not.

A holiday. A vacation, as the Americans have it.

I prefer that word - vacation. To vacate one's life.

Vacate: Leave, give up, cancel or annul.

It sounds more permanent than a mere holiday.

It would be wrong. In every way, it would be wrong to do to a child - a baby - what I had done to me: To be begrudged, and ultimately abandoned.

Yes, much better to sever that now, and go before 'it' can know me.

Nature versus nurture.

Is it truly in my genes? Or was it exposure to it that implanted it there?

A bit of both, perhaps. Either way, it'll surely be better for everyone concerned if I am not present to pass it on, and add fuel to a flame that may otherwise be extinguished or peter out of its own accord.

I resent!

I resent my mother for leaving, and my father for disliking me, and Gilly for where I am in life.

Yet there is only one common factor in it all - me.

Am I the problem?

Is it myself I hide from through drink...?

...a fork of lightning flashes across my brain...

...Living a life I know I don't want, but am too afraid to do anything about. Drink allows me to fantasise, but the cold, sober light of day illuminates all of my resentments.

We live in a caravan now, because we couldn't pay the rent on the cottage. The disco work dried up when the weather got wetter, and Gilly couldn't go to work.

No maternity pay, so she signed on. It was better if I didn't work, from a benefits perspective. The paltry amount I was earning from DJing wasn't worth the effort. Then there was the cost - buying records, new stylus, etcetera. When the motor went on the turntable, it never got replaced. I'll fix it in time for the summer season. The same with the speaker. It probably only needs a new fuse. I'll have a look at it.

If I can afford it.

There's no work. Unemployment is the highest it's been in half a century.

I do the odd side-job, cash in hand, which I try to stash away and not tell Gilly about. She gives me a guilt trip for every penny I spend.

She doesn't understand. I need to escape and unwind. A few pints every night is hardly going to make a big difference.

Everything's about the baby, and what 'it' needs. Well, what about what I need?

"I saw Beverly today," Gilly says, and I know where this is going.

"Oh right," is my dismissive reply.

"She said you did a job at the Club House on Monday."

"That's right."

"Where's the money, Nick?"

"It was only a couple of quid."

"Fifteen, Nick. It was fifteen quid."

"I had to pay a debt. There wasn't much left after that."

"What debt?"

"I owed a bit down the pub. And I need a new fuse and stylus for the disco gear. I might be able to get some work over Christmas, with parties and so on."

"We need a cot, Nick. The baby can't sleep with us for ever! And clothes. The baby needs clothes! And we can't carry on bringing up a baby in a caravan!"

"I'm not fucking stupid, Gilly, I know that. I'll fix the gear and earn the money. It was fifteen quid, that's all. I can earn that in a night over Christmas and New Year."

"Let's see the money, then?"

"It's in a safe place."

"Yes! The till behind the bar is a safe place!"

I glower at her.

"Be careful, Gilly," I warn her.

"From what you've told me, you're turning into your dad," she says nastily, and I've lashed out before I can think about it.

Storming out the door, slamming it as I go, and walking across the field in the direction of the pub I only left forty minutes ago.

Stopping at a phone box and searching through my wallet for a scrap of paper on which is a number.

A code I know so well, as I spin the dial and connect to Tredmouth.

Home.

"Hello? Is Amanda there? Yes, tell her it's Nick. Nick Cherry. We're old friends."

As I wait, I see the red mark on the side of my hand holding the receiver. It was a slap, not a punch. I'm not like my father.

More of a push, really. No harm done.

"Hi, Amanda, how are you? Me? Not too bad at all. Hey, I was wondering if you still wanted to catch up. Remember how we said we would? No, no, still in Tinbury. But I'll be up there at the weekend, perhaps."

Shit, how will I get there? The van was sold months ago. It was sitting idle most of the time. I don't have enough money for the train. I'll get it. It'll be fine. Where there's a will, there's a way!

"Yes, yes, I had a couple of drinks. Do I sound that bad? There was a party at the radio station. You know what those things are like. Oh, really? Nobody told me you'd rung looking for me. No, no, I still work there. I'll be getting my own show soon enough. Someone must have been joking with you!

"Well, look, I've got to come up to Brakeshire at the weekend, so, what do you think? Ah, I see. Yes, no, I fully understand. Good for you. Right, well, have a safe trip. Enjoy it. Maybe next time. Hello...?"

...the barmaid slips me a couple of free drinks, bless her.

"If I can slip you anything in return," I propose to her, and she giggles in her saucy way.

It's just a bit of harmless flirting - a bit of fun. A couple of snogs and a grope or two is as far as it's gone. She's bubbly and funny. She makes me feel good.

And she feels good.

She's going to be a model and an actress, and I'm going to be a DJ. That's our angle. Most people you meet at the seaside are killing time, waiting for their big break.

She's been in a couple of things. Small parts in television series - blink and you'll miss her, type stuff. That's how you get started in the acting lark.

"You fancy a big part, do you?" I say, and she laughs at that. "You're only twenty. Plenty of time," I further tell her.

It's bollocks. She'll never be an actress or a model. At least, not in the way she thinks. She hasn't got that je ne sais quoi. Nor does she have any worthwhile connections. She actually pays money to some local Agent who takes a hefty percentage of the poxy scraps of work she has managed to land.

"I've got another audition next week," she tells me in a whisper, her head checking where the landlord is.

"Good for you. What's it for?"

"It's not really what I'm looking for, but my Agent says it might lead to other things."

"Well, what is it?"

A DIFFERENT MIX

"It's a bit.. You know... It's a photo thing. For a magazine."

"What kind of magazine?"

"One of those magazines," she says, and widens her eyes at me.

"Oh! Right."

"It's decent money, though. If I get the shoot. And you never know, do you? It could be a break. My Agent thinks so."

"You've certainly got the assets for it," I tell her.

"You don't think it's wrong?" she asks, leaning on the bar with her arms folded beneath her ample bosom.

"No. Look, I come here to have a drink and relax. The fact you're here makes that more pleasant. I get to look at you and chat to you. And we've had a bit of fun together. The landlord makes a lot out of your 'assets', while you get paid a pittance. So, if you can get a bigger slice of the pie by basically doing the same thing, fair play to you, I say."

"Yeah! That's right. Men look at me, anyway!"

"I have contacts at the main television station in Brakeshire," I boast, matching her conspiratorial tone. "I'll put in a word for you, if you like. I'm due to go up there any day now."

"Really?"

"Yes. Keep it between us, though."

"Oh, I will. I definitely will. Another drink?"

"Go on, then. I'll have to owe you. I couldn't get to the bank, as I said."

"Don't worry about it."

I stick around till closing time, milking her for free drinks as we plan her future together.

More accurately, I plan my own immediate future, and my desire to sample for real what all and sundry shall soon be able to gaze at in full-colour, double-page spread...

..."Will you really get me in at the television station?" she bleats.

"Of course," I assure her. "I wish I'd thought of it before."

We're in the Club House at the caravan site. I kept the key, from back in the days when I used to DJ regularly. I had an extra cut, just in case.

Pulling her to me, I roughly ram my hand under the leg of her pants. Dirty cow. She's sopping wet - gagging for it.

Off they slip, down her legs and over her shoes - high heels for a bar job - her feet must be killing her, but she's young and fit; she can take it.

She can take this, too, as I slam into her avariciously - all the way - taking her breath away.

All those little pricks, wanking themselves senseless soon enough, looking at what I'm looking at, but never knowing how it actually feels.

This is what it's all about, life. We're young, doing what young people do - getting it all out of our systems before we settle down. This is what I should have been doing, instead of being tied down to Gilly, wasting my best days...

...The caravan's quiet. She'll be asleep. She's always asleep - constantly tired. Too tired for sex, even. She can't blame me for dipping the barmaid. I have needs.

Another drink is what I need, replace some of the fluids I sweated and shot out. Filled her right up!

I count the money as I drink from the bottle I took from behind the bar. Scotch. My dad's tipple after the beer. A nightcap. Or two or three. It won't hurt. It's not as if I have to be up in the morning.

I'm not stupid, me, I only took a few notes from the till. I doubt they'll even notice. Twelve quid is the sum. Enough for a train up to Tredmouth. I'll stay at uncle Russ's, if I don't stay with Amanda. I'll pay it back, as soon as I can. Replace it, so they'll never even know.

The Scotch was even smarter. I took an empty, and part filled it with the full one hanging on the Optic. Ha! They owe me that - all the work I've done for a few quid here and there. Let them ring an electrician out the local paper, and see what it would cost them.

I'll give Gilly a fiver. See, I'm nothing like my dad. He wouldn't do that. He wouldn't have done it for me and my mum. Uncle Russ had to bail us out. We'd have starved otherwise.

Yes, I'm nothing like my father.

I'll wake her up. Check on her and the baby. 'Here you are, Gilly. Get yourself something nice. Or something for the baby,' I'll tell her.

I rinse my dick in the plastic-tasting water in the kitchen before I do. You never know, she might be grateful enough to repay the kindness.

It's long overdue.

She's not in bed. They're not in the caravan, her and the baby.

Had I known that, I'd have brought that dirty barmaid back here for a proper seeing-to.

Ah well, she'll come crawling back.

Right on cue, a rap rattles on the caravan door. I locked it when I came in. Still, she's got a key. Probably too dark for her to see. I should leave her there - teach her a lesson.

Another rap. Alright, give me a minute!

It might be the barmaid, back for a second helping. Who could blame her?

I'll do what I can for her with the television people. I'm a man of my word, after all.

A policeman stands at the door. Another waits a few yards away by a panda car.

"Can I help you?" I say.

"Are you Nicholas Cherry?"

"That's me. What's happened? Are Gilly and the baby okay?"

"Have you been in the Club House tonight, sir?" he asks, ignoring my question.

"No," I lie. "Is this about my girlfriend? We have a young baby."

"No. Do you have a key to the Club House, Mr Cherry?"

"No... I mean, yes! Yes I do. It's somewhere. Do you need it to get in?"

"May I see it, please?"

"Sure, if I can find it. I haven't used it in a while. I'm a DJ. I do the discos during the holiday season."

"Have you had a lot to drink tonight?"

"A couple of beers. I just had a whisky, actually, before getting my head down." The stolen whisky. I wish I hadn't mentioned that. I feel it flush my face. Did he see it? "That was when I noticed my girlfriend wasn't at home. I'm really worried about her."

"Were you with anyone tonight, sir?"

"No... Well, yes, I was at the pub. The barmaid there will vouch for me."

"Donna Kirkman?"

"Yes, yes, that's her."

"She claims you took her in the Club House here."

"Oh! Well, not quite, but kind of. We just went into the hallway part. Not the actual main bit, if you see what I mean."

"How did you get in the hallway?"

"Erm, it was open. Why? Look, I go in there all the time. I help with the electrics, and, as I said, I do the discos. I don't understand what's going on? Are Gilly and the baby okay?"

"May I see your wallet?"

"What for?"

"I'd like to take a look, to see how much money you have in there."

"Why? I can tell you, there's a few quid. Look, I did a little side-job," I say as if he'll understand - making it sound like a little fiddle, rather than a crime as such. "Everybody does it."

He smiles. Yes, he understands. I'm no criminal - hardly worth their time and effort, coming all the way out here.

"How much money do you have on you, Nick?"

Yes, we're on the same wavelength. He's calling me Nick. I'll probably get a gig out of this, doing the police Christmas party.

"Not sure. About ten or fifteen pounds. The job paid a tenner."

"If I can just take a quick look."

"No problem," I say, feeling more confident as I tug my wallet free.

He walks away to the police car and utilises the headlights. A hushed conversation takes place between the two plods.

On his return, he says, "and I need to see that key, Nick. Please."

"Sure, sure. I'll just have a look. It's probably in the drawer in the bedroom."

It's not. It's in my fucking pocket. But I'm not letting him know that. As I charade a rummage, I break a nail levering it off the ring I carry.

He's in the small sitting area when I return, holding the bottle of whisky I drank about half of.

"See your problem, Nick?" he says, and makes it sound like a question.

I shake my head.

"When you were in the pub tonight, a full inventory was carried out at the Club House. All the Optics were topped up and a float left in the till. It's for a party tomorrow night. I guess they've got someone else doing the disco."

Of course, of course, of course! That was why I got the side-job, fixing the fucking fridges. Shit, shit, shit. What did Donna tell them? And how do they know about her?

What the fuck's going on?

"Okay, I took a little nightcap from the bar. I'll happily pay for it. I was going to. Tomorrow. First thing. Look, if anything else went missing from there, she must have taken it."

"Who?"

"Donna. It must have been when I went to use the toilet. Yes! She was over by the bar when I came back. I remember. That was what led me over there, and I took a bit of whisky. Let me speak to the owners. I know them. They know me."

Stop it, Nick! Just fucking stop it! What are you doing?

I stand in silence with my mouth open - whatever bullshit I was about to blurt left unsaid.

The list of charges don't even lodge in my brain - illegal entry, trespass, theft.

I'm a thief. A cheat. And a liar. According to the record, I always will be. It's a relatively small town, Tinbury. Word

A DIFFERENT MIX

will get around. It'll go to court, and be written about in the local paper.

And Gilly and the baby are gone. I know they won't be back...

...I roll from my bed and dash to the toilet in my home in a quiet street in Tredmouth, arriving just in time to spew a noxious mix of coffee and all I've swallowed in recent times.

A little of it leaked onto the hand that clamped my mouth.

Sinking to the bathroom floor, my breathing heavy - my mind attempting to discern fact from fiction. It all feels so real - so terrifyingly real.

Gilly went to California with her husband, I remind myself. She went there, because I didn't show her enough love. I chose Amanda and the path I trod; the life I actually lived.

This life.

There was no baby. No violence. No barmaid called Donna. No theft.

I was not like my father.

Am not!

I am not like my father.

A love of music came from my uncle Russ and my mum's side of the family. That is the essence of me.

My genes are constituted of a different mix, further shaped by decisions I have made - by the life I have lived.

34.

- Following the news, we're heading back, back, back in time - sponsored by Knight & Day, where you can find the antique watch of your dreams. And this morning, we're counting down the top ten from 1969! Where were you - what were you doing? Drop us a line and let us know.
- This is Nick Cherry, and you're listening to Tred FM on this damp Monday morning. Thanks for being here.

"I thought you might drop by on Saturday," Dave says.

"Ah, sorry, Dave. I had a full on weekend. Perhaps another time."

"I'll be there this Saturday."

I nod to let him know that I heard him.

"What were you up to?" he pushes on.

"Oh, this and that. I did manage to squeeze in a walk. I took a trail north towards Wrenbrook, then east to Millby. I saw a murmuration."

"Fucking hell! I hope you reported it."

"Starlings, Dave."

"What, they killed someone?"

"No... A murmuration."

"Oh, sorry, I was thinking of crows."

"What?"

"Nothing. What do you know about home delivery?" he asks for no reason I can fathom.

"I was born at home, but I don't remember it very clearly," I reply.

"I meant food."

"Oh. Well, there's a firm advertises on here. It's big business these days, I think."

"Is it any good?" he asks.

"I don't know. I've never used it. Why?"

"Ah, a friend of mine was asking. With you living on your own, I thought you might know a bit about it."

"I still cook meals, Dave. Besides, there's usually something going on, so..." I let it drift.

When did I become a fibber?

They aren't lies like I imagined myself telling in my latest dream. They aren't told for malice or personal gain. They're simply my way of filling out my life, and making it seem more interesting than it is.

There's a selflessness about my little white lies, as I don't want anyone to worry about me or feel obligated in any way.

I wouldn't describe myself as lonely. And I don't think I'm depressed.

Am I?

How do you know?

Depressed: In a state of general unhappiness or despondency. In a physically lower position, having been pushed or forced down.

Yes. In the latter sense, I am indeed depressed. Pushed down and lowered. But none of that is of my making. I didn't get the breaks. The cutbacks led to where I am.

Plenty were let go - redundancies and early retirements. Not me. I'm still here, doing what I love - doing what I've always wanted to do.

Yes, I may have been reduced, but I'm not quite on the scrapheap yet. There's still time.

Eddie Noakes didn't last this long, despite his shares in the company. He flogged them when the takeover came, and was out within a day.

Nor did Ray Nuno. As good as he was, he was off the air before he hit my age. Whatever happens now, they have to give me three months notice, so I shall be doing this when I turn sixty in June.

Thirty-four years of presenting a show and playing music for the masses.

I called Ray when I heard he was being axed.

"I'm sorry, Ray. You're the best DJ I've ever heard."

"Thank you, Nick."

"When do you finish?"

"I already have. They said I could carry on for the next six months, till the new schedule in October. But I figured it was best to step down now."

"Crikey! That quick."

"Yes."

"I'll never forget, Ray. I'll always remember it was you who gave me my first break. 'On My Radio' was the first song I ever introduced. Thank you."

I heard Ray Nuno smile down the phone line. "You never forget the first song, Nick. But it's the last one that will haunt you."

"What was it?" I asked him.

"You didn't listen, then?" he retorted teasingly.

"No, sorry. I would have, if I'd known."

"It was Eddie Cochran, 'Somethin' Else'."

"Ray, that was your first…"

"I know. Genius, eh?"

That was our last proper conversation. I was busy hosting a popular show. I always had it in mind to get in touch and see how he was doing, but never seemed to get around to it.

- *The highest new entry - Lulu, 'Boom Bang-A-Bang'. And at number ten this very week forty-nine years ago, it's only Donald Peers with 'Please Don't Go'. And don't go anywhere, because we'll take a peer at the weather after this.*

"Banned by the BBC in 1991, Lulu was," Dave comments.

"Really? People were still playing it by then?"

"Yes. Gulf War."

"Right. I remember it winning Eurovision."

"Joint winner," Dave corrects me.

"Didn't Cliff win it the year before?"

"No, he only came second. A travesty! Sandie Shaw won it the year before that with 'Puppet On A String'. Mind you, she fucking needed to after Kenneth McKellar's ninth place finish in '66 with 'A Man Without Love'. The lowest placing for the UK up to that time, a record that would stand until 1978 when Co-Co finished eleventh. Cheryl Baker was in the band, and, of course, she'd make up for the abysmal shit-show by winning it in '81 with Bucks Fizz."

All I can do is stare at him in utter disbelief. Or is it disappointment?

"Why, Dave?" I eventually say.

"Phonographic memory." He adds, "it's a real thing. Some people just have it."

"How are the kids, Dave?"

"Doing alright. They look in on us every weekend."

"And the grandkids?"

"Yes, they seem fine. It's hard to know. They always have their noses stuck in a phone these days."

As I get older, I often think about not having any children. It's probably selfish, but I crave the comfort that would come from having someone keep an eye on me - someone to pop round every weekend for a cup of tea and a natter.

Gilly being pregnant in my dream, and the baby I imagined us having, somewhat haunts me. My career got in the way. Then, later, I became too set in my ways to want children.

We did try, Amanda and I. Halfheartedly on my part, as time began to catch up with us. That failure, I think, was a part of why things disintegrated the way they did. That, and hitting forty. As well as other things.

I wondered if I might be sterile. It kind of suited me to think that I was, as it meant Elaine's child wasn't mine.

Amanda got what she wanted in the end, because Amanda always got what she wanted.

She had a baby at forty-two. With a man called Martin who was at least a dozen years her junior.

I think I thought myself out of it. Perhaps sperm know. They sensed my reticence, and didn't try hard enough.

She suggested going to a fertility clinic, and I made the right noises about it. Then did nothing and hoped it would go away.

Dave has it all; the loving wife and family. Do I envy him?

No, how could anybody envy Dave?

I watch him as he pokes his finger in his ear, inspects it, sniffs it, and wipes it on his jumper.

Oh god!

I see it all of a sudden. Such a sadness in his eyes. His beard a fuzzy mess. His hair in need of a cut. His clothes un-ironed, straight from the dryer. The tired bags beneath his eyes. The strain etched on the bits of his face still visible. And he's a bit gaunt - his clothes hanging scarecrowly from him. He's definitely lost weight.

If I didn't see him four times a week, the difference in him would shock me. As it is, it's been revealed to me gradually over weeks, and is less marked as a result.

It's amazing what you see when you actually bother to focus on something other than yourself.

"Is everything okay, Dave?"

He stares at me, his piggy blue eyes blinking just once. And I think I detect a little moisture at the edges.

He goes to speak, but swallows it before it can leave his mouth.

"Absolutely fine," he says instead, and I know he isn't. "Back on in five, four, three..."

35.

We don't talk about it, because we're men and we have to 'man up'.

Bury it, hide it from view, and it'll all go away. Brush it under the carpet. Pull the curtains over it.

Swim with the tide, roll with the punches and let sleeping dogs lie.

Chin up, stiff upper lip, keep your pecker up.

Look on the bright side, every cloud, glass half full.

People see it as weakness, if you show your feelings.

Nobody likes a misery guts.

But, but, but...

Misery loves company.

The truth is, I don't want to embarrass him. So I don't push.

And I'm afraid.

I'm scared that if he goes down that road, I'll feel compelled to tell him about my life - my situation. Not in a competitive way, but because if he knows how shit my life is, he might feel better about his own.

If he really wanted to talk about it, he would.

- Up five places to number five, Dean Martin, with 'Gentle On My Mind'. And at number four, it's only Cilla Black, 'Surround Yourself With Sorrow'.

There's a huge great elephant sitting in the studio.

Dave confronts it. "Tina's been a bit out of sorts, Nick."

"Ah, I'm sorry, mate. I thought there was something."

"Not to worry, we'll work things out. Thanks for asking."

Excellent. We dealt with that. I knew it would be something and nothing.

"I'm thinking of buying a caravan," Dave surprises me by saying next.

"Good for you," I reply enthusiastically, keen to talk about normal things. "Are you going to live in it?"

"No."

"Holidays, then?"

"No, not really."

I'm confused. "Then, why do you want a caravan, Dave?"

"It's up for auction next week. It's down in Tinbury Head."

"There are a lot of caravans down there."

"They used to use it for the Road Shows and things," he further explains, and I blink rapidly as dots connect in my brain.

"Hang on. How old is it?"

"It's from the eighties. Well, the actual caravan's older than that, but it was fitted out in the early-eighties."

"Bloody hell!"

"What?"

"I helped build it. Well, if it's the same one, I did. I don't think there was ever another. And, if it is, it was put together in 1979."

"You're pulling my chain?"

"No, it didn't have a toilet. What are you going to do with it?" I ask.

"Fix it up. I need a project, and if I can get it at the right price..."

"Is the charity bingo not satisfying you?"

He smiles. That's better. We're back to the banter.

I continue. "If you do get it, I'd like to have a look."

"I was wondering if you fancied coming in with me?"

"I'm not going camping with you, Dave."

He ignores me. "You know your wiring and whatnot. We could get it up and running. Maybe even sell it on and make a profit. It's a safe enough investment. The estimate is less than the value of the gear in it."

"What condition is it in? It's been standing around for years, I bet."

"It needs a bit of work."

"How much work?"

"Quite a lot."

"Where has it been?" I ask.

"It's stood in a barn for twenty-five years. Not out in the elements."

"Have you seen it?"

"Only pictures. I'll send you the link," Dave offers.

"Okay," I'm surprised to hear myself saying.

"Five songs about caravans. Thirty seconds. Go!"

"Ah, erm, 'Caravan Of Love', Housemartins. There's a jazz standard called 'Caravan', if I'm not mistaken."

"By?"

"Ooooh, erm, was it Duke Ellington?"

"Yes it was! Back of the awning!"

"The Doors, 'Spanish Caravan'."

"Good work."

"I'm struggling," I concede.

"Twelve seconds."

"Ah, oh, eee..."

"Eight..."

"'Trailer For Sale Or Rent', Roger Miller."

"That's 'King Of The Road'. Nul point!"

"Bugger."

"Five, four... You missed Caravan, 'Where But For Caravan Would I?'."

36.

"I think you're making a mistake," Ray Nuno said to me. "Stick it out here. A chance will come along. Get your own show, and learn to walk before you try running. Don't be too impatient, Nick."

"But I think there's more likelihood of that happening back in Tredmouth."

And I was right. Amanda and I were seeing a lot of each other since Gilly had gone. I was spending plenty of time up in Tredmouth, staying at uncle Russ's. I'd drive up in my van every chance I could, before heading back south for the disco and radio work.

Nothing had really happened between us. It was platonic. We'd hold hands, and kiss when we met and parted, but it had never gone any further. A peck on the lips rather than a peck on the cheek. So, something more than friends. But she had never let it progress.

She intimidated me, to some extent. Socially, she was a level or two above. Even when she'd been a hairdresser in Oakburn, I'd found her a daunting prospect. She had a superior way about her, and moved in all the right circles.

Whereas I was still trying to get a break and make my way, Amanda knew precisely where she was going, and how to get there. Her path in life seemed to be more clearly defined than mine - it was an easy trail to follow.

And such was her sense of purpose, I began to see my path inextricably tied in to hers.

Tredmouth, too, had a hold on me. Perhaps not a hold, but it was the place I felt an urge to conquer - to be seen as a success.

Undoubtedly that tied into my childhood. Particularly with regard to my father.

In truth, too, I found it difficult to be in Tinbury Head when Gilly no longer was.

My relocation took place after a talk with Eddie Noakes. Amanda, as always, facilitated the meeting.

"How long have you been DJing?" he asked me over a drink.

"Seven years on the discos. And I've been standing in for Ray Nuno for the past three or four."

He raised his eyebrows at that. I knew a little of his rivalry with Ray. It was long-standing, back to the mid-sixties. They'd both gone for an interview on one of the big pirate stations.

In short, the younger Nuno got the job, and Noakes had his nose put out of joint. A couple of years on, and the Marine Broadcasting Offences Act came in, putting an end to it all.

Nuno came back, and ended up working for the same parent company as Noakes. Out of spite, Noakes was instrumental in ensuring Ray was packed off to a small station down at Tinbury Head. Even then, Ray made a great success of it, landing television work through the crowds that flocked to the beach every year.

Through me, Eddie Noakes saw an opportunity to deal his old nemesis a blow.

I've often considered that it may have been the reason Eddie brought me in at Tred FM.

Still, I had my first contract of employment. A wage!

And I finally landed Amanda.

I didn't see it at the time, but those two things were always tied. One was never going to happen without the other.

Where Ray Nuno was all about substance, Eddie was all about image.

"Look the part. That's where they get it wrong. They think because they're on the radio, how they look doesn't matter. Well, take it from me, it does. It's all that matters. You are what you see in the mirror, and that'll come across on the airwaves. If you look good, you'll sound good. If you feel sexy, you'll come across as being sexy.

"Have the right woman on your arm and your cock, and always say you know, even when you don't. Never, ever admit you don't know something!"

Again, I contrasted his words with those of Ray - "it's fine to admit you don't know something. How else do we learn and grow?"

But Noakes seemed the more relevant as the mid-eighties approached. The world was changing.

In addition, my contract named me as Eddie's stand-in, so it made sense for me to heed his advice and allow myself to be moulded.

It shames me to think I chose him as my Best Man.

The best man I knew, Ray Nuno, came to the wedding. He sat smiling, happy for me. In the evening, I tried to find him so we could catch up, but he'd slipped quietly away.

As I sit here listening to the unknown record, I know there are plenty of people - most people - who would take my achievements and be more than happy.

The truth is, I've never worked hard in my life. Not really. Not when I compare it to what others have had to do to get on, or simply survive.

Ray Nuno, though. Whilst he never made the big time, and enjoyed national success or hosted Top Of The Pops, I often wonder if I might have achieved more had I listened to him.

Or would my career in broadcasting have ended when his did - before it had really begun?

With the song in mind, I go to bed and wish for that insight...

37.

...Ray suggests it one night in the studio. "I could be your manager. It makes sense. I have the contacts, you're a fresh voice. And I know the business."

"Okay."

I don't even think about it. Why would I? I owe everything to Ray Nuno. He got me the evening slot - seven till nine. My own show, playing new releases five nights a week - the stuff that probably won't make the chart. But it's the good stuff. The indie and alternative music I actually listen to.

Listenership is beyond everybody's expectations. And it's a young crowd - a different demographic to the daytime audience.

I've been approached - taken out for dinner and wined and dined. A London station are keen to bring me in. The catchment area is millions. A national called me. They want to talk.

Since Gilly decided to head off to California, I've dedicated myself to my work. For four years I've lived and breathed radio. Nothing else matters.

Even the discos are pegged back. I play about one a fortnight, mainly to test new records and gauge the audience reaction. Such is my renown, I earn more for one night now than I did for a dozen nights when I first moved here.

I don't even have to buy the records. I get sent everything in advance. Bands send me cassettes by the sack-load. Labels listen to my show in hope of finding the next big thing to sign.

"You don't have to leave here," Ray suggests. "You can syndicate your show, and sell it to a score of other stations."

"I don't know enough about it, Ray. What would you do?"

"That. Be a big fish in a lot of small ponds, rather than a small fish in a big pond. Less chance of getting eaten alive by the sharks. Sell the show rights to a dozen stations at five hundred a week. That's six grand. A week. Three-hundred thousand a year."

"That's, erm, that's quite a lot. What about you? What about Tinbury Sound? I owe them, and I use their equipment."

"I get a percentage as your manager and representative. The station gets a kick-back which I'll set up. Give them ten percent of your earnings. Any more than that, and you may as well set up your own studio, or rent one."

"It's tempting. But the nationals, Ray..."

"They'll stick you on a dead slot in the middle of the night. How many listeners do you think you'll get? And they'll make you play at least some playlist controlled chart music. Is that what you want?"

"No."

"Look, I have contacts in America and Australia. People I worked with back in the pirate station days. This could be huge, Nick."

I drum my fingers on the desk.

"Go on," he encourages me. "Ask whatever you want."

"Why haven't you done this for yourself, Ray?" I say, and project my awkwardness through my facial expression.

"Good question. It's the right question. Don't look so guilty. The truth is, by the time it was possible, I was too old. Punk changed everything, Nick. It opened everything up. It was never just about the music. It was about the structure, and how things were done. Just look at the record labels and shops that began around that time. Independent distribution came. Radio, too. It changed overnight, and began broadening its line of vision. I'm not sure any of what I'm proposing was possible even a decade ago."

"And you're certain this is my best option?"

"No, Nick, I'm not. I won't lie to you. But my gut tells me it is. I like the idea of maintaining control. And I much prefer having twenty stations - many paymasters - as opposed to one. That way, if you lose one, you still have nineteen."

"Let's do it, Ray."

"Are you sure?"

"Yes."...

...I'm huge. I'm a star. I can earn five hundred a night playing records at one of the big nightclubs. A grand for two hours spinning records at a festival. Five thousand dollars for six hours work at a massive gathering in America - all expenses paid.

Offers for television work come in all the time. I hosted the first episode of a new show called 'Coming Up Next', a showcase for independent and unsigned bands tipped for the top.

Voiceovers take up a lot of my time, but pay well enough. My heart, though, is still in radio. My daily show goes out all over the world.

I'm the voice of 1988, according to one prominent monthly music magazine. Copies of which I sit signing in a huge record store in London - flourishing a black marker pen all over my own face on the cover.

The media love me - they can't get enough. My opinion matters. I can make or break a band with a few words.

"Nick!" they cry, desperate to get my attention.

"Nick!" people shout, so that I might turn to them as their cameras click and flash.

"Nick!" teenagers scream at me.

I get sent things in the post. Underwear and pictures of young women - pouting and telling me that they love me and want to meet me.

Some, male and female, write long letters, a few of which I have time to read. Occasionally, I reply.

They tell me what a difference I made to their lives by introducing them to their new favourite band.

Some claim that I saved their lives, all because, through me, they found something in a band or singer or song or lyric that changed their perspective on life.

It's vital, the work I do!

She's nice. About eighteen, though it's hard to tell. Old enough, at any rate. You have to be careful. Some look a lot older than they are.

She has a face and body worthy of worship. And it's all on show, that body. Not much left under wraps.

"Thank you, Nick," she says as I sign a magazine for her.

"An absolute pleasure," I reply, and give her my best smile.

God, I can feel myself getting aroused beneath the table I sit at. Best not stand for a while!

I hope she sticks around till the masses have departed. We'll go for a drink somewhere off the beaten track, away from the glare of cameras and the stare of eyes.

I have a flat in London. It might be best to go there. I sign the next magazine, a long line of young people snaking through the shop and all the way out the door.

How long will this take? I could be here for another hour or two yet.

Will she stick around?

Nothing on tonight, and I wouldn't mind having nothing on tonight, pressed up to her naked body.

My eyes furtively follow her as I sign blindly - a scrawl across my own face.

She really is beautiful.

"Nick!" a voice calls.

I turn instinctively. A flurrious machine-gun of frames being captured.

"Is it true that you raped your stepmother?"

They're getting every nuance of my reaction. I'm frozen - unblinking - mouth half open - black pen suspended in midair - mind racing as I process the question.

Three seconds is all it takes. But it feels like much longer.

"What?" is all I can say.

"Your stepmother, Nick. Elaine. Is it true that you forced yourself on her?"

"No! That's an outrageous statement!"

"She claims you're the father of her child. An eleven year old girl. What do you have to say about that?"

I'm rising, pushing my way through the crowd, desperate for air and space in which to think.

I know. I know in a flash precisely what's going on. Elaine is looking for her fifteen minutes of fame and a payday like no other - a chance to rise on the back of my decline. She's still with my father, so he's either in on it, or she doesn't care about that.

Money. It'll all be about money. Why didn't she come to me? We might have worked something out.

Ah, because she wants it all - money and the limelight. She'll have taken her tale to one of the tabloids. I bet they do a glamorous shoot of her. Well, as glamorous as she could ever hope to be.

They'll make her look like an innocent victim - me as a big, bad sexual predator. Despite the age difference, they'll dress it up like that.

What other things will come out of the closet? What other skeletons will step forth and rattle their bones?

The pretty girl is right here, at the door. My god, she's beautiful.

She's processing it all, just as I am.

And now I see it. The look of disgust. I'm already judged before I can have a say.

And she turns away.

Shit, it was better in the record shop. Outside, there are no limits - no restrictions.

It's a set-up - a plethora of news channels tipped off and in position.

A television camera is thrust under my chin, filming upwards, making me look arrogant and bigger than I am - making me look like a bully who towers over his victims and looks down his nose at them.

I can already see it playing on the news and emblazoned on the front pages, along with headlines that pun my name or what I do.

The work will already be drying up. The phone will cease to ring, once the journalists stop calling after the carcass has been picked clean.

I have to say something. I have to defend myself, or I'm done. Finished. I'm only fucking thirty. I'm the victim here.

My feet stop moving. A deep breath, and I spin to face my accusers.

"Nick!" they plead, all wanting the exclusive - the viewers - the advertising.

"You've got it all wrong!" I say to the first camera as I sink to my haunches.

"Did you have sex with your stepmother?"

"Yes. I did. I regret it... I was eighteen!"

"Did she have your child, Nick?"

"I don't know. It's possible."

"Did you rape her?"

"No! Definitely not. She came on to me... I was drunk. It was my eighteenth birthday," I say as I rise to my feet. I'm shaking.

"She says you were very aggressive, Nick. That you forced her to perform acts. She says she begged you not to. That you were insatiable."

"No, that's not..."

"How many times did you have sex with her?"

"Erm, twice. It was only one occasion, but we did it twice."

"Where was this?"

"In my family home." It was no home. Not really. It was no family.

"One time was on the coffee table, is that right?"

"I don't remember."

It was. I do remember.

"Did your father ever know about what you did?"

What I did?

"Erm, I don't know. I don't think so."

"He knows now," someone calls out, and a sinister roll of laughter passes through the crowd of journalists and curious members of the public.

The beautiful girl is one of them, but she doesn't cackle. She stands at the back, looking on with disappointment plaining her face.

I see her drop the magazine I signed in a bin, before turning and walking away.

"Is it true that you made her clean you with her mouth after each occasion?"

"No! Yes, I mean. Not like that... I didn't make her."

"Even after you made her have anal sex with you?"

"No! Absolutely not!"

I'm off again. This is not right - not true.

"Nick!" they call after me, but in a very different way to how they did even an hour ago. Now it's vulturous.

I picture her - Elaine. That filthy, slovenly woman. And that was twelve years ago. What must she look like now?

What will people think of me? My mum and uncle Russ. Even my father. And Ray Nuno. What will Ray think of me? Will he still want to be my manager?

Then there are the millions who listen to my show...

...I wake up, sit upright, and see my ashen face looking back at me in the mirror. My black, petrified eyes try to make sense of everything as my pupils shrink.

"Ughhhh!" I moan as it all sinks in. The record on the platter downstairs. My wish for fame and fortune, and following a different groove in the pursuit of it.

Trying to fathom where it all went wrong.

It didn't go wrong. I was never quite hungry enough. As a result, there wasn't sufficient for others to be envious of.

Milkmen don't even know who I am.

Nobody listens to the radio anymore. Well, not local radio in Brakeshire.

They tune in to the national stations, or play their own choices via streaming services or downloads.

It's all lost.

The unpredictability and randomness of life is largely gone. People want control. They want to listen to what they want to listen to when they want to listen to it. They want to have all their tastes and beliefs confirmed by the media, not challenged by them. They desire only to be exposed to that which they already know.

Nobody discovers these days. Not really. They swallow whatever it is they're force-fed.

I didn't force Elaine. She came on to me. I was eighteen. She was pushing forty. She knew precisely what she was doing that night.

But it's still there. It exists because it happened.

I can't undo what's done.

They say life is a rich tapestry. But pull on a loose thread, and the whole thing might come unravelled.

38.

"Where's Dave?"

"No idea," replies the young guy behind the glass.

"Well, why are you here?"

"Standing in. I think he called in sick, or something."

"Dave's never sick. He's not missed a day in twenty years."

The guy shrugs.

"He'd have rung me," I mutter to myself, and I wonder if he's not sick at all, but down in Tinbury Head looking the caravan over.

We always coordinate our holidays. It's most unusual.

My chair is, for once, perfectly comfortable.

"Have you touched this chair?" I ask the Producer. I think his name's Kyle. It begins with a 'K' sound, I believe. I saw him in a meeting a few weeks back. He's new.

"No."

"Right, what do we have today?"

"As far as I can tell, it's just the usual routine."

"And do you know what the usual routine is?"

"I've familiarised myself with the format," he replies mechanically.

"Kyle, right?" I decide to check.

"Callum," he corrects me.

"What's the oldies year, Callum?"

"Erm, 1989," he informs me, after glancing at his screen.

"Really? I thought we were on a sixties week?"

"That's what it says here."

"Is it any good?"

"I don't know. I was only four."

"Okay. Well, what week are we doing in 1989?"

"It says March the twelfth."

"But today is March the twentieth. So we should be on March the nineteenth to correspond. Unless there was no chart that week for some reason." I don't say it nastily.

"It's what the computer says."

"I think the computer might be wrong, Callum."

He stares at me as if I'm insane.

"What do you want me to do?" he asks. I detect nerves.

"Ah, don't worry. Nobody will notice," I say to him nonchalantly, and smile to let him know how trivial a matter it is.

"Oh no, erm, Mr Cherry?"

"Yes, Callum? And, please, call me Nick."

"Nick, we've got a huge problem!"

"It's okay. Calm down. Tell me what it is."

"It's the highest new entry."

"What about it?"

"It's already in the top ten. Madonna. 'Like A Virgin'. It's a new entry at number two. What are we going to do?"

"Prayer."

"Erm, okay, if you think it will help." He actually puts his palms together and closes his eyes.

"No... The song is 'Like A Prayer' by Madonna."

"That's right!" he confirms after opening his eyes and inspecting the computer screen. "How did you know?"

"I've been doing this a long time. Is this your first time riding solo?"

"Is it that obvious?" He's going to lose it any second.

"Hey, Callum. Everything will be fine. I'll cover anything that goes wrong. You can do this. If you make a mistake, it's not a problem. That's the only way we learn."

"Okay. Thanks, Nick."

"What's the next highest new entry?"

"Number fifteen. Soul II Soul featuring Caron Wheeler with 'Keep On Movin'."

"Then we'll go with that. Okay? We'll keep on movin', Callum, no matter what."

"Yes."

"Blow your nose."

He does. With his microphone still on.

"How long, Callum?"

"One minute."

"Right. Name five songs with a colour in the title. Go!" I say by way of relaxing him and sharpening his mind.

There's a really long silence.

"What about 'Blue Monday' by New Order?" I suggest.

"Yes. 'Blue Monday' by New Order," he repeats.

"And, say, a song by The Rolling Stones?" I guide him.

"I do know of them."

"Painting a colour. On a door... Or a rooster, maybe?"

He shakes his head at me. "Why would they paint a rooster?"

"They wouldn't. The Beatles, then - a submarine, perhaps?"

"Yellow!"

"Way-hey - there you go! Well done."

"You're on in ten seconds, Nick," he says robotically, and I know he'll be fine.

- Morning. Nick Cherry here on this dry and unseasonably warm Tuesday morning. Hope you're well. Callum is in the Production seat for Dave, and it's a pleasure having him and you with me. Drop us a line and tell us why you're up at such an hour.

The song comes in perfectly, and I see him relax a little as his shoulders drop. He smiles at me, and raises a thumb.

A DIFFERENT MIX

He's off to a better start than my first time standing in for Ray.

We get through it. Brief perfunctory chats break up the monotony of the music and adverts and weather and news.

"Any emails or texts, Callum?"

"There's one from a man who is looking forward to the chart from 1989."

"Why's that?"

"Because it was the week his daughter was born, and he sat listening to the chart show while his wife was in labour."

"That's nice. I think I'll read that one out, even though it's the wrong chart. Can you forward it, please?"

He does.

"There's another from someone called Timbo Quimbo."

"Probably best to ignore..."

"He says he was seventeen that year, and clearly recalls lining up outside your house waiting for his turn with your wife."

"Right."

"Is she a teacher of some kind?"

She wasn't. No sooner were we married in 1985, than she gave up being anything.

My broadcasting career began in earnest in October of '84. Monday the first, to be exact.

The inaugural song I played was 'Jeepster' by T. Rex. It was where it had all started for me, and whilst Sharon was long gone, Amanda was the girl whose love I was a jeepster for.

My universe reclined in her hair. Or, at least, in the hair that she styled.

Two days later, on the third, I span 'Somethin' Else' by Eddie Cochran. It was for Ray, but also to mark what would have been Cochran's forty-sixth birthday.

I could play what I wanted back then. As long as half of the songs came from the current chart, the remainder were whatever I chose. Not that anybody checked. If the listeners were there, it was fine.

Both professionally and personally, my life went largely unchecked.

When Amanda and I divorced in early-2002, I couldn't argue with her case. She had enabled me to become a DJ. All I had achieved was, on paper, down to her. From introducing me to Eddie Noakes, to pushing me on and buying the big house in Wrenbrook. The achievement was hers as much as mine. More so, probably.

Isn't it evidenced by the fact that, since her, I've stood still in life?

But I should have known what Amanda was like. I did know. But I chose to ignore it, or to think I could fix her. Or even that she'd fix me.

I'd quickly learn - you'll never fix someone who can't even see they're broken.

- Down from number two to number eight this week in 1989, Michael Ball, and 'Love Changes Everything'. Doesn't it just. We'll be back with the rest of the countdown in but a moment.

39.

Amanda had it. Eddie Noakes had it.

They both loved themselves above all others. And when you're like that, you're not capable of loving anyone but yourself.

Worse still, when you're so inward looking, you don't see anything outside of the self.

I honestly thought selfishness and self-obsession were advantageous traits to possess, having come from a family where a certain level of self-loathing was the norm. I saw it as confidence and self-assuredness. However, it was anything but.

Callum did well. I told him so at the end, as Jason Donovan's 'Too Many Broken Hearts' played us out.

He's thirty-three, in his first proper job. He's the future. Him and the up-and-coming DJs filling the daytime slots - all quiet non-offensive efficiency. I'll put in a word for him - see if I can get him on one of the bigger shows.

Not that anybody listens to me anymore. And I'm not just talking about the public.

I anonymously slope in and do my show, as I hope to survive. That's the extent of my ambition now, for I am fully conscious of the fact this is going to be my last stint on the radio. Once this show's gone, so am I.

How different it was the day I bought my metallic blue 1984 Vespa!

It was brand spanking new, with two whole miles on the clock, as a result of my test ride.

I'd always wanted one, ever since I was a kid and had been taken for spins round Tredmouth on the back of my uncle Russ's.

Not a Lambretta. No, it had to be a Vespa. His was white.

Amanda wasn't happy. She'd have preferred a car, and for what it cost, we could have got something decent second-hand. But it had been my dream since childhood, and during my time at college with Harry, as we sat watching old films on his television. And it was rekindled in Tinbury Head when the Mods came down for the roadshow.

I saw myself riding it, like Jimmy in Quadrophenia, with my girl, Amanda, on the back - me clamped between her legs, the vibrations turning her on, and the wind on our faces waking us up to a world of possibility!

Amanda never once went on it. I mean that she never even so much as sat on it, let alone went out for a ride. She called it, "an undignified way to travel."

"Besides," she added, "wearing a helmet will mess my hair up, and the wind will make my mascara run."

It was the only positive when divorce came. The Vespa wasn't even mentioned as being something she wanted. It had sat motionless in the garage for ten years by then, but seeing how I had no car all of a sudden - or a garage - I decided to fix it up.

Amanda was attractive. And she appeared sexy. But it was all an act, that sexiness. In fact, there was a calculated coldness in her.

Every single facet of her life was stage-managed to best present herself as she wanted to be seen. Sex was a part of that.

Oh, and envy. There was such terrible jealousy of anyone who had all the things in life she coveted for herself.

I was a means of her getting it all. At least, that was her plan. I failed, of course, by not becoming quite what she had hoped for. Not even close.

Tred FM was as far as it ever went for me.

The aroma from the baker's piques my sense of smell. There is no better scent in the world than freshly baked bread.

"Morning," I call out.

"Morning Nick. Usual?"

"Please."

"Enjoyed the show today!" He always says that. I'm not sure if he actually listens. Whenever I come in, the radio is tuned to BBC Radio Two.

Ten minutes on, and I'm pulling up at my home, the loaf still warm.

Amanda would never have bread like this. She thought it antiquated not to buy a sliced loaf sealed in plastic, with a use-by date at least a week in the future. On moving in together, one of the first things I had to do was buy a decent bread knife.

It was this bread knife! I've had it for as long as I've been broadcasting - its serrated edge still perfectly functional. The crust and a small slice, where the loaf tapers down, fall on the board.

Unsalted butter, thinly spread. Nothing else, because I am a plain man who enjoys simple things in life. That is my inherent nature.

I thought I wanted more, so looked to achieve that through other people. Amanda, primarily. We each used the other. Her for my earning potential and escalating celebrity. Me for her connections and apparent substance and ambition.

It was fake. Much like a loaf of bread with too much or too little of something in the mix, huge air-pockets were hidden beneath the crust, where nothing existed.

From the moment we got together, the staleness began to set in. But I was blind to it, because I'd waited so long for her and had given up so much. Gilly, primarily. And Ray Nuno.

I didn't want to be wrong. Since years before, when she'd cut my hair at the salon, I'd had designs and desires.

She made me wait, as she strung me along. And I think she did that because she knew there was no substance beneath the crust.

This is my bread and butter.

As I eat, I notice the slight discolouration in the white flesh of the slice. An imperfection. Life isn't perfect. It would be fairly banal if it were. The failures, I think, give us a point of comparison. We need downs to appreciate the ups - bads to highlight the goods.

It's the imperfections that make a sunset beautiful. It's the clouds in the sky that provide a backdrop for the projection.

I eat on and cut myself another slice, that brown stain a little bigger. I'm still hungry - an appetite for more continues to buzz within me.

One more. I'll have one more slice with the rest of my coffee. A slice of life! Tranche de vie!

Tranche: Any part, division or installment.

That's all they are - parts of a whole. Episodes in a serialisation. Alter one, and the remainder of the narrative has to be different.

Concomitance.

It's here in this eucharistic bread I consume.

But I stop consuming it, and spit the mouthful I have into the sink.

Picking up the loaf, I scrutinise it.

At first I can't make it out, but a dig with my fingers exposes the yellow and black body of the wasp baked in the dough.

Well, what remains of it. A little has been swallowed by me.

The rest of the loaf gets dropped in the bin, and with a resolute sense of purpose, I go to the room and cue up the unknown record.

Ambition. It was hers, Amanda's, the notion of having the house in Wrenbrook that was some way beyond our means.

It was for the future; for the kids we'd never have. It was all based on me ascending and earning more. The fact I didn't irked her, and kept her eyes open for other possibilities - a better option.

It wasn't my kind of place, Wrenbrook. It's a sleepy little village pepper-potted with white painted houses with structurally irrelevant black beams on show, lush green lawns and 'old' county money.

The day we moved in, we must have brought the age demographic down by about thirty years.

Peer pressure added to the debt, as Amanda spent borrowed thousands on furnishing the place.

I didn't grumble, and never once refused. I was so keen for her to be happy. Happy with me, I mean.

It tied me down, that house, and meant I could never take a risk. I opted for the security that came with stability, and allowed a status quo to tether me.

We bought at the peak in 1989, and it would take ten years for the price to reach that level once more. Heating the place in the winter was frightening, as was the general cost of upkeep.

The outside was the primary focus, because that was what people could see.

It was no different to a radio broadcast in those days. To the consumer, it all appears slick and calm. But a look inside the studio can reveal anything but.

I miss that chaos, though. Everything now is computerised and low-risk. There are no physical records for me to pop on a platter and rotate through the dead wax until the needle meets the cut groove. Now, Dave presses a button.

A Disc Jockey is a misnomer. There are no discs. I don't jockey.

No crackles and pops add character. Even CDs could get stuck once in a while, and make life interesting.

Recently played records aren't removed from one of the turntables, and stacked on the desk ready for filing away post-show. Bits of paper aren't flung back and forth, holding hastily scribbled notes to be imparted to eager public ears.

Dave sits behind a glass screen and observes me in my goldfish bowl, around which I float and go nowhere.

A mere twenty years ago, he was in the same room as me, breathing the same air, the rustle and bustle of paper and activity being transmitted through the microphone and adding a sense of...

Depth, I think. Imperfection and art and beauty.

And laughter and character and a humanness.

It was dialogue, not monologue. A conversation both internally and externally with the listener. An interactive broadcast where people were made to feel a part of it.

That word gets bandied around these days.

Interactive: Influencing or having an effect on each other.

And now: Allowing a two-way flow of information between a computer and a computer-user; responding to a user's input.

We sold that house in Wrenbrook in 2002. Just before the property boom. Still, at least the place I'm in has appreciated. When it's sold, there'll be a pile of cash to be left to nobody I can think of.

But I can't consider changing it. Any of it. Amanda is synonymous with my life in broadcasting. I've always conceded that she was instrumental in my rise. She was the yeast in my dough.

To undo Amanda, as I've seen in the other attempts to change my life, would, I fear, be ruinous. I can't run the risk of seeing myself again as anything but a DJ on the radio.

And so I wish for something else entirely.

What was it Dave said?

"What do you wish you hadn't done in life, Dave?"

"Nothing."

"Nothing?"

"No. It's all a journey, see. It all leads you to where you are."

I wish I could go back to how things were, spinning physical records and roadshows and audiences and such wonderful happy memories.

I'd take all of the downside to re-experience those highs. I am, I can see, defined by what I do.

With that, I switch off and head up to bed.

I'm eager to sleep and revisit those times, whether they turn out for better or worse.

It stops me sleeping initially, as I play through a mental highlights reel of my life. Laughter predominates - with Ray Nuno and Dave. And even before that, doing the discos at Oakburn Technical College and at the Haven Bay Caravan Park...

...When I wake up, I've slept as soundly as I have in a long time.

No dreams and vivid visions pervasively tortured me.

I smile up at the ceiling, and know it's because I don't really have regrets about any of that.

They were the best of times.

I am Nick Cherry, the DJ.

40.

Dave hasn't been in for two days. It's unheard of. I ring him after the Wednesday show.

"Everything alright, Dave?"

"Hello Nick. Yes, everything's fine. Good of you to call and check."

"Are you ill?"

"Me? No, no, right as rain."

"Rain's a bit shit, remember?" I remind him.

"Not if you live in the desert," he counters perfectly reasonably.

There's a pause. There's something not right.

"Dave, what's wrong?"

"Tina's a bit up and down, that's all. And my car's in the garage till Friday - a problem with the fuel-injection system. I'll be back in tomorrow morning, so I'll see you then. I'll get a taxi."

"Perhaps you should leave it till next week," I suggest.

"No, I need it, Nick. The work, I mean. The studio and everything."

"Fine. If you're sure."

"I am. I'll see you then."

"Hey, any news on the caravan?" I ask before he can disconnect.

"I've not had much chance to think about it. It's up for auction tomorrow."

"Where?"

"Down in Tinbury Head. The station, Tinbury Sound, has been taken over by one of the big media companies. It was in financial trouble. Anyway, they're looking to flog off anything they can, and close down the local operation. In the future, it'll just play syndicated stuff from London."

"Ah, that's a shame. I knew a lot of people on that station back in the day."

"It's how things are going, Nick - the way of the world."

"It's not right, though."

"No, it's not. It's shit is what it is."

"Do you want to go down and have a look?" I propose.

"Tomorrow?"

"Yes. We'll head off after the show. Perhaps a change of scenery will do us both a world of good. What time's the auction?"

"Midday."

"We'll go down on the Vespa. She could do with a good run."

There's a very long silence.

"Dave?"

"Yep, hang on a minute."

"Dave?"

"Right, we're on the 7.42 fast train from Tredmouth to Tinbury. It gets us in at just after nine. You can still bring your baby motorbike if you want, and put it in the fucking bicycle rack. We can get some breakfast and go and take a look. See if it's even worth bothering with. And I appreciate it, Nick. I know how busy you are."

"There's nothing I can't reschedule. I'll mix things around a bit. See you in the morning."

For the first time in a very long time, I have something to look forward to.

We'll get the caravan, and we'll fix it up. I'll borrow some money if I have to. I have no idea how much it'll sell for. Between Dave and I, we have all the skills required. And Trevor Goods, over in Palmerton Chase, can do any mechanical and body work it needs. It's a caravan. How hard can it be? It doesn't even have an engine.

The symmetry of that pleases me - the fact Trevor's father, Bill, found and fixed up my first van over forty years ago.

Again, I find myself smiling fondly back at a memory, as Bill Goods regaled me with stories about his record collecting, and helping Darren with the disco. He knew Tommy Histon - he'd stayed at his flat!

He seemed so old, but was probably only mid-thirties.

Reminiscences swamp me lately, ever since I bought that record. It's as if it's trying to tell me something - to steer me down a track I can't clearly see.

If I can just reset my bearing and find my way.

Perhaps the path I'm searching for lies in Tinbury Head, just as it did when I was starting out.

41.

- A very good morning to you, on what's set to be a beautiful March day. Dave's back with us, and I must thank Callum for stepping in and doing a fantastic job.
- In the second hour, we'll have the chart from 1991, which is fairly recent in the great scheme of things. So drop us a line - tell us what you were doing twenty-seven years ago. In the meantime, here's Ed Sheeran.

"We should set a limit," Dave proposes.

"On Ed Sheeran?"

"On the caravan."

"Let's have a look at it first, and see what's salvageable."

"If we get it, Nick, whether we strip it down or fix it up, there's a fair amount of work to be done."

"I know. I'll free up some time. Perhaps we spend a few hours working on it every Saturday. It'll be fun."

"I can't do Saturdays. Bingo."

"Of course. I wouldn't want you to miss that. Sunday, then?"

"Sunday," he agrees. "In the morning."

"Tina doesn't mind you doing this?"

"I told her about it."

"What did she say?"

"Nothing. But I know she doesn't mind. She's always said I need something other than her and this place. It doesn't do to have all your eggs in one basket."

There's the sad look again. It's difficult to believe they're struggling, as they've always struck me as the perfect couple. But it can be hard, I suppose, being together all the time. The kids have flown the nest, and Tina lost her job a couple of years ago. It probably explains the charity bingo, because I can't imagine what else would make him do that. It feels a bit desperate - like an excuse to get out.

I did similarly for years, as I pretended everything was fine and dandy. Amanda and I would go to various functions, and portray ourselves as the perfect happy couple. It was all a facade.

When we eventually split, most people who knew us were shocked. Nobody saw it coming. Then word of my affair spread, and it was all very neatly explained.

Amanda got the sympathy, and through that, the attention she needed. But the truth was, it wasn't even an affair as such. The marriage was already over. We'd discussed it, and agreed to split at some point. But we continued cohabiting, albeit in separate rooms, while we tried to work out how to manage everything. We carried on for years like that, eating meals together and attending parties.

I was forty-three. I hadn't had sex in years. I'm not even sure how long I went without. Two or three, I guess, after we gave up on our attempt at starting a family.

There was a girl at the station. She was there training us on the new computer system. She was half my age. Twenty-one and hormonal in 2001. September, to be precise. The tenth of the month, to be even more specific. Her name was Diana, named for the Princess, as so many were who were born around the time she was.

She was flirty with me, as she sat close to my side and walked me through the new soulless system. Her leg touched mine, but I didn't read it. My confidence on that score was low, as a result of my barren life.

I was the popular host of the DriveTime Show - three hours from three till six. I'd made the slot my own, even out-rating Morning Brake a couple of days a week. It was the peak of my career. Never before or since did I have such an audience.

Diana's slim leg pressed against mine, the smoothness of the skin on her thigh bewitching; as my eyes kept dropping to look at it. Just to look at it, and imagine where it led to under the hem of her short black skirt.

And the boots, buckled up the outsides, and nibbling at the skin around her knees.

She leant across to press two keys simultaneously, and her appley breast barely changed shape as it met my upper arm.

Still, though, I believed she was unaware of her actions, and oblivious to it all. I was safe. I was a man twice her age - old enough to be her father. She was young and less inhibited. They were, weren't they - young people? That generation.

"Where are you from?" I asked her, having noticed her accent.

"Nottingham," she replied, smiling at me and showing the white teeth she'd had for not much over half her life.

"Is that where you live?"

"No. I went to Oakburn Tech, and studied computers, so I know this area. I think that's why I got sent up here. I live in Hertfordshire now, and travel all over the country doing this."

"I went to Oakburn Tech. Electrical Engineering."

"Really?"

"Yes. A long time before you were there, though."

"Not that long," she beamed, and re-snapped her long blonde hair in a tie.

I became aware I was admiring her chest, it being thrust out towards me with her arms either side of her head.

"Where do you stay? In a hotel?" I asked and averted my eyes.

"I am this week. A lot of our work is in the London area, so I commute most days."

"It must be boring, being stuck in a hotel miles from home."

She said it then. "Why - do you fancy keeping me company?"

"If you like."

That Monday night there was a band playing over in Jemford Bridge. It was on the other side of the county, some forty-five miles away.

An invite had arrived on my desk, as they did for just about every band gigging in Brakeshire. I didn't even bother playing the guest-list card, such was my desire to keep things low-key.

The gig gave me a handy excuse to give to Amanda for my absence, not that it was required by that stage. But checking out a band was something I did fairly regularly, so aroused no suspicion. It was also something I knew she would have no interest in.

I picked Diana up in my Audi. If it was possible, her skirt was even shorter than the one she'd worn to work that day. Her hair was let loose, and crimped in oceanic waves. She looked sensational.

For my part, I wore a vivid burnt orange shirt with black jeans in an attempt to look younger than I was.

The band were okay, but trying too hard to be The Strokes, who had just released their debut album. There wasn't much of a crowd, with it being a Monday night.

I had one drink, because I was driving. Even that can't be offered as an excuse. Similarly, when she produced a spliff, I declined.

She was all over me, and all I saw, heard and otherwise sensed, was sex.

An article would appear in the paper the next day. A photo of the band in the music round-up section. And right there, stage right, in grainy full colour, was me, with my tongue in the mouth of a gorgeous blonde twenty-one year old girl called Diana.

It didn't mention my name. The writer of the article, and the photographer, evidently didn't recognise me. And it wasn't as if we were front and centre. It was a snap of the band that we happened to appear on the edge of, lit up by a combination of the flash and the stage lighting. That bloody orange shirt shone like a Belisha beacon - drawing the eye.

It should have been lost. Had the picture been cropped down another half an inch, we'd have been erased. And it wouldn't have detracted from anything had that been done.

Oh, I admit it, I had sex with her back at her hotel. A quick in and out because I'd not had intercourse in years.

I was home before midnight. One beer before bed. Amanda already gone up to her room.

And the next day, September the eleventh, I rose, breakfasted, showered, dressed, worked, and headed into the studio as I normally would.

It was different, though. I was excited at the prospect of seeing Diana again. That tug in the gut. I hadn't known it for years. Since the early days with Amanda. And with Gilly. And before then, with Sharon.

A rush of adrenaline or something, that makes everything in the world seem okay and not so bad after all.

There's nothing like it, those early days of a new relationship, when an anticipatory excitement clashes with the doubts around imminent change, and churns the mind and body.

I heard the news on the radio as I approached Tredmouth. It must have been some time between two and half past. A plane flew into a building. It was miles away. In New York. Even so, what a thing to happen.

It was reported as a terrible accident, that first one. When the second one hit, things began to dawn on people. And then those buildings came crashing down. Thousands dead.

A numbness came with it - that such a thing was possible.

I parked and entered the building.

My show was cancelled for the day. They were running a constant news stream from the parent company in London.

I was told I may as well go home, but I didn't. I looked for her - Diana. Even amidst that carnage, I sniffed an opportunity for her and I to slip away and carry on from where we'd left off the night before.

By three in the afternoon, just as my show should have been starting, a report came in of a plane crashing in Pennsylvania.

Where next, London?

If it can happen in rural Pennsylvania, it could happen here in Brakeshire. Nowhere was safe. Everywhere felt vulnerable.

What did I do? Did I rush back to my wife and home? No. I decided, if the world was about to go down in flames, I'd do well to be in a hotel room with a stunningly sexy young woman.

That's why I felt such guilt once the dust and ash had settled.

Here's the thing - this is the bit that gets me. Had it not been for the news that day, Amanda would never have bought the Brakeshire Evening News. It was the only time in all the time we were together that she purchased that particular newspaper.

As if the television wasn't enough, she felt a need to have a physical tangible thing before her mind could accept it was real.

And there, pushed towards the back, almost lost amidst everything else hastily reported that day, was me in a burnt orange shirt she'd picked out for me the previous June.

She was one of very few people to spot and recognise me. Nobody at the station connected the dots on Diana - not with her frizzed and crimped hair. Nor from the angle from which the photograph was taken, with her face pressed against mine.

With that picture, Amanda had the means to get everything and leave me with next to nothing. It was all she'd been waiting for.

As for Diana, she headed back home that day, and I never heard from her again. Mind you, I didn't attempt to contact her. And I refused to disclose her name in the divorce.

Rather, I admitted to everything, and allowed myself to be cleaned out. My guilt and shame dictated it all.

Life from that moment became... Difficult, for want of a better word.

With immediacy, I had to find somewhere to live.

An affordable place to live. As breadwinner and mortgagee on the house in Wrenbrook, I still had to repay the loans loaded with interest. We were struggling as it was.

A grotty flat in Millby was all I could stretch to, resulting in a twenty mile commute on my Vespa. As winter arrived, I travelled by train. But that was so expensive, I may as well have rented a more costly place in Tredmouth.

That said, I liked the fact I had a few miles between me and my former stomping ground. It forced me to see it as a fresh start.

But I didn't begin again. I continued exactly as I had been, albeit without Amanda and the nice house in Wrenbrook.

A year on, and I bought my home in a symbolically quiet cul-de-sac, where I've lived a fairly anonymous life ever since, keeping my head down and toeing the line, and clinging on to the little I have left.

42.

- *Standing still at number six, that was Stevie B with 'Because I Love You (The Postman Song)'. When we come back, we'll cross the road to number five, and a bit of Chesney Hawkes. Oh yes! And then a couple of your emails.*

Dave blows his cheeks out. Words are unnecessary.

We plod on, playing the tracks, most of which we'd never choose to play.

And we run the adverts and report the news and weather headlines.

Every single one plays on fear. A beautiful fresh, dry and breezy March day, is dressed up as being a Wild Fire Hazard Day.

Synched to that comes an advert for insurance - fire and theft.

The news is grim and terrifying, as global events are made to feel as if they're happening in every town and city and village. Even in Brakeshire.

Mass shootings and poisoning are the focus, followed by a timely advert for house alarms.

- *The Clash, 'Should I Stay Or Should I Go', dumped from the number one spot. It was their only UK number one single, and it was a reissue, almost a decade after its initial release.*

- *And filling the void? Here it is, the number one single this week in 1991, making the short step from number two - Hale And Pace And The Stonkers with 'The Stonk'. We'll be back on Monday. Thanks for being with us. Have a stonking day, and a wonderful weekend.*

Dave won't be finished till six, having to sit by and ensure the Gentle Pop pre-recorded broadcast that fills the air before Morning Brake is transmitted without a hitch. I sit with him and watch him bring in locally relevant adverts in the gaps.

My god, it's nut-numbingly anaemic. I know most of the music we have to play is bland, but there's no energy in any of it.

It can't survive, I think to myself, and not for the first time.

One day soon, the ticking clock that is my time on the air shall stop. There shall be no warning. I don't hear the ticks, because I'm so used to them being there in the background. Only when they're absent, shall I realise they were even present.

I don't know why they keep me on. They feel sorry for me, I suppose, having been here for so long. And I'm cheap, so not much of a drain on the budget.

Dave's safer than me. He still needs to sit in the chair and twiddle his knobs and bring in the adverts and news and weather on cue. It all requires monitoring and levelling. In time, though, his clock will cease, replaced by microchips and a programme.

"You know what, Dave. I might drop the Vespa at home and get a taxi back to the station. That way, we can have a pint somewhere and not have to worry."

"Fine by me. I'll head over and get some breakfast at the cafe near the station when I'm done here. See you there."

Less than fifteen minutes later, with the traffic light this time of day, I'm parked up and in my home. I wash my face and brush my teeth, and decide I have time for a coffee. It's only five to five.

I put a record on. The same record. The one that hasn't left my turntable for twelve days.

Hell hath no fury.

Right away, I got the feeling Amanda had been waiting for her chance. And there it was, on page sixteen of twenty-four in the Brakeshire Evening News. Just before the classifieds and adverts for jumble sales and tattooists.

And she wiped the floor with me. There was no explanation allowed on my part. It was, she claimed, inexcusable, and so why even bother listening to any excuse?

Slowly, I began to see that any apology or explanation was the last thing she sought. She desired everything to be just as it was. She wanted out. But on her terms. And I handed it to her on a printer's plate.

She waited three months before Martin moved in. That, she deemed, was a reasonable amount of time. When I say three months, I mean precisely three months.

On December eleventh, 2001, he moved in to the beautiful detached house in Wrenbrook, with its high hedges and manicured lawns, and the patio and swimming pool that cost a fortune and I was still paying for, and would be for another few years.

I saw him once, about four months after we split, driving my Audi through Tredmouth. The numberplate and Tred FM sticker gave it away. At first I thought he may have bought the car. But as Amanda emerged from the passenger side, I connected the dots.

They looked happy. In a perverse way, it made me happy to see that. He took her hand, and I spied on them from a street corner, curious to see where they were going.

As they cleared the line of parked cars, I noticed Amanda's small baby-bump. No sooner had they entered a building, than I skulked across the road and read the sign on the front - Prenatal Care Clinic.

The dates swam around my head. How pregnant was she? I knew it wasn't mine. It had been a lot longer than that. I recalled Elaine, and the way she'd been that Christmas I stood outside and watched through the window. It had been six months since my eighteenth birthday.

Amanda looked less far gone than that. Perhaps three or four months? It was before he moved in. It couldn't have been too long after we split. Did she already know him by then?

Sure enough, she gave birth in June. A boy. They called him Adam.

"It's wrong, what she did to you," Alice, a mutual friend said to me at a party some months on.

"Well, it was me who..."

She cut me off. "Nobody who knew blamed you for that, Nick."

"What do you mean?"

"Martin," she said, as if it explained everything.

"What about him?"

"She was seeing him for years, behind your back."

I'd thought about it. How quickly it all happened. But she was so angry - so protective of our image as a couple, I'd dismissed it.

"Yes, I know," I lied, not wanting to concede how ignorant I'd been - how much it stung.

"It was disgraceful. He's using her, you know?"

"They seem happy enough. She's happier than she was with me." And I gave her my self-deprecating smile of resignation.

"You mark my words, Nick. You know how they met, don't you?"

"No," I admitted, not sure I wanted to know.

"He was a gardener. A bloody gardener! Well, slightly more than that, but it's the same thing. He came round the house to do some work - planting and suchlike. Well, he certainly planted his seed there, didn't he?"

I laughed lightly. I recalled him then. I had a feeling I'd seen his face before. His family owned the Garden Centre near Norton Basset, midway between Wrenbrook and Oakburn. It was a grotty place, but we'd picked up some annuals for the borders. He was the son, and drove a small truck delivering orders.

When was that? The summer of the World Cup. France. 1998. Christ, had it been going on since then? Yes, something did change around that time. Things hadn't been stellar before, but a downshift crunched the gearbox around that time. It was when the sex finally fizzled out.

Alice raked on. "She told me once, you know? I wish I'd told you, Nick, but I thought she was my friend."

"Ah well, I don't suppose it matters now," I said discouragingly.

Alice didn't want to be discouraged. She'd had a few drinks, and a falling out with Amanda. "They used to laugh at you. He'd come round in the afternoon every weekday he could, on the pretence of tending the beds."

I remembered. Someone came once a week, and pulled any weeds and cut the grass. Was that him? I never saw him. It was always when I was at...

"He'd listen out for you on the radio. As soon as you came on the air, he knew the coast was clear."

Fucking hell. All the neighbours must have seen his truck.

"He'd park over the back, and sneak in through the garden. I shouldn't tell you this, really."

"It's ancient history now," I said dismissively, "shall we get a drink?"

"Well, they'd lie in bed and have you on quietly in the background. Just to make sure you were still on the radio, and wouldn't come back unexpectedly and discover them! When she told me that, she laughed! I found it quite disturbing, to tell you the truth. Who would do that?"

"Amanda, evidently," I replied, and made an excuse to leave her company.

I didn't get another drink. I headed out of the venue, and kept walking through shards of icy rain. I went to the place where the rivers merge, and the current is vicious.

Looking down from the bridge into the torrent, I became fixated on the fact I cannot swim.

They tried to teach me. At school, I mean. Not my parents. My parents never bothered.

I'd blindly scramble my way across a width with white floating pads beneath my arms, water filling my nose and mouth - that awful fucking chemical water in the local municipal swimming pool - piss and remnants of shit rendering the need for those additives.

It was a psychological thing. It still is. I love the sea. Being by the water is one of my favourite places to be. My time in Tinbury Head was so pleasant because of it. Well, that and other things.

However, I cannot swim a stroke. Remove that buoyancy, and I will sink like a stone.

Remove me from the radio, and likewise, I shall sink without trace.

That was all that kept me afloat that night on the bridge, as a voice from over my shoulder asked, "aren't you Nick Cherry, the DJ?"

"That's me," I replied, all smiles and happy-to-be-here once more.

"We love your show. Will you sign something for us?"

"With pleasure!" And we laughed as we hunted for a pen and I scribbled my name on a Tred FM sticker I fortuitously had in my coat pocket.

What do I wish for, as the second side of the record plays to its awfully beautiful conclusion - that beautifully awful finale?

It was the time when everything changed, 2001, 2002.

Not just my marriage, and the global aftershocks of the events on September the eleventh, but all that materialised from those training sessions with Diana.

The computers came in to broadcasting, even at a local level, and nothing would be quite the same again.

If I'm honest, I fell out of love with radio to some extent from that day forward.

I wish I'd not gone out with Diana that night to the gig.

That way, I might have left Amanda on my terms, and been a lot, lot better off than I am now.

43.

We got the caravan for nine hundred and twenty pounds. Mice included!

Trev Goods is set to drive down with a trailer and haul it back to Brakeshire. Dave believes the speakers alone are worth at least a grand. It was impossible to test the components, but it had been stored under cover for a quarter of a century. I was pleasantly surprised by the lack of corrosion throughout.

Everything is arranged, and Dave and I had a couple of pints and a bite to eat in a pub I remembered from nearly forty years ago.

I saw no familiar faces. I kept a look out for Ray Nuno, thinking he may have nostalgically dropped by. He'll be well into his eighties, if he's still alive. I've heard no mention of him dying, but I'm barely involved in the industry these days.

"It's usable, you know? It wouldn't take much to get her up and running," Dave says, repeating what he said in the pub, as we sit on the train on opposite sides of a formica table.

"So you said. But then what?"

"I don't know." He drums his fingers.

"You want to do this, don't you, Dave? You want to operate it."

He smiles his gnarly old closed-mouth smile, his beard pushing out at the sides of his face.

"Why?" I ask.

He flexes his forearms as he pushes his splayed hands down on the tabletop. It creaks a bit. A deep breath drawn through his nostrils fills his lungs for the onslaught.

"We're not getting any younger, Nick, and I'm not fulfilled by what I do any more, and I know you aren't either. It's fucking shit, is what it is, playing shit music on a shit station in a shit slot to people who don't give a shit about any of the shit we do.

"It's a fait accompli - a matter of time - before we're out on our fucking ears, and then what? We toddle off to sit on our arses watching shit television all day to fill the shitness.

"What have we got to lose? A few quid? I can only speak for myself, but I can always sell the house and move somewhere cheaper. The kids are grown up and doing well for themselves, so they don't need anything, and me and Tina are at a stage in life where we don't really want much beyond a holiday once a year - nothing too exotic - and a few home comforts.

"I need this, Nick. I want to take control back, and I honestly think there'll be demand for it. It's where we started, you with the mobile disco, and me flying by the seat of my pants in a live environment, spinning actual records we get to select. And some of them would stick from time to time, and we'd have to cover that and improvise. I miss it. I miss the buzz of it all. And I want to revisit it before I get too fucking old and daft and tired to be able to. It feels like a last chance, Nick.

"So, are you in?"

"Let me think about it, Dave. How is Tina?"

"She's got to have her leg amputated," he calmly reports. He's so calm, the import of it is almost lost.

"Bloody hell. I'm sorry. Why?"

"She got a clot. She's been in hospital now for... I don't know how long it is. It's been shit. She had a mild stroke. She won't be dancing again. And that's it, really. That's what got me thinking. My Tina can't do what she loves. We can! We have an opportunity right there, in that caravan, to do the thing we love - the only thing we know how to do."

"Why didn't you tell me, Dave?"

"I don't know. We don't, do we? We bottle all the shit up and deal with it ourselves. It's a generational thing. And I didn't want to kill the mood. You always seem so upbeat, I suppose - always happy."

Wordlessly, we look at each other for several seconds. I see all the pain in him now; the strain of having to cope. Yes, he has family, but he's the 'dad'. The father. The man who is expected to hold it all together. It's why he wanted to know about food delivery, because he's having to feed himself while Tina's out of action.

"This caravan idea, Dave?"

"Yep."

"I'm in. Let's do it."

"Okay," he says, and shakes my hand.

"God, I'm tired. I've not slept since yesterday afternoon."

"I've had my three hours."

"When are they going to remove Tina's leg?"

"If it went to plan, about two hours ago."

"Dave... Didn't you want to be there?"

"No. No I didn't. Besides, there's nothing I can do. I needed this today, to take my mind off it. I'll go there straight from the station."

I nod my understanding, and close my eyes...

44.

...she's gorgeous. But so young.

I can't work out if she's being flirty with me. Is she serious?

Whether she is or isn't, it's nice to be in close proximity. She leans across, her thumb and middle finger stretching to hit two keys simultaneously. Her breast rests against my upper arm, her face close to mine.

My eyes drink in the silky skin on her thighs, her skirt pushed up ever so slightly, a dark tunnel leading beneath the hem - just a few inches to navigate.

"Where are you from?" I ask her, my mouth close to her ear.

"Nottingham."

"Is that where you live?"

"No, not now. I went to Oakburn Tech to study computers. Now I live in Hertfordshire, and travel all over doing this. I suppose that's why they sent me here, because I know the area."

"I went to Oakburn Tech. Many years ago, of course."

"Really? It couldn't have been that long ago."

She leans back and re-fixes her hair in a tie, her arms up by the sides of her head.

My look of admiration is barely disguised, as I go from her breathtaking face down to her pert tits poking forward under her white blouse. Something about her expression hints at an orgasm.

"Where are you staying?"

She twists her mouth saucily.

Quickly, I add, "I meant, do you still have friends around here?"

A DIFFERENT MIX

"Work pays for a hotel, so I stay there. And, no, we all moved away after college."

"I hope you're not bored. There's not much to do in Tredmouth."

"It's okay. Why, do you fancy keeping me company?"

I laugh. "My wife might have something to say about that."

"I only meant a drink!" she claims, and blushes ever so slightly. "You can bring your wife with you."

She shows me another shortcut on the computer...

...the radio reports it as I drive to work. A plane flew into a tower in New York. Bloody hell. Imagine that. The navigation equipment must have been faulty. Still, you'd think the pilot would have seen.

Instinctively, I glance up at the sky through the windscreen of my Audi. All appears normal. It was probably some computer fault. That's the trouble with computers, we put too much faith in them these days.

A second plane hits another building. It changes things. Or does it? It could still be down to the computers.

No. There's talk now. There's talk of something more sinister at play. But nobody really knows.

A numbness comes with it. How could people do this to other people?

I park up and briskly walk to the building. I'm not sure I want to be in a building on this day. It's hardly a high-rise, but even so.

My show is cancelled. They're going to dedicated news coverage via the parent company in London. The only other time it happened was when Princess Diana died. But that was a Sunday. By the Monday, my show went ahead, with instructions to play low-key music and be sympathetic.

I catch Dave in the control room. He has to stay on and keep the feed going. The adverts will still be broadcast. More than ever, given the increase in audience.

Despite an urge to switch off the radio and drive home in silence, I can't stop listening. Buildings tumble. A plane in Virginia. Another in rural Pennsylvania. If it can happen there, it can happen anywhere! Even Brakeshire.

To prolong my journey home, I take a scenic route, passing by Tredmouth Racecourse, and winding through overhung lanes, a grey sky frowning through lush green fringes. So different to the blue skies in New York and Washington DC I saw on the news.

The world goes on. My life goes on, no matter what. I think of Diana, and wonder if I misread it all yesterday. Was it wishful thinking on my part?

China Crisis. 1983.

Diana was a toddler when that came out. What on earth would she see in me?

Music. I need to hear music. But a scan through the stations only finds more of the same.

It's not that I don't care about what's going on, but I've always been a 'keep my head down and hide and hope it all goes away' kind of person.

It explains why I stay with Amanda. Risk averse. Better the devil you know. Don't rock the boat or go out on a limb. It'll all be alright in the end.

I'll go home and play a record. A vinyl record, rather than a CD. A bit of crackle and hiss to make it real and let me know this isn't all some nightmare I'm having. The world never has been perfect, after all.

A small truck forces me to slow down on the lane running to the west of the picturesque village of Wrenbrook.

We've done well for ourselves. And things are getting a little easier. The mortgage isn't such a burden as it was, thanks to a pay rise for making the DriveTime show so popular.

My eyes look to the right, to the well-spaced houses, one of which is ours. I pick it out by the roof and evergreen hedge line.

A man walks over the field. A farmer perhaps. It must have been his truck. His head is down, studying the sandy soil. Like an ostrich. Does he even know what has transpired this day?

Two minutes later, and I'm pulling into my driveway

Home sweet home.

Christ, I hope things are back to normal tomorrow - that I can present my show and not have to be here.

But I know, deep down, that things will never be the same again...

...the computers have been up and running for less than a month before it all goes wrong. It's a shame, as I planned on playing Eddie Cochran's 'Somethin' Else', it being October the third - it would have been his birthday.

The song always makes me think of Ray Nuno. And without fail, thinking of Ray puts a smile on my face.

I ask Dave what's wrong with the system.

"No idea. It's all gone to shit," is his professional opinion.

"What are we going to do?"

"Broadcasting isn't a problem. We can still get a show out. But I can't run any music selections, jingles, adverts, or any other shit. It's one track only, and I can't mix anything. If it isn't live out of this building, we're fucked."

"I could just talk for three hours."

He gives me a look. "Or we run with the back-up show we laid down as a precaution."

"We did, didn't we?"

He nods. Dave doesn't trust computers. He insisted on us recording a show to slot in, having envisaged this very scenario.

"I'll check with the Director, but assume we go ahead, Dave. Can you get it ready?"

"No problem."

And that's what happens, as it buys three hours in which to fix the glitch.

I drive home, listening to myself present DriveTime on the radio. It's a strange experience. The traffic, weather and news are brought in as normal, and, apart from any bang up to the minute observations on my part, nobody will know it isn't live. He's a clever man, Dave.

The house is quiet as I step inside. A radio plays somewhere - a song. It takes me a second. The Zombies, 'Time Of The Season'.

She's listening to my show. It makes me so happy, that knowledge. Perhaps there's hope for us after all.

I'll surprise her, I think, as I tread lightly up the stairs, using the radio as my guide.

It's coming from the bedroom she uses.

I go to tap. I don't know why. It's our house, but it's her room.

Before my hand can connect, the door opens. It takes me by surprise, as I heard no feet approaching.

"Can we switch him off now?" he asks, looking back at the bed.

He turns towards me. His face vaguely familiar.

The rest of his naked form isn't. His bare feet made no sound on the wood floor. His penis is erect, leading the way, almost touching my groin.

I see the confusion written all over him. How can I be in two places at once?

Over his hirsute shoulder, I see Amanda's face. Anger and embarrassment. Plus something else.

Fear.

Yes, that's fear washing through her.

I wheel away. Down the stairs. I need to get outside where I can breathe and think.

Sliding open and pushing through the patio door, I pace around, expending energy and dissipating anger.

He comes to find me. Not her. The fucking cowardly bitch.

"I'm sorry," he says, and I remember where he's from. A Garden Centre we visited. A grotty place up by Norton Basset. He planted some trees and other stuff after the pool was completed. I didn't want to use him, but Amanda thought it good to employ a local company.

"You weren't supposed to find out," he says.

As an afterthought, he adds, "like that."

No, he was right the first time. I was never meant to know. Hence the radio being on, ensuring it was safe.

Thoughts ricochet around inside my skull.

"Do you love her?" I ask him.

He glances at the house and garden. "Yes."

"Then she's all yours. But all this? The house - the garden - they stay with me."

Oh, now I see the game. Real anger that flushes his face and sharpens his eyes to points.

He tries to swallow it.

"She thinks she's pregnant. She says it's mine," he says as if it explains something.

"Well, it isn't mine," I assure him. "Where's your car?"

"Truck," he grunts, and points over beyond the evergreen hedge skirting the rear.

"You'd better go and get it. Trust me, Amanda won't walk across there. Pull in the drive, and she'll be ready by the time you return."

It's so quick, the shove.

He's a strong man, working with his hands all day - digging the earth. And he's a fair bit younger than me.

The unexpectedness is what really catches me out. I step back, trying to stop myself from toppling, but my foot finds nothing but air.

And then water, as I flip over and into the pool.

I can't swim. I panic. My eyes close, then open, bulging. I've already swallowed water because I thought it would be oxygen.

Through the wavy line of vision, I see him looking down at me.

He smiles, the evil fucker.

Amanda must have told him I can't swim. I bet they laughed about it, and the fact I'd agreed and paid to have a pool put in.

My feet connect with the bottom, and I push, propelling myself towards the light.

Lungs screaming and burning, my chest seemingly hollow. I see him leaning down, getting closer, the sky as a backdrop, where all the air in the world is held.

He's in with me. He's not a lunatic after all. He's jumped in to save me. But it wasn't necessary. I was heading the right way, at an angle whereby I could grab the rail at the side.

Any advancement stops. Looking down, I see him, his hair floating around in the water - his hands holding my ankles and anchoring me.

I kick.

More water taken in. Feeling woozy.

He's stronger than me, digging the earth all day and lugging trees on his broad hairy shoulders.

And everything goes black...

...I feel myself jerk to wakefulness as a breath is urgently sucked in.

"Bloody hell. Are you alright?" Dave asks, as I take in my surroundings - the motion of the train, and formica table - Dave looking at me over the top of his book on the history of traditional Eastern European folk music.

"Bad dream."

"You were well away. It's all that partying, Nick. You need to slow down. What were you dreaming about?"

"I was drowning. It must have been being by the sea."

"Right. We're due in to Tredmouth in five minutes. Songs about the seaside. Go!"

"Donovan, 'Sand And Foam'."

"'Sun And Sand' by Rainbow Ffolly."

"Oooft! Obscure. Small Faces, 'Donkey Rides, A Penny A Glass'."

"'Puppet On A String'," is Dave's next attempt.

"Why? Because of Punch And Judy?"

"No, you twat. Sandie Shaw."

45.

It's a whim. I stop to pick up a bunch of flowers. It's only when I get to the Vespa that their cumbersomeness dawns on me.

Being close, I leave the Vespa and walk the few hundred yards to the hospital.

I ask for her at the reception, Tina.

A smiling nurse directs me.

"Didn't you used to be on the radio?" she asks.

"I still am. Nick Cherry," I remind her.

"That's right! I knew I knew you. Never forget a face, me. Would you mind just signing this?"

"A pleasure," I say, and juggle the flowers.

Looking down, I see it's a visitors book.

On I go, to the ward, my Converse boots squeaking on the highly polished floors. They're not great for the mild bursitis in my hip, but they look good.

"Hello, Tina," I call out as I enter her room. "How are you feeling?"

"I'm fine, Nick. How good of you to come! I know how busy you are. Are they for me?"

"Yes. I'd have come sooner, if Dave had bloody told me."

I see the arch beneath the sheets, holding the cloth over the space where her leg had been just two days ago. As an excuse to avert my gaze, I look for somewhere to put the bouquet.

"Leave them on the side, Nick. I'll get a vase from the nurse. Thank you. Very thoughtful. They're beautiful! You're just in time."

"Just in time for what?"

A DIFFERENT MIX

"Dave's radio show. It's so kind of you to let him go in early and use the studio."

I think of the setting on my seat every morning. "It's the least I can do."

"He grumbles, because that's his way, but it gives him something to do, and still be close to me. You missed the bingo. Twelve o'clock in the canteen. He's raised over five hundred pounds, you know?"

"Has he? What for?"

"He's trying to revive the hospital radio station. It was closed down a couple of years back - cutbacks. Anyway, they were using it for general announcements. You know the type of thing - what's on the dinner menu tonight, and so on. Well, as soon as Dave heard it, he asked if he could do a show every Saturday afternoon. Then he started the bingo."

A speaker by the headboard splutters to life. One on the dot, I note from the clock. Typical Dave.

- Afternoon all. You're listening to Dave, and it's one o'clock on a Saturday, which means only one thing - it's time to play some of your requests!

I hear his beard rub against the mic. He always does that in the studio. He gets his mouth too close. Then there's a sound of him swallowing his coffee. A little burp follows that.

- Oops, shit. Sorry about that. I spilt a bit.

Bloody hell, he's terrible.

- Right! Here's a little song for you. It's been requested by Jade, who is seven years old, and is recovering from her latest round of treatment. She wants it played for her mummy and daddy, who come to... Ah, well, see, they come to see her every single day, and they spend hours here with her.

- Saturdays are the best, Jade says, because, when she's well enough, she can go to the canteen and play bingo, and then they can sit and listen to this very show what you're all listening to now.

There's a long pause. Come on, Dave, you're losing the audience.

- She says... Er, let me see now. Yes, she wants her mum and dad to know that they mustn't be sad...

- See, the thing is, Jade's got lots of friends here, and so she wants you not to worry about her. And it's okay if you don't come every day. As long as you come on a Saturday for the bingo and whatnot.

- Ah, erm, Jade also wants her mummy not to get upset when her hair falls out again. Jade quite likes being bald, because it makes her look more like her daddy!

- Right! Well, here we go then. This is 'In A Room' by Dodgy, from 1996, which is when Jade's mum and dad met and fell in love.

"I might just grab a coffee," I say, my voice at a strange pitch.

I fumble with the door handle and step out into the corridor.

As I squeak my way along, I hear the radio playing out from every room and ward. It's piped into the hallway, and it echoes out of the canteen, where families and friends and off-duty staff and complete strangers lay down their devices and sit together around tables, smiling as they listen along.

46.

It's been three years, and Tina's dancing again on her prosthetic leg.

Nobody should have to stop doing the thing they love.

For my part, Tred FM let me go when Covid came along. I was furloughed for a few months, and then offered a package. I didn't hesitate in taking it.

My mortgage is finally paid off, and I have enough from my pension to live well enough. It isn't as if I need much. I still ride my Vespa, and buy fresh bread when I can.

I always check it for wasps.

As for the final song I played, I don't recall what it was. It wasn't my choice, so it didn't matter.

Besides which, I'm still on the radio.

In the time before the virus, Dave and I - with help from Trev Goods - had the caravan fully functioning. No sooner was it, than there were no functions for us to DJ at.

But all the pieces fell into place, just as they tend to in life, if you follow the natural course and allow things to be.

Tredmouth General Hospital went into strict lockdown, and we were denied access. Undeterred, we set up in the car park, and plugged into the internal speaker system through the external control room.

It's been invaluable to so many people - those with Covid, and those who have to be there for other reasons.

I read out messages from loved ones, back and forth, and play requests every Saturday at one, and Sunday morning at ten.

The other shows, five evenings a week, are mostly filled with our choices - Dave and I. Sometimes we theme them, and come up with a playlist, digging records out from our respective collections.

Some of them once belonged to my uncle Russ, his name still written on the paper sleeves or labels.

Recently, I came across the 'unknown section' in my collection. I don't tend to buy so many of those nowadays.

My hand rested on the single I bought in March of 2018. Out it came, and on the deck it went. I was lucky again, landing on the sparser A-side first.

Reflection came to me through it, just as it always has. But, when I went to bed that night, I slept soundly.

There was no desire for anything to change.

47.

- Evening, Nick and Dave here, coming to you live and loud from the Caravan In The Car Park!
- I can tell you the weather. It's not raining. But you knew that, because you can't hear it hammering down on the caravan roof.
- Tonight's theme? With restrictions soon to be eased, we've only gone and come up with a playlist of songs to reflect that.

My finger finds the switch on the direct-drive turntable, where the record lies, perfectly cued up - the stylus having been advanced through the dead wax, and dialled back a little to offer a small run in as the motor gets up to speed.

- 'Summer Breeze' kicks things off tonight. And Dave insisted it be the Seals And Crofts version from 1972.

Dave works his magic, muting my mic feed and bringing the music up on the mixer. And I'm on my feet in the caravan, the side dropped down to let the breeze in and out.

And I dance. I actually dance! It's a little sway in time, and my fingers click, as I look over at Dave squeezed in a nook at the front.

He's busy. Occupied. Doing what he does. But his bearded chin nods in time, and a smile pushes his face out so he resembles Yogi Bear.

I see the light in his eyes when he looks up at me. That spark, I know, resides in mine, as our smiles broaden and we both sing along.

"Have we got anyone phoning in tonight, Dave?"

"Yes. A patient. On the cardio ward. No mobiles in there, so they've set up a landline. I'll call up at the midpoint and patch in.

"I'll run a jingle, then the pre-recorded 'thank you to the NHS' pieces from the florists and the bike shop, then you're back on. Roughly ninety seconds."

We make a few quid out of the adverts, but it all goes on records and maintaining the gear. Some of our own money gets injected, but we're not far off break-even. People make donations, too. The bingo ceased when social gatherings were stopped.

The hospital agreed to us using the existing hardwired network, and I extended that into the newer wings so we have total coverage.

People don't have to listen. There's an on-off switch. But we're told that most do. Since Covid, just about everyone tunes in.

We pay a nominal fee for broadcast rights, being a registered charity. Dave wants to stick an antenna on top of the caravan so we can be picked up by local residents, but we'd need a licence for that. It's all a bit too much bother.

"Five," Dave calls out, and counts down the seconds on his fingers. A pointed digit brings me back in, his hands sliding the levels up and down.

- *Thanks to our friends at Beth's Bloomers and The Chain Gang for their continued support. We want summer to stick around, so here's Mungo Jerry.*

We carry on, Dave and I, in our little bubble.

We'd do this even if nobody listened, because we can't do anything else. Rather, we have no desire to do anything else. It's no different to me in my bedroom when I was twelve, thirteen, fourteen.

A DIFFERENT MIX

I've only ever wanted to be a DJ.

48.

- *'Itchycoo Park', by The Small Faces, from 1967. It's time! We've got a phone-in. Hello, can you hear me?*
"Yes, perfectly."
The voice is a little strained and raspy; the breathing laboured. It will be, I suppose, being on the cardio ward.
- *What's your name, and what song would you like to hear tonight? I'm told it's for someone very special?*
"It's for an old friend of mine."
He has to stop and I hear the hiss of an oxygen mask.
- *What's your friend's name, sir?*
"Nick. His name's Nick."
A shudder passes through me. There's something in his voice...
- *Okay, so a song for Nick it is. And what's your name?*
"My name's Ray. Ray Nuno."
But I already knew that.

Dave squats by my side, removes the record I was set to play, and cues a replacement. He looks along the groove and spins it back to where it begins.

- *Oh, Ray... How wonderful to hear your voice. How are you?*
"I'm on a cardiology ward, Nick."
I chuckle.
He continues. "I knew it was you on my first day here. Before I heard your name. I was barely conscious, but I knew it was Nick Cherry on the radio."
- *How?*
"I recognised the sound of your smile."
I have to swallow and reset.
- *I owe you everything, Ray.*

"In that case, play a record for me, pal."
- Anything. Why don't you introduce it?
"Because you're the DJ, Nick Cherry. Remember the first show you did?"
- Of course. I stood in for you.
"I was perfectly well that day. I feigned a sickie to get you on the air. Now, do the thing you do best, and introduce that record, before you lose the audience."
I never knew that.

A quick glance down at the seven-inch on the turntable, and I settle in to the microphone.

One on one, just as if he and I are sitting across a table in a pub having a cosy chat.

He taught me that. He taught me everything I know that's of real value.

- Forty-one years ago, on a Friday in January of 1980, a wonderful, kind man gave me my break on the radio. More importantly, he gave me the most precious thing any person can give to another - his time.

- You never forget the first song you played, just as I've never forgotten the man who made it possible.

- This is for you, Ray Nuno.
- Selecter, 'On My Radio'.
- Thanks for listening.

The end.

ALSO AVAILABLE BY THE AUTHOR:

The Cut

***** Andy Bracken writes with evocative ease to conjure the moments and minutiae of everyday life that make his characters tick. Acutely observed, with sensitivity and wit, his cast is relatable in a powerful way. Crate digging and vinyl collecting, the love of music and what it means to the protagonists, forms the core of this lovely book. Touching, moving and funny.

***** This is a funny, heart-warming story of a man and his loves. Andy Bracken is the best author you don't know yet and he's written a book that will be brilliant forever. The writing, characters, story and soundtrack are faultless, his technical skill draws comparisons with Alan Sillitoe.

His ability to communicate real human experience in an unflinchingly honest and relatable way, scoping the bathos, pathos, wonder and insanity of human experience, makes this book unputdownable. The Cut is laugh out loud funny, cry onto the pages moving and shout at the cover engaging.

He sails through the saucy, tawdry, gaudy, ordinary, glorious stories of our lives and it's a joy to read. It uses music, records and the habits of collectors as a backdrop but the foreground is full of lovable, and unlovable, characters and the colourful incidents and seismic events that define their lives and loves.

Andy Bracken really is a brilliant writer, support this book, his others and him, and tell the World that his work is here!

Worldly Goods

***** What a lovely, uplifting, heartbreaking, funny, wistful and wise story. I fell headlong into this book - the characters were believable and human, and I found myself identifying with each of them - their joys and sorrows, their longings and regrets.

There were moments that brought me near tears (I actually wiped one or two away on the second to last chapter). I recommend this book to anyone, especially any of us who still collect records.

Thank you so much for this wonderful volume! Easily worth more than 5 stars!

***** 'Worldly Goods' is simply fantastic! Any vinyl collector will feel right at home with the tale Andy spins across its 290 pages.

It will make you laugh. It will certainly make you cry. Andy is skilled at slowly letting the reader become familiar with the characters and watching them grow and mature. And this growth is so subtle that you admire characters like Danny Goods and his father Bill Goods. And you only learn about Bill through his letters to Danny six years after his father's passing, what a beautiful and poignant journey of discovery!

Folklorist - The Tommy Histon Story

***** 'Worldly Goods' was full of charm, nostalgia, warmth and a sense of belonging to one's family, but 'Folklorist' is a tale of mystique, darkness and magic.

A story of a loner; a loner with inexplicable innovative talents that belonged to another time, a time ahead of his own.

This is an engrossing read, and the writing, the pace, the decision to inject interviews, stories etc. on Tommy from the future at regular intervals, before returning to Tommy's own time, enhances the legend brilliantly.

There is a troublesome darkness in Tommy's soul that sets him apart from others. He is one almost not of this world. And yet, deep inside, lies a sweet soul who desires no other purpose in life than finding someone to love for the first time.

All cool music lovers and followers of cult musicians, myths & legends must read this!

A truly superb book and one which left a huge impression on me.

***** In an ideal world, 'Folklorist: The Tommy Histon Story' would be a #1 seller. It's a great story, extremely well written. It's emotional and moving, and you won't be the same after you read it. At least for a while.

It's about a musician who was never understood (well, barely noticed, actually) in his time, and was always ahead of the game. We have the privilege of reading about a unique talent written by another unique talent; the writer Andy Bracken.

This is the fourth book by this author I've read. And they keep getting better. There's no way that you won't identify, somewhere in his books, with some of the characters' thoughts and attitudes.

Bracken's capacity to write about feelings and emotions is compelling. And he knows how to tell a story; always a good story.

His previous book, 'Worldly Goods', was my favourite book of 2019. If someone loves records and has a record collection, well, 'Worldly Goods' is unmissable.

And now we have 'Folklorist'. This book must be read by every serious music lover. And, by the way, any serious reader of modern literature.

Book of the year, again!

Thank you for taking the time to read this book. It is very much appreciated, and I sincerely hope you enjoyed it.

A **Morning Brake** Publication.
Contact: morningbrake@cox.net

Other works by Andy Bracken:

Novels set in Brakeshire and elsewhere:
- A Different Mix
- The Cut
- Equilibrium
- Folklorist: The Tommy Histon Story
- Worldly Goods
- Across The Humpty Dumpty Field
- Reflections Of Quercus Treen and Meek
- The Book Burner
- Clearing
- The Decline Of Emory Hill
- What Ven Knew
- Gaps Between The Tracks
- Beneath The Covers

Non-Fiction:
- Nervous Breakdown - The Recorded Legacy Of Eddie Cochran

Printed in Great Britain
by Amazon